RESTORED

JOANNA CHAMBERS

Restored

Eighteen years ago, Henry Asquith, Duke of Avesbury had to leave his kept lover, Kit Redford, in order to devote himself to raising his young family. Now, a lifetime later, his children are moving on and for the first time in years, Henry is alone.

During a rare visit to London, Henry unexpectedly happens upon an old friend of Kit's and learns that Kit did not receive the financial pay off he was entitled to when Henry left him. Instead Kit was thrown out of his home and left destitute. Horrified, Henry begs Kit to see him and allow Henry to compensate him. But Kit, who now owns a discreet club for gentlemen of a certain persuasion, neither needs nor wants Henry's money.

"Perhaps you should earn the money you owe me the way I had to earn it? On your knees, and on your back, taking my cock like a whore."

Kit thought he had put his old hurts and grievances about Henry behind him, but when he sees Henry again, he discovers that, not only is the old pain still there, so is the fierce attraction that once burned between them. When, in a moment of fury, Kit demands a scandalous form of penance from Henry, no one is more surprised than Kit when Henry agrees to pay it.

As Kit and Henry spend more time together, they learn more about the men they have become, and about the secret feelings and desires they concealed from one another in the past.

Henry realises he wants to build a future with Kit but can he persuade his wary lover to trust him ever again? And can two men from such different worlds make a new life together?

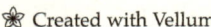 Created with Vellum

I

LONDON, JULY 1808

KIT

It was after one o'clock in the morning when Henry finally arrived at the little house in Paddington Green.

Kit had dined and bathed and was curled up in a velvet-upholstered armchair by the fire. He'd been indulging in his favourite daydream—walking through some idyllic stretch of English countryside with Henry by his side, his faithful, beloved companion—but he must have dropped off, because he woke with a start when a familiar deep voice said, "Christopher? Are you sleeping?"

Kit blinked, briefly discombobulated, then scrambled out of his chair, his smile bursting out over his face as he took in the welcome sight of his lover standing in the doorway of the cosy parlour, elegant in his evening clothes. God, but Henry looked magnificent. His wide shoulders filled his black evening coat most satisfactorily.

"You came," Kit said happily, rushing forward to greet him.

Henry closed the door behind him and stepped towards Kit, eyes glittering as he took in the loose, midnight-blue robe that only partially concealed Kit's lithe body.

"I'm rather later than I hoped to be," Henry said, sliding

his hands inside the robe and up over Kit's shoulders. The movement was a caress and a disrobing in one. The fabric slid off Kit's shoulders and down his arms, puddling round his feet like a sapphire pool, the silk gleaming in the candlelight like water.

Henry gazed at Kit's naked body with unhidden pleasure. "I'm glad to find you still up. I was afraid you'd have gone to bed and I'd have to rouse you."

Kit's smile was so big, it made his face hurt. All the hours of impatient waiting were forgotten now that Henry was here. Just being with him again made Kit's heart lift.

Deep down, he knew that he was being foolish. He was just a kept boy. His desires were quite irrelevant to the question of when Henry chose to use him—the man was at liberty to show up when he wanted, and if Kit had any sense, he'd treat their time together as work. But it didn't feel like work, not with Henry.

And Kit didn't feel like a whore when they were together.

Kit pressed his naked body against Henry's clothed one, winding his arms about Henry's waist as he lifted his face for a kiss.

"I've missed you," he told his lover truthfully, though he smiled teasingly as he said it. He always made sure to keep things light with Henry. Henry had so many responsibilities and obligations in his life—he came to Kit for relaxation and pleasure, and Kit prided himself on providing just what Henry needed.

"Have you?" Henry rumbled, his lips curving into a smile. His big hands moved possessively over Kit's slim body, one sliding down to caress Kit's left buttock. "Or has your arse been missing my cock?"

Crude words, but the teasing warmth in Henry's voice and the glint of humour in his eye made it a lovers' shared joke. Kit gave him a sly look and pushed closer. "Perhaps a little of both."

Henry's chuckle made Kit giddy with happiness. He loved being able to make this serious man—so terribly serious at times—laugh.

Henry leaned in close, his satin breeches brushing against Kit's sensitive naked flesh, his warm breath gusting over Kit's cheek. "Shall we reacquaint them then?" he whispered into Kit's ear, making him gasp with laughter and hunch his shoulder. "My cock and your lovely arse?"

"God, yes," Kit breathed and turned to press his lips to Henry's. Henry groaned and pulled him closer, pressing his tongue deep into Kit's mouth, kissing him so thoroughly, Kit's head began to swim.

When Henry drew back he said, "Here, or upstairs?"

Kit's answering laughter was soft. "Here first," he said. "Bed later." And God but he loved the way Henry's eyes glittered at his words.

Henry was a lusty man, and Kit knew he loved that Kit's appetite was as insatiable as his own.

Before he'd entered Henry's protection Kit had sometimes had to fake the strength of his own urges with his clients. Oh, he'd always been able to get it up—he was a young, healthy male, and was fortunate that his profession of servicing other men aligned with his own preferences—but it was only with Henry that his personal desires had ever matched those of his protector. Maybe even surpassed them.

With Henry, though, everything was different.

"Let's get your coat off," Kit said.

He helped Henry off with his skin-tight coat, then unbuttoned his ivory silk waistcoat and unwound the elegant froth of linen about his neck. When Henry went to undress further, Kit stopped him.

"I like you with some clothes," he said, and Henry grinned because he did too, when Kit was naked. He let Kit tug him toward the armchair Kit had been sitting in when Henry first arrived, let Kit unbutton his breeches and push him into the chair, landing with an *oof* of good-humoured laughter that turned to a groan as Kit sank gracefully to his knees.

Henry drew out his cock as he watched Kit fold his body down into the submissive pose. The strength of Henry's desire was very evident from the stone-hard shaft and weeping, rosy head. Not to mention Henry's hiss of almost pained pleasure as Kit leaned forward and took his thick cock deep into his throat. Kit loved the noises Henry made, and the sliding curve of his big hand as he palmed Kit's golden head.

"Oh, Christopher," he breathed. "You are so very good. So very beautiful."

Kit's moan in response was heartfelt. Because yes, this may be *service*, but it was still a pleasure. His pleasure and Henry's both.

He stayed there, on his knees, for a good few minutes, enjoying Henry. Enjoying his lover. Henry, who had somehow become, in ten short months, Kit's entire world. His keeper and master.

The master he could reduce to a begging heap with his mouth.

"Oh God, Christopher—stop," Henry pleaded at last, "before I spend in your mouth. Let me inside you."

Kit raised his head. Henry's expression was abandoned, full lips open, cheeks flushed, dark hair in disarray. His big body was sprawled out in the chair like an offering. Kit loved that sight—loved to see this powerful, beautiful man dazed with lust.

Let me inside you.

He loved that Henry didn't order him around, as though Kit was his slave. That he asked Kit for his favours, as though they were true lovers.

That when Henry said his name, it felt as though he was speaking of something—someone—he adored.

Scrambling to his feet, Kit clambered on top of Henry,

straddling him so they were face to face. He'd oiled himself earlier in readiness for Henry's arrival, and so it was that he only had to grasp the man's shaft in his hand and lower his body slowly down, taking Henry's beautiful cock into his body in a slow, undulating slide that had them both gasping.

"Kiss me," Kit demanded once Henry was fully seated inside him, and Henry obliged, taking Kit's mouth eagerly as his cock pressed deep and his strong hands settled on Kit's hips, urging him to rise up and sink down on Henry's thick shaft.

Kit was near sobbing with pleasure by now. Henry fit him so well. With each upwards stroke, the blunt end of his cock grazed that sensitive spot inside Kit that made him practically combust. He loved each brutal, tender stroke, and the scrape of Henry's evening beard against his chin as they kissed. Henry's strong fingers digging into his hips. The evidence of Henry's passion would be written on Kit's body tomorrow in pale blue smudges, and Kit gloried in it.

Henry tore his mouth from Kit's. "Christopher," he gasped. "I can't hold back any longer. Let me see you spend. Please."

Kit groaned and let his climax take him, his hand working his cock as his lithe body moved, his spend exploding from him in blood-warm pulses, spattering Henry's chest and neck. And then Henry was coming too, his hands holding Kit firmly in place as his cock pumped seed into Kit's body, flooding his arse.

They sagged against one another, foreheads damp, breath mingling as they panted. At length, as their harsh breathing quieted, Henry turned his face, kissing Kit's cheek, and stroking his hair with a gentle hand. It felt so perfect—Kit had to bite his tongue to stop himself blurting out something foolish. Henry's tenderness always did him in, these after-gestures so sweet they made his eyes sting.

At last, when he felt he had himself under control, he

pulled back to look at Henry. Henry's head was lolling against the back of the armchair now, and his smile was lazy, his eyes warmly contented.

"You look happy," Kit said softly.

He wished he hadn't spoken when he saw Henry's smile wilt a little and his grey gaze cloud over with something Kit recognised as guilt. He knew that Henry loved their time together, but he knew too that Henry was devoted to his family... and that he saw his need for Kit as a weakness.

It made Kit afraid that one day, Henry would decide he should not come any more.

And that day may come all too soon. In two months, their year's contract would be at an end, and it would be for Henry to decide whether to renew it.

Henry forced his smile back, raising his brows teasingly. "How could I not be happy?" he said. "When I have the most beautiful boy in London, all to myself?"

Kit saw the move for what it was—Henry swerving away from that brief moment of heartfelt intimacy, reaching for something light and easy instead.

"Christopher?" Henry said tentatively. "Is something wrong?"

A lump rose in Kit's throat, and his heart grew heavy in his chest, even as he reminded himself of Mabel's long-ago advice:

"Always be agreeable; never complain. You are your protector's refuge from his other cares. If you can be that, he'll keep you in luxury, and when you part, you'll still be friends."

Their bargain was really very simple: Kit's smiling service for Henry's gold. The truth was, Henry had neither asked for, nor did he want, Kit's affection.

"No, nothing's wrong," Kit said softly, forcing himself to smile. "Quite the opposite. Everything's wonderful." He began the awkward business of uncoupling himself from Henry and getting back to his feet. Henry didn't press the point, but Kit felt the man's gaze on him as he lifted his robe from the floor and slid it over his shoulders again.

Kit made himself turn, made himself smile at Henry invitingly and lift his eyebrows. "Are you coming to bed?"

The last remnants of Henry's frown dissolved, his eyes warming with humour. "Yes, but I'll need to sleep. I'm weary to my bones." He yawned, then stood, tucking himself inside his breeches again before heading for the door.

Kit bent and picked up the coat and cravat Henry had discarded. He did not like to leave their discarded clothes on the parlour floor for the servants to tidy away. The house had only one live-in servant, Hodge, an old retainer of the Asquith family who Henry trusted implicitly and who slept in the butler's rooms, just off the kitchen. Hodge retired to his rooms each evening, only coming out to admit Henry when he visited before returning to his own quarters. The other servants went home each evening after tending to Kit's needs.

Kit extinguished the candles in the parlour, then followed Henry out into the hall and up the short flight of stairs to the master bedchamber where Henry was already wearily pulling off the rest of his clothes.

Kit picked up each discarded item and carefully hung them in the wardrobe, twitching the crumpled fabric straight to encourage the creases to fall out.

By the time he crawled into bed, Henry was already breathing rhythmically, his eyelids closed.

"You look exhausted," Kit murmured, pressing a kiss to Henry's broad shoulder.

"Been up since five," Henry mumbled. "Long day."

Kit leaned over and blew the candle beside the bed out, letting darkness swallow up the room. "Good night."

Henry gave a little grunt of contentment and turned onto his side. In less than a minute his breaths had slowed and lengthened as sleep took him over.

Kit couldn't sleep though. He lay awake in the darkness, Henry's words playing over and over in his mind.

"I have the most beautiful boy in London, all to myself."

They weren't terrible words. He hadn't called Kit his whore or belittled him in any way. And yet... Henry could have been speaking about a prize stallion, or a beautifully-tailored coat, and Kit couldn't rid himself of the sudden, lowering conviction that he was just a *thing* to Henry, perhaps a much-cherished thing, but still, a *thing*, not a person.

Why did he keep torturing himself by allowing himself to imagine otherwise? How else could he expect Henry to think of him? For Christ's sake, when they'd met Kit had been wearing nothing but a skimpy, near-transparent tunic and had been sprawled over the lap of one of the several men who, at that time, were vying to become his new protector.

He'd been selling himself. Advertising his wares and handing out a few free samples. Letting the goods be well and truly examined.

Well, that was the kind of man Kit was. One who could be bought outright with gold.

"I have the most beautiful boy in London, all to myself."

Kit made himself face the truth. He *was* a thing—an object to be used. And for now, he was Henry's, fairly bought and paid for. Paid to provide services; to fulfil Henry's desires, not his own.

He had to remember that.

Henry wasn't looking for someone to love. He had a wife. A woman to whom he was—in his own words—*devoted*. Four children whom he adored. They were his life.

Kit was just the beautiful boy Henry fucked twice a week.

And if Kit had been foolish enough to lose his heart to the man—to his client for God's sake—that was his own damned fault.

2

HENRY

As usual, Henry left just before dawn.

Christopher was still sleeping when he climbed out of bed, and for a minute, Henry just stood there, staring at Christopher's comely face, relaxed and peaceful in sleep.

Henry's chest ached.

He set the heel of his hand against his breastbone and rubbed there, but it did nothing to ease him.

These last months, his feelings for Christopher had started to alarm him. The young man haunted his thoughts ceaselessly, and Henry's growing fondness and protectiveness towards him had begun to feel like something far more profound than the light affection he'd decided would be acceptable in an arrangement of this nature.

This was not how it was supposed to be.

He did not want these feelings. He did not *need* them. He had entered into this arrangement to deal with other needs—physical needs he had denied too long. He had expected it to be uncomplicated. Christopher was lusty and willing, a hedonist as well as a beauty, and Henry wanted to slake his desires upon the man's body. That was all it was ever meant to be. All it could be.

Henry sighed and turned away to fetch his clothes, noting that Christopher had neatly hung them up for him last night when he was so tired it was all he could do to take them off before he fell into bed.

Moving quietly, Henry took his clothes into the neighbouring dressing room so he wouldn't disturb Christopher as he dressed.

Once he was ready, he briefly considered going back into the bedchamber to wake his lover to say goodbye, before reminding himself that he needed start exercising some discipline over his unruly feelings. Instead, he left the dressing room by the door that gave onto the corridor outside, and briskly descended the stairs.

He rang the bell in hallway and soon enough, Hodge appeared to unlock the front door and let Henry out, quietly closing it behind him, and shutting him out of Christopher's life for another few days.

Outside, dawn was not so much breaking as creeping, the greyish sky gradually lightening by degrees.

Henry set off for home on foot. His coachman had dropped him off the night before. Henry never asked him to wait—it was little more than two miles back to the townhouse, and he didn't mind the walk. It gave him time to assume once again his ducal persona and the weight of the everyday obligations associated with his real life.

But as he walked home this morning, it was not the life he was returning to that he thought of. It was the man he had left sleeping in the little house in Paddington Green, and the fact that it would be three long days before he saw him again.

Henry had decided at the outset of his arrangement with Christopher that he would allow himself to visit the man twice each week. That would meet his physical needs while ensuring that his other responsibilities were not affected. He had not expected to spend the days in between each visit longing to see the man, his concentration ruined by speculation over what Christopher was doing while Henry was away. Worse than that, each time they were reunited was too intensely joyful.

It wasn't supposed to be like that.

Lustful, yes. Passionate, yes. But *this*?

He wasn't supposed to be watching the boy sleep with his damned heart in his throat.

Had his father not warned him about this? Precisely this?

"Take lovers by all means—but don't lose your head over them, Henry."

Was he losing his head over Christopher?

Perhaps it was because this was the first taste of freedom he'd had in years, and Christopher made him feel young and carefree. Not that Henry was so very old—only nine-and-twenty—but when he'd been Christopher's age, six years ago now, he'd been married with a child of his own and a second on the way. He'd already held the ducal title for three years, following his father's sudden death. At three-and-twenty, Henry's life had been full of responsibilities.

It wasn't all responsibilities though. In Caroline, Henry had found his dearest friend, and the children were the light of his life. The love he felt for his young family was calm and pure and abiding, very different from the muddled, almost agonising feelings Christopher inspired in him. Again, Henry thought of the advice his father had given him on the day he had told him of the marriage he'd arranged between Henry and Caroline. The old duke was already dying, and was anxious to see Henry settled.

"Take your pick of whoever tickles your fancy, my boy, but mind this: save your romantic feelings for your wife."

Henry had taken that advice to heart. During their brief courtship, Henry had treated the shy, reserved Caroline with a gentle gallantry that had been almost chivalric. The love that had grown between them had been devoted and pure.

As Caroline said, they did not need to share a bed to love

13

one another.

Henry had realised early in the marriage that Caroline had no real interest in bed sport, but it was only after the birth of their fourth child, Alice, that he had learned how deep her aversion truly went. It had come out when he'd gone to her one night, several months after Alice's arrival, thinking she must be wondering why he had stayed away from her so long. But when he'd removed his robe and slipped into bed beside her, she had begun to sob.

It had all come out then, in a storm of terrible weeping. She loved Henry, but she hated *this*. She wanted no more children, and she wanted no more of the physical intimacy between them.

As she had sobbed out her confession, she had apologised over and over, saying that she was a terrible wife and that she knew very well that if Henry was like other husbands, he'd have beaten her just for saying such things to him.

And all Henry could think was that, if he had ever truly desired her, perhaps Caroline may not have hated the marriage bed so much. Overcome by guilt and, shamefully, a crawling sort of relief, he'd taken her in his arms, met her wild, grief-stricken gaze, and assured her that he would never want to divorce her. He valued her for far more than her body. And it had been true, every word. She was the mother of his children and, by then, his dearest friend in the world. He had hated seeing her pain.

And he'd had his own secret desires that he'd never confessed to her.

Later, when Caroline was calm, she'd told Henry that he should feel free to go elsewhere to have his physical needs met. She did not expect him to remain celibate. She would look the other way, and they need never speak of it. She asked only that he be discreet, treat her always with respect, and break off any arrangement if she asked him to do so.

He had promised her, then and there, to abide by her

rules, assuring her that he was devoted to her in all the ways that mattered, and that no lover he took would ever usurp her.

He'd felt so confident about those promises, envisaging a future in which he would silently slake his lusts on a parade of faceless men. After all, up until then, his experience with other men had amounted to little more than a series of forget-table encounters with accommodating whores.

But he had not envisaged meeting anyone like Christo-pher Redford. Had not thought it possible to feel such compelling desire for anyone—a desire so intense he would agree to spend a fortune setting Christopher up in his own house, with a handsome allowance, and a generous severance arrangement—just so Henry could have him all to himself for one year.

A year that would soon be up.

What was he to do in two months' time? Let Christopher go, or continue for another year? God knew he did not want to give Christopher up, but was he flirting with danger if he continued?

"Take lovers by all means—but don't lose your head over them, Henry. Whether they're women, or men, or both, it matters not. Whatever morality lessons powerful men may espouse publicly, the truth is that nothing is forbidden to men of our station. However, one must be responsible about one's actions. We cannot allow the common man the same licence. Can you imagine the effect on society?"

Henry could still see his father's chilly smile.

"It is different for us. Men of our class carry a great weight of responsibility in this world, and so, such outlets are permissible for us, within limits. By which I mean that you must keep in mind the need for proper discretion at all times, and always remember where your loyalty lies. Take your pick of whoever tickles your fancy, my boy, but mind this: save your romantic feelings for your wife."

Henry knew, without a doubt, that his father would not

have approved of his arrangement with Christopher Redford. The old duke would have told him to end the arrangement when the year was up.

But Henry wouldn't be doing that. He couldn't. The thought of never seeing Christopher again made him feel physically ill. And the thought of Christopher with anyone else was... well, it was intolerable.

By now Henry was nearly home, turning onto Curzon Street and walking towards his own house. As he approached, the lock scraped and the door swung open, a sleepy footman stepping aside with a slight bow to let Henry pass.

Henry nodded a greeting.

"Your grace," the man murmured. Henry handed off his hat and cane then headed upstairs to bathe and change into fresh clothes.

His bedchamber was dim and shadowy, thanks to the thick drapes that kept out the morning light. He crossed to the window and yanked the drapes aside, only to startle when he turned around and realised there was a person lying in his bed, sleeping.

Caroline?

She never came to his bedchamber—and it had been several years since he'd visited hers—but here she was, a small, slight figure in the middle of the mattress, her long, loose hair covering her face.

Puzzled, he approached the bed carefully, sitting down gently and reaching out to carefully comb her hair back from her face.

She stirred and turned her face, and he saw it was blotchy and swollen from what must have been recent tears. His gut hollowed with dread.

Please, don't let it be one of the children.

Caroline blinked her eyes open. There was a long moment when she seemed entirely normal, entirely well. And then some horrible realisation seemed to come over her, and her blue eyes filled with tears.

"*Henry*," she gasped. "Oh God, Henry."

She scrabbled up onto her knees and launched herself at him, burying her face in his shoulder as she began to cry in great wrenching sobs that sounded as though they'd been dragged from the depths of her soul. Henry stared at her in shock for a moment before folding his arms around her and pulling her trembling body close.

"What's wrong?" he said urgently.

She felt both familiar and strange in his arms. It had been so long since they'd touched each other like this. The rose-water scent of her soap was like an old memory.

She pulled back and met his gaze, her face wrecked by tears.

"What is it?" he breathed, terrified.

She didn't say anything, only reached for his hand and lifted it to her breast, guiding it with her own. Pressed his fingers against the soft flesh.

When he felt the lump, he understood, and their eyes met.

"What's that?" he breathed, but he knew—he could feel it, under his fingers.

"Just like Mama," she said thickly, and now Henry felt tears spring to his own eyes. Caroline's mother had died a few months after he and Caroline had married. It had been shockingly quick, and Caroline had been distraught.

"I can't bear it!" she half-sobbed. "The children are so young. You are going to have to be everything to them, Henry. From now on."

"Don't talk like that!" he exclaimed. "How do you know? Have you even seen the doctor yet?"

"Of course I have!" she cried, and she pressed his hand against her breast again, forcing him to feel the hard, uncompromising lump.

He swallowed against the sudden thickness in his throat,

fighting for control. When he felt he could speak again, he said as calmly as he could, "Was it Doctor Jenkins? He's not the only one—".

"I've seen two," Caroline interrupted dully. She closed her eyes briefly, gaining control over herself, before she added quietly, "Dr. Jenkins and another man he called for. They both said the same—they believe there is little they can do, other than provide pain relief."

"But surely there's something, some treatment—" Henry said, his voice cracking with disbelief. After a moment's hesitation, he added weakly, "Surgery?"

Her mother had undergone surgery—to no avail—and it had been agonising.

Caroline shook her head swiftly.

"We'll get another doctor," Henry interjected desperately. "My dear, you can't give up. The children—"

"I know!" she broke in, her voice low and fierce. "You think I don't *know*, Henry? The thought of leaving them breaks my heart!"

And then she was crying again, and so was he. Till he had no tears left and felt like an empty husk.

"I want to go home," she said. "Today. I want us all to go home to Avesbury House. Just us and the children." Her fingers tightened on his. "May we, Henry? Please?"

He did not hesitate. "Of course. Whatever you want, my love. The doctors can come to you there and any treatment you need will—"

She interrupted him. "You will have to leave everything else behind."

"Darling, it's fine," he interrupted. "I don't mind—"

But she carried on, apparently needing to say more. "You will have to leave your young man behind," she said. "You will have to give him up, Henry."

She was talking of Christopher.

Henry's throat closed. He couldn't speak at all.

"I know you will miss his company," she added, "but, my dear, it is time to put your toys away. We must think of the children now. They will need this time with us together—what little we can give them—and then after, you will have to put them first, Henry. Before your own desires."

Somehow, Henry managed to swallow against the rocks in his throat.

"I know," he whispered, stroking her hair. "*Sssh*, I know."

But she was too caught up in her own urgency to quiet. "Promise me, Henry," she begged. "Promise me you will put them first, always."

"I promise," he said, though it felt like a wild thing was clawing his heart to pieces. "We will go home, and I will be very glad to do without Parliament and all the hubbub of London to have this time with you and the children. And as for my—my friend—" Somehow, he managed to quirk a smile, despite his sore, raw heart. "He will receive a parting gift and he will be perfectly content when I explain. I can arrange things so that we leave tomorrow—"

"No!" Caroline interrupted. "No, Henry, *today*. We must leave today." She began to weep again, and he stared at her helplessly.

"All right," he said. "All right. Don't cry, my dear. I will speak to Parkinson, and he will arrange everything. We will leave today, if you wish."

"Thank you, Henry," she whispered.

He pulled her close again, and in that moment, grief swamped him.

He grieved for Caroline, and for their children—for the sorrow that would soon be coming their way. But he also, shamefully, grieved for himself.

For the loss of Christopher.

For the loss of the young man who Henry's heart had fastened upon, despite his better judgment, and who he did not at all wish to lose.

II

LONDON, APRIL 1826

18 YEARS LATER

3

KIT

Kit was running his finger down the long list of entries in the expenses ledger, totting up pennies, shillings, and pounds in his head, when the door of his office burst open and a small and very grubby person rushed inside.

"Mama!" the small person cried. "Look!" He held something between his closed, cupped hands—God only knew what, but it would be alive, Kit was sure.

"For heaven's sake, Peter, what is it now?" Clara, his mother, asked wearily.

A former governess, Clara had been working for Kit at his club, Redford's, for six years now. Peter had a nursemaid, Betty, but Betty had taken ill yesterday. And so Clara had brought Peter to the club with her today, so that, with the help of Kit and the kitchen staff, she could look after the boy as she worked.

It was not going very well.

Clara set down the bundle of invoices and delivery notes she had been sorting through and turned in her chair to face her small son, whose lip had already begun to wobble alarmingly. Her eyes widened at the sight he presented.

"Peter, how on earth did you get so dirty?" she exclaimed,

rising from her chair and hurrying across the room. "You look as though you've been rolling around in a cellar!"

"I have!" Peter assured her.

Clara closed her eyes.

Kit bit back a laugh and said in the gravest voice he could manage, "Peter, you were supposed to be sitting in the kitchen quietly with Mary."

"I know, Uncle Kit," Peter said reasonably, "but I was playing with Gimlet"—Gimlet was the kitchen cat —"and she ran off, so I followed her down the stairs to the cellar, and it was dark and dirty at the bottom, which is how I got so mucky."

Clara groaned. "Can't you sit still for a minute even?" she gritted out, her thumb and forefinger pinching the bridge of her nose.

Peter coughed then, a wheezy sound that made Clara's expression change from one of irritation to anxiety. He'd had a weak chest since he was a baby, and Clara worried terribly about every cough and cold. She dropped to her knees beside him. "You shouldn't go into damp, dusty places," she scolded. "They're bad for your chest."

Peter nodded and wheezed again.

"And cover your mouth when you cough," she added, frowning.

"Yes, Mama," Peter said, though he kept his hands where they were, cupped around whatever it was he held.

"Clara," Kit said gently. "Why don't you take him home?"

Clara gave him a helpless look. "I've barely done anything today."

"It doesn't matter," Kit assured her. "I can manage to hold the fort for a few days till Betty recovers."

"Are you sure?" she asked, her expression worried.

"Of course. Before you came along I used to do everything myself, if you recall"—he grimaced—"not that I'd want to go back to that for more than a few days."

Clara gave a watery smile. Then she stiffened her shoulders and turned to Peter. "Right then, my lad. Let's go and clean you up first.

"But Mama!" Peter said, thrusting his closed hands in her direction. "I haven't shown you my spider yet."

"Oh no!" Clara exclaimed, horrified. "Is that what you're got? A *spider*?"

Peter's lip wobbled again. "Yes, only it's stopped moving and it feels all squidgy—I think I might have *squashed it*." When he went to open his hands, Clara yelped, leapt forward, and clapped her own around them.

"Not here, darling!" she cried, while Kit pressed his lips together to stifle his laughter.

Peter's eyes welled with tears. "I wanted to show it to you and Uncle Kit," he mourned. "I was going to have it as a pet."

"Never mind," Kit said gently, "spiders don't really make very good pets anyway. But maybe we'll get a little cat, like Gimlet, for our house. What do you think?"

Peter beamed, his tears magically disappearing. "I would love that, Uncle Kit! Can it be my cat?"

"Yes, but it will have to sleep in the kitchen, and it might not be for a few days. Now go with Mama and get cleaned up."

Peter's eyes shone. "Did you hear that, Mama? Uncle Kit's going to get a cat and it's going to be *mine*!"

Clara rolled her eyes. "Yes, I heard. Now, keep your hands closed while I fetch my things."

She crossed to the hat stand in the corner, while keeping a sharp eye on Peter, and quickly tied on her bonnet and shawl before ushering Peter towards the door.

"Will you be home for dinner?" she asked as they left.

"Yes," Kit said. "I'll see you later."

It was very quiet once they were gone. Kit and Clara didn't talk much as they worked, but there was a very different quality to the silence in a room when you were alone.

Before Clara and Peter had come into his life, Kit supposed he had lived a rather solitary existence. He had friends—quite a number of them, actually—and he took pride in treating his staff at the club well. But after he had given up the game and opened Redford's, he had always lived alone, perfectly content in his private rooms above the club.

And then, one day, Clara had walked into his life, begging for employment.

Kit had been making inquiries about taking on a clerk. He'd wanted someone bright, efficient, and discreet who would not be shocked by the nature of his business—not an easy combination to find, he'd discovered.

Somehow, Clara had learned of his search and, one freezing winter morning, she'd arrived at his door, practically blue with cold. He hadn't known quite what to make of her, this genteel, highly educated young woman with a stubborn tilt to her jaw and a glint of desperation in her eyes. She had struck Kit as entirely unsuitable, and he had been in the middle of gently turning her away, when her eyelids had fluttered closed and she dropped to the ground in front of him.

When he had discovered her pregnant state, and seen too that she was clearly unwell, pale and underfed with a persistent cough, he'd found himself giving her the position on a temporary basis. And then, when he'd seen where she was living, he'd insisted she move into his apartments above the club.

A few months later, Peter had arrived, and Kit had been astonished by his own attachment to this tiny new scrap of humanity. Realising that a late-night club was no place to bring up a child, he'd purchased a new townhouse in Marylebone, and they'd moved there together, telling the neighbours that Clara was Kit's widowed sister, and Peter his nephew.

Odd, to find himself with a little family of his own to take care of. If anyone had asked him if he wanted such a thing, he'd have said no, of course not. But life surprised you sometimes.

Kit worked on for another two hours after Clara and Peter left, poring over ledgers, and sorting through the invoices. At last, though, deciding he'd had enough, he put everything away and locked the office up.

The club occupied two full townhouses, numbers fifteen and seventeen Palfrey Terrace—though there was only one official entrance at number fifteen. Kit's office—and the private rooms above it where Kit used to live—were situated on the upper floors of number seventeen. The respectable rooms in the club—the reception and dining rooms, card rooms, kitchen and storage areas—were all confined to number fifteen. The notorious back area and private rooms, used for assignations, were situated on the lower floors of number seventeen. These could be accessed from number fifteen by a discreet corridor between the two houses that could be quickly hidden should the need arise.

Most of Kit's patrons spent a little time in number fifteen when they first arrived, enjoying a drink or two, perhaps some dinner, or a few rubbers of whist, before they headed through to the private areas. There was a large back room there where thirty men could comfortably gather, and nearer fifty could be accommodated at a squeeze. And there were a number of small, private chambers for more intimate encounters. Many of the patrons chose to associate only with other patrons, but Kit allowed a small number of carefully selected prostitutes to ply their trade at the club, catering for those patrons who did not wish to meet their needs with their peers.

Kit was extremely selective about the men he would allow to sell their services at Redford's. Above all else, they needed to be trustworthy. In return for their discretion, Kit's doormen provided security, and Kit took only a modest ten percent of their earnings, a fraction of what most brothels would take. The men could choose their own clients and work as little or as much as they chose. All in all, it was a far better arrangement than most prostitutes could hope to get, whether in a brothel or working the streets, and Kit never had any shortage of men asking to join the select group who worked at the club.

He made it a rule, though, never to be intimate with any of them himself. It wasn't that he looked down on them—on the contrary, he was friendly with them all and had helped a couple of them to find other employment, most recently Tom Atkins, who was training to be a footman in Kit's own house.

The reason he avoided any liaisons with the whores himself, was that he'd vowed when he left the game not to allow money any influence in his bedchamber again, directly or indirectly. Which ruled out anyone he came into contact with at the club.

For the last few years, he had found whatever companionship he needed at the house of an acquaintance in Clapham who hosted monthly supper parties for men like him. Men seeking someone to fuck for the night—and only for that night.

After locking up the office, Kit made his way downstairs to carry out a quick check of the back room and private chambers. He made sure that all the rooms were tidy, with fresh sheets on the beds and clean towels and ewers of fresh water in place. He checked that the floors had been swept and that the airing cupboard was piled high with clean linens for the swift room-turns needed after each assignation. Satisfied, he made his way through to number fifteen, where he spoke to the kitchen and serving staff and did a last walk around of the public rooms. Finally, he let himself out of the back door into the alley behind the club... only to nearly jump out of his skin when a figure peeled away from the wall to his left and moved towards him.

"Bloody hell!" Kit gasped, pressing a hand to his chest. Then he saw who it was, and his jangled nerves calmed. "*Mr. Sharp?* What are you doing loitering here?"

Jake Sharp's smile was sharp-toothed. "Waiting for you, of course, Kitten."

Kit grimaced. "Please don't call me that."

"Why? Don't you like it?" Sharp asked, all innocence. "It suits you."

Kit rolled his eyes. "I can see you're in one of your absurd moods," he said and began to walk away.

Behind him, Sharp chuckled and began to follow him. "Maybe it's because you remind me of the tabby kitten I had when I was a boy. He was a lovely thing. Big innocent green eyes, just like you—though, I must say, he was a sneaky little devil."

Despite his intention of ignoring Sharp, Kit glanced over his shoulder at this, arching a brow. "I hope you're not suggesting *I'm* a sneaky little devil?"

Sharp laughed, and Kit couldn't help his own lips twitching in response. Sharp wasn't a particularly handsome man, but he had *something*, that was undeniable. Something that made him seem somehow twice as alive as other men, and far bigger than he really was. In truth he was only a couple of inches taller than Kit and not much broader through the shoulders, but the way he carried himself... he seemed to loom over Kit. And then there was that unsettling spark in his amber gaze that spoke sometimes of merriment and other times of chilling menace.

Kit shivered, and hoped Sharp didn't notice. He wasn't entirely sure whether his awareness of Jake Sharp was rooted in attraction or fear, but one thing he knew: he had no intention of investigating further. After all, there was every reason to plump for fear. That would certainly be the rational conclusion.

As the second oldest son of Lenny Sharp, Jake Sharp was

part of the city's criminal aristocracy. His father had reigned over a sizeable empire of thieves, whores, and thugs in the heart of the Rookeries. Sharp's older brother had taken over that empire when Lenny died, while Jake—more clever and far more adaptable—had spread his wings. Using money borrowed from his brother, he'd opened his first gambling club, not in the Rookeries, but in a respectable part of town, a fancy gilt-trimmed place with an expensive French chef and an impressive wine cellar. A place where serious gamblers played deep.

Very deep.

Since then, Sharp had opened two more places. One, located in Knightsbridge, was patronised by men of the Ton, men who would lose ten thousand in a night without blinking—whether they had the money to meet the debt or not—and who expected to be served the finest French brandy while they did so. The other was just a few minutes' walk from Redford's. It wasn't quite as fancy inside as the one in Knightsbridge, but then, it was a slightly less rarified location, and the patrons there were more concerned with how appealing the whores were than the quality of the brandy.

Sharp moved closer to Kit. "I don't know whether you're a sneaky little devil," he said, his smile growing sly and secret. His slow, careful movements made Kit simultaneously feel that he couldn't step back and that he desperately wanted to, like he was being stalked by a tiger. "But," Sharp went on, "you're certainly a pretty one, I'll give you that."

Kit eyed the man curiously. Jake Sharp had been singling him out for attention for some weeks now. Powerful and feared as he was, he didn't even bother to hide his preference for men. Sharp knew one of the prostitutes who worked in Redford's and had told him that he very much fancied a tumble with Kit—much to the amusement of Kit's employees at the club, who teased him relentlessly about it. But though Kit laughed easily whenever the subject was raised, he suspected Sharp's supposed interest was not really in Kit himself—or at least, not only in him.

Kit tilted his head to the side, considering Sharp. "Tell me this, Mr. Sharp. Why were you waiting for me out here?" he said. "I'll wager it wasn't to pay me compliments about my eyes."

Sharp chuckled at that. "Why not? They're lovely."

Kit shook his head. "Shall I tell you what I think?"

"By all means," Sharp invited, smiling delightedly.

"I think you'd like to acquire Redford's. Is that a fair guess?"

Sharp's expression was unreadable. After a moment, he said, "Well… if you were minded to sell, I would certainly be interested in discussing the matter."

Kit nodded. "Thank you for telling me. However, I have to advise you that I have no wish to sell."

That wasn't quite true. Kit was not, in fact, entirely averse to the idea of selling Redford's at some point. However, the timing had to be right, as did the purchaser. Kit had attracted an enviable list of members over the years, all of whom paid considerable annual fees, thanks to his reputation for complete discretion and trustworthiness.

The list was worth a fortune. All those names. All those secrets.

Kit could not hand that list over to just anyone. He may have opened the club with a view to making money, but that didn't mean he had no scruples—he would not betray the trust that had been placed in him by his patrons.

Until he found an equally discreet and trustworthy successor, he would not be selling Redford's. And based on what he knew of Jake Sharp—admittedly not a great deal—he did not think Sharp was that person.

Kit turned to go, but Sharp reached out, detaining him with a hand on his arm. His gaze was reproachful. "It's not very polite to be deliberately misleading, Kitten."

Despite Sharp's mild tone, a shiver went up Kit's spine. He hid his unease behind a tight smile. "As flattering as it is to be compared to a kitten," he said sweetly, "I feel bound to point out that I am one-and-forty—far too old to be compared to an infant cat."

"I beg to differ."

"Then we shall have to agree to disagree, Mr. Sharp."

Sharp sighed. "I wish you'd call me Jake."

"And I wish you'd call me Mr. Redford," Kit replied, "but we can't always get what we want, can we?"

Sharp laughed then, and for a moment he really was handsome, his teeth seeming very white against his olive skin, and his light-brown eyes sparkling with humour.

"Have supper with me tonight," he demanded, his gaze fixed on Kit.

Kit shook his head. "I'm afraid I will be dining early at home this evening, then returning to the club till the early hours."

"I'll come here then," Sharp replied, undeterred.

"Regrettably," Kit said smoothly, "you are not a member of Redford's. So I will be unable to admit you."

Sharp chuckled. "Oh, come on, Kitten. You could give me a membership right now."

"I'm afraid not," Kit replied. "The rules of the club require at least two references from existing members—"

"But you *own* it," Sharp interrupted, though thankfully he seemed amused rather than offended. "You can do as you please, surely."

"Not so," Kit said implacably. "If I do not obey the rules, how can I ask others to do so?"

Sharp eyed him for a moment. Then he gave a rueful shrug. "Very well. I will just have to obtain the references, I suppose."

"I'm afraid so," Kit said smoothly, even as he wondered how many of his own patrons would be prepared to give the man a reference in return for writing off some gaming debts.

"Until then," Sharp went on. "How about you join me for supper another evening. Tomorrow? Friday?"

"Mr. Sharp—"

"I know what you're going to say," Sharp interrupted. "But I don't believe for one moment that you have to spend *every* evening at Redford's—and even if you do, there is nothing to stop you taking an early supper with me one evening before you go to the club, is there?"

Kit sighed. "I'll think about it," he said finally.

"Friday then."

"I only said I'll *think* about it."

"All right," Sharp agreed easily. They had reached the end of the alleyway now, and emerged together onto the main street. "Let's speak again in a few days."

Kit sighed. "Very well, but I warn you: you should not expect to receive a different answer."

Sharp only grinned that sharp-toothed grin again. "I'll call on you," he promised, and then he was walking away, swinging his cane and whistling as he went.

And since Kit was only human, he could not help but notice how very fine the man's arse was.

As Kit made his way home, he found himself mulling over Sharp's words.

I don't believe for one moment that you have to spend every evening at Redford's.

Whatever the man's real reason might be for pursuing Kit, he was right about that much.

When Kit had first opened Redford's, he'd relished spending his evenings there. Of course, he'd only lived upstairs at the time, but it wasn't just for convenience. He'd been making the place his own, stamping it with his character, as surely as he'd covered the walls of the card rooms in that damned expensive Chinese dragon wallpaper he'd liked so much.

The truth was, he'd loved finally having something all of his own. Until he'd opened Redford's, Kit's existence had centred solely around satisfying the whims of others, with all the unsettling potential for sudden change such an existence entailed. It was a life that had left him with an insatiable hunger for some solid, unchanging foundation in his life.

Redford's had provided that foundation.

Lately, though, his single-minded devotion to the place had begun to wane. Perhaps it was partly because, over the last several years, he had become much more financially comfortable. He'd finally paid off a sizeable loan he'd taken on when he'd opened the club, and several investments he'd made had done very well indeed. He now had a nice cushion of capital that was enough to provide a comfortable income on its own, quite aside from Redford's.

Moreover, since taking Clara on, he didn't have to be such a constant presence at the club. It had taken him some time to let go his iron grip on every detail of the business, but slowly, gradually, he was getting there. In the last year, as he had begun to lean more heavily on Clara, he had discovered he had time again. Time to visit old friends. Time to go walking in his favourite spots—down by the Serpentine and around Green Park, even all the way up to Hampstead Heath a time or two.

He'd begun to secretly draw a little, carrying little notebooks and pencils with him that he'd pull out when he sat down by the river or under a tree to idly sketch whatever little things he might spot: a simple flower, a horse chestnut bristling out of its prickly coat, a waterfowl floating docilely down the river.

The annoying thing was that, the more time he had to

himself, the more time he wanted. He'd even found himself wondering whether he needed to attend Redford's as often as he did in the evenings—something he'd once considered vital, reasoning that his members needed to see him to trust him.

Kit was so deep in his thoughts, he didn't realise he'd arrived home.

The door swung open before he could so much as place a finger upon it, and Tom stood in the doorway, grinning. Six foot one inch of pure muscle, his teeth flashing white, his perfect smile only very faintly marred—or perhaps perfected —by the slight crookedness of his left front tooth.

"What d'ye think, guv?" he asked Kit, blue eyes sparkling.

Kit blinked at him, not understanding. "What do I think of what?"

Tom huffed in exasperation. "The new livery!" he exclaimed, gesturing at the ensemble gracing his form: midnight-blue coat and breeches trimmed with dark-gold braid and large gold buttons.

"Oh, of course!" Kit said, stepping back to admire him more fully. "Oh, yes, Tom, that's very handsome indeed. The dark blue is wonderful with your eyes." He stepped forward to pat the lapel of the coat, then smiled. "Now you look the part."

"I reckon so," Tom said, standing aside to let Kit enter, then closing the door after them and following Kit into the hall. "Give me your hat, guv."

Kit cocked a brow at him. *"Give me your hat, guv?* Hmm. You've a bit of work to do before I can say you're acting the part." He took his hat off and handed it to Tom. "Are you really sure you want to do this footman lark?"

Tom flushed slightly. "Course I do." he said. "Standing around looking handsome is right up my street—don't need no brains for it, do I? I know I forgot to talk right when you come in just now, but that's just on account of me getting a bit

35

giddy over my new garb." He cleared his throat decisively, then added in a quieter and more polished voice, "May I take your hat, sir?"

Kit quirked a smile. "That's much better, but for the record, I disagree with you on the brains bit. Clara and I have rumbled you—you're very quick."

Tom flushed with pleasure. "I don't know about that, but don't worry—if it's true, I can hide it."

Kit chuckled.

"Anyways, I reckon it'll be easier for me to remember how to behave, now I've got the proper duds," Tom continued. "Should keep me right."

Kit clapped him on the shoulder. "Good man. But keep up the lessons with Clara. It won't do you any harm. Now, I'm going up to my sitting room. Could you ask Mrs. Saunders to send up some tea?"

"Right-o, guv." Tom cleared his throat. "I mean, yes, sir."

Kit suppressed a sigh. However bright the man was—and Clara thought he was very bright indeed, notwithstanding his complete illiteracy—the role of footman was plainly not coming easily to him.

Kit made his way upstairs to the small, cosy room that was his own private space. The house had a formal drawing room too, where they could receive visitors, but when he was alone, he always chose this room. The walls were painted primrose, and two matching walnut bookcases stood on either side of the fireplace, the mellow wood glowing in the late afternoon sun. Small as it was, the room was dominated by a decadently plush chaise longue upholstered in antique gold damask. Several fat cushions in the same fabric were piled up at the head end.

It was rather like a throne.

Closing the door behind him, Kit gave a happy sigh and began unbuttoning his coat. Once he had it off, and had rolled up his shirtsleeves, he removed his boots, then padded over to one of the bookshelves in his stockinged feet, reaching for the plain wooden box sitting there—his writing slope.

Humming contentedly, Kit carried the box over to the chaise longue where he settled himself down, placing it on his lap. After fussing with the cushions, he leaned back to unlock the box. It opened out into a wedge shape, high at the back and sloping down to less than two inches in height at the front edge, a perfect elevation for writing or drawing. The slope itself was covered in tooled red leather, and there were several ink bottles stored in the cubby holes at the rear of the box. The writing implements were held in a small side drawer, and some of Kit's notebooks were kept in the document compartment hidden beneath the slope.

Kit pulled out the topmost notebook and turned to the next clean page.

He was thinking about what to draw when the knock at the door came.

"Come in," he called.

Tom popped his head round. "Your tea, sir," he said in the lofty voice he used when he was making his best effort at being a footman.

"Excellent, Tom, bring it in."

It was not, of course, only tea. Alongside the tea was a plate of toasted crumpets. Mrs. Saunders was incapable of sending a tray to Kit without adding something to eat.

Tom set the tray down and poured a cup for Kit, adding milk without waiting for Kit's direction. He didn't hand the tea over though. Instead he stood there, staring at Kit, a disapproving expression on his face.

Kit smiled at him. "You can leave the tea on the table. I can reach it from here."

Tom frowned and pressed his lips together as though trying to keep himself from talking.

Kit raised his brow. "That will be all," he said sweetly.

Tom closed his eyes and for a moment, Kit thought he was

37

going to manage to stay silent, but then he opened them and blurted. "You're going to get ink on that sofa and ink stains is worse than port wine to get out." Then he turned on his heel and stalked out, muttering under his breath about idiots who didn't know the first thing about cleaning furniture.

Kit watched him go, smiling ruefully, then turned back to his notebook.

It was well over an hour later before he raised his head.

Again, it was a knock at the door that roused him, and he blinked, almost dazed, noticing the still-full cup of tea on the table and the untouched crumpets.

"Come in," he called.

This time it was Clara.

Kit's brows pulled together when she entered. Clara never ventured up here, treating this room as Kit's private enclave. She had forbidden Peter from entering too, despite Kit saying he didn't mind. She insisted that Kit needed at least one room in his own house to himself. Kit always reminded her that if he did not want her and Peter around, he would say so, and she would smile and nod. But the truth was, he did rather like having this one little room to himself.

Looking at Clara now, though, he could see that something was wrong.

"Clara," he said worriedly, "what is it?"

It was only after the words were out of his mouth that he began to notice the other signs that pointed to her distress: her face was pale, her expression pinched into anxiety, and her light-brown hair—usually so neat—was coming down on one side.

She gave a faint sob, then looked horrified, as though she hadn't expected to do that.

Kit quickly set the writing slope aside and rose, going to her and drawing her fully into the room. He guided her to the chaise longue and sat her down, settling himself beside her.

"Has something happened?" he asked, trying to sound calm even as his heart began to race with alarm. "Is it Peter?"

When she shook her head, he could not hold in his sigh of relief. "Then what?"

"It's—honestly, it's silly. I feel such a fool," Clara said. But her voice shook and he could feel her trembling beside him. It was difficult to believe this was Clara, who was as solid and sensible as the day was long.

"Tell me."

Clara swallowed. "I took Peter to the park on the way home. He played with two other little boys for a while, while I talked to their mother—then Peter was hungry so I took him to get a bun at the baker's shop. We were walking home when it happened—" She broke off and took in a long, shuddering breath.

"Clara? What happened?"

She turned her head and met Kit's eyes, her own wide and shocked. "We were—I was—there was a man—" She choked out a cry.

"Are you all right?" Kit demanded, alarmed. He ran his gaze over her anxiously. "Did he hurt you?"

"No, nothing like that, but he was..." She met Kit's gaze with her own wide-eyed one. "This will sound quite mad, I fear, but I think he was *following* us, Kit!"

Kit frowned. "Are you sure?" Despite his words, he instinctively believed her—Clara was the most level-headed person he knew.

Clara dropped her head into her hands. "I—I don't know, I really don't, Kit! Why would he follow me? But yes, that's what I thought. He kept his distance, but he just walked behind us, all the way home. Thankfully Peter didn't notice." And then, unbelievably, she began to cry.

Kit blinked, astonished. Clara had experienced more than her fair share of tribulations in her life, but this, he thought, was the first time he had seen her cry.

Belatedly, he realised that rather than stare at her, he should be comforting her. Carefully, he put his left arm around her and pulled her close. She fell against his chest and began to sob, while he stroked her hair, murmuring soothingly as she cried her heart out.

At length, she quieted, only small, irregular hiccoughs shaking her body. His shirt front was damp from her tears.

"Better?" Kit asked.

She nodded, raising her hands to wipe at her eyes. Slowly she straightened, moving away from him.

"I'm so sorry," she said, looking anywhere but at Kit. "I don't know what came over me. It was probably nothing. He never even spoke to me. I feel like a perfect fool now, burdening you with this nonsense. I probably just panicked and convinced myself."

Kit gazed at her doubtfully as she rose to her feet, smoothing first her skirts, and then her hair. "I'm glad you told me," he said carefully. "Even if it was nothing."

She sent him a relieved smile, and he smiled back reassuringly. But inside, he felt uneasy. Clara was usually so unflappable. She was all phlegmatic common sense. Not at all the type of person to panic, not without good cause. To see her this distressed alarmed him.

And he could not help but wonder whether—despite her own protests to the contrary— her instincts had been entirely correct.

4

HENRY

Henry woke to unfamiliar sounds.

He was used to his quiet suite of rooms at Avesbury House, in the depths of the Wiltshire countryside; used to waking up to quiet birdsong and gentle sunshine and not so much as a creak of the floorboards until he chose to ring for someone.

It was very different here, in the townhouse in London. It was a well-sized property, but compared to the sprawling country pile that was Avesbury House, the Curzon Street house was positively cramped. As well as Henry himself, his daughter Marianne and her husband Jeremy, and Freddy, his younger son, there was a hoard of servants, whose activities began shortly after dawn and appeared to involve walking up and down the stairs and corridors nearly continuously. Moreover, the clattering of horses and carriages from outside, accompanied by the voices of servants, tradesmen and delivery boys began absurdly early and did not let up till late into the evening. Henry liked to sleep with the window open at home at this time of year, but the noise of the city made that impossible, so that, when he woke up, he felt muggy-headed and altogether out of sorts, before he'd so much as thrown his bedcovers off.

Henry sighed and sat up, rubbing his hands over his face. He was turning into a curmudgeonly old man. Seven-and-forty and as set in his ways as a septuagenarian.

Difficult to believe he had once loved living in London so much that he hadn't been able to imagine living happily in the country again. He had returned to Wiltshire with Caroline and the children eighteen years before, expecting to be tearing out his hair with boredom within a few months. Until then, he had been a fond but slightly distant father to his children, a role that seemed to have been decided for him and with which he had passively played along without ever questioning it. But over those months, as Caroline had gradually declined, he'd realised he would have to do his best to make good the hole her death would leave in their lives. He would have to be both father and mother to them.

Once Caroline had passed away, he hadn't been able to bear the thought of London, with all the clamouring crowds and commotion. The children had been heartsore, and so had he. And, of course, by then he'd known he had no reason to return.

Christopher had never answered his final letter.

So he'd let the London house to tenants, arranging to stay in hotels for his occasional unavoidable trips to town. Curzon Street was a fashionable address—too fashionable for a man who had never had much interest in polite society to begin with and who had absolutely none after his wife's death. The children loved being at home. They loved their horses and playing by the river and running wild. And they were safe there. Henry had hired the best governesses and tutors he could find to avoid sending any of them to school for those first few years after Caroline's death.

How quickly the years had passed since then. One moment, his children had been small, and now—quite suddenly, it seemed—they were all grown. And here he was, back in the townhouse in Curzon Street.

Sighing again, Henry threw back his bedcovers and rose from his bed, rubbing wearily at the tense spot between his brows. It had been warm last night with the window closed, and he had been restless. But there was no point lying in bed all morning hoping to fall asleep again—that would certainly not happen.

Making his way to his dressing room, Henry shook his head over the swift passage of the years, wondering—as he occasionally did these days —whether he had built too much of his life around his children.

In some ways, he'd had no choice. They'd needed him badly after Caroline's death. Some fathers might have withdrawn from their children, becoming an even more distant figure, but Henry had drawn closer. In truth, their demands had kept him going in those dark and difficult days. They had given him a reason to wake each morning and shaped each day with purpose. He had not wanted to be apart from them.

And later, after little Alice's death, there had been years when he'd been too frightened to leave them alone. It was terrifying how quickly disaster could strike. He had taken one short trip to Salisbury—the first time he'd left the children since Caroline's death—and when he returned three days later, his youngest child was in a high fever from which she had never awoken.

Henry poured the water from the ewer into the washing bowl, sluiced his face with it, then straightened, meeting his own gaze in the looking glass

The man facing him was familiar, but a little older than he expected.

Time had sped past at an unholy rate. For years, Henry had been the centre of his family—he still was, he supposed, but now his children were drifting away from that centre, leaving him feeling somewhat redundant.

George, his eldest, was soon to be five-and-twenty, a serious, quiet young man. A good man, Henry thought, but lately, a melancholy one, and for reasons he could not discover. George preferred to spend his time in Wiltshire. He was the most self-contained of Henry's children and the one he worried most about. Marianne, his sunniest, easiest child, was three-and-twenty, happily married and pregnant with her first child. It was for her sake he was in London now. And Freddy, at two-and-twenty was... well, Henry wasn't quite sure about Freddy. He appeared to be unwilling to have any kind of discussion about his future with the father he had once adored and chattered away to about everything under the sun.

Henry's children were, each of them, quite grown, and busy with their own lives. And of course, that was how it ought to be, only sometimes, he could not help but wish for those older, easier days when they had clamoured noisily for his attention.

Only one of his children would always be with him. Alice, who had passed away two years after her mother, at just five years old.

Some losses eased with time. These days, his grief over Caroline's death was just a faint ache. But even now, fifteen years later, Alice's loss had the power to overwhelm him.

As the years wore on, it felt like Henry was the only person who remembered her, his darling youngest girl. Guarding her memory had begun to feel like a sacred responsibility. One that both pained him and was, somehow, the pinnacle of everything he had ever been: Alice's father.

Henry thought of her every day—that was something no one else knew, not really. He spoke to his other children of Alice from time to time, and they would humour him with kind words and memories of their little sister. But he knew they did not really understand how altered—how *fundamen-*

tally altered—he had been by her death. That he had lost a part of himself that day that could never be made good.

Caroline would have understood, and while he was glad she had been spared that grief, sometimes it was hard to bear alone. To have no one who shared the depths of his sorrow, or missed Alice as he always would.

His sorrow would always be there, but he was fortunate to have joy in his life too. And if he was a little melancholy just now over the slowly growing distance between him and his children, perhaps those feelings were the impetus he needed to force himself out of his comfortable existence.

Like a fledging trembling on the edge of the nest.

Henry eyed the grey temples of the man in the looking glass.

A rather elderly fledging, in his case.

Sighing, he turned away and went to get dressed.

Marianne and Jeremy were in the breakfast room when he arrived downstairs.

Henry had made a wedding present of the townhouse to his daughter and her new husband prior to their marriage, and Marianne had promptly redecorated the place from top to bottom. The old breakfast room, which had been a rather dark and chilly room at the back of the house, had been turned into a music room, and the new breakfast room, which got the morning sun, was warm and cheerful.

"Good morning, Papa," Marianne greeted him, smiling brightly.

"Good morning, darling," Henry replied fondly, dropping a kiss on her dark head. He was taking the opportunity to enjoy as many of these affectionate moments as he could while he had her. Soon she would be gone—Marianne and Jeremy planned to leave London within the next two weeks for Jeremy's estate in Kent, where the baby would be born. Indeed, since Henry had arrived in London two days ago, all Marianne seemed to talk about was how eager she was to go, and how busy and uncomfortable London was at this time of year.

Henry smiled at his son-in-law. "Good morning, Jeremy."

"Morning," Jeremy returned. "Did you sleep well?"

"Yes, thank you," Henry lied, as he made his way to the sideboard, where he filled a plate before returning to the table where Marianne was pouring his tea. He watched as she added the precisely correct amount of milk and passed the cup and saucer to him.

She was the only one who ever got it just right. It was a thought that made him happy and sad at once.

He smiled brightly at her. "So," he said. "Do you have any plans for the day?"

"Two morning calls," Marianne said. "A duty one to Aunt Tilly"—she pulled a face, making Henry smile. His older sister, Mathilda, was something of a trial to say the least —"and one to see Becky Sanderton—do you recall Becky? We came out the same season and got on famously. She's marrying Auberon Smyth in the autumn. He hasn't got two feathers to fly with, but she tells me it's love." She rolled her eyes. "Then I'm going into town to get some lace and ribbons to trim some of my old gowns with—the dressmaker is letting them out." She sighed. "Clothes are such a tedious business when one is in an interesting condition."

Jeremy looked mortified, a faint flush across his cheeks. Henry had to check a smile. Poor Jeremy always got so embarrassed when Marianne made even subtle references to pregnancy or married life in front of Henry.

"Well," Henry said, "how about I relieve some of the tedium by taking you to Gunters for an ice after?"

Marianne brightened. "That would be lovely! Though I'd rather go to Mercier's on the Strand. They make the most wonderful pastries and confections there." She smiled happily. "And it's close to the haberdashery I'm going to."

"Excellent," Henry said. "I'll come and meet you there then. What time?"

She thought about that. "Two o'clock? I shouldn't keep you waiting much beyond that and if I'm delayed at the haberdashers, the carriage will be outside for you to wait in."

"I'm not so old that I can't stand outside a shop for a few minutes!" Henry protested, only half-pretending to be offended.

She laughed. "I'm only judging you by my own standards, Papa. These days I get very cross when I have to stand around."

"*Hmmm*," Henry said. "Well, I'll give you the benefit of the doubt this time—and look forward to our visit to Mercier's." In truth, he was very much looking forward to getting her to himself for a little while.

Just then, the door opened and Freddy entered the breakfast room. He gave a sort of grunt which Henry supposed was intended as a greeting and went straight to the sideboard.

"Good morning, Frederick," Henry said pointedly when Freddy joined them at the table. "Did you sleep well?"

Freddy nodded, but his expression was pained and he looked distinctly green about the gills. Plainly, he was suffering from the effects of the previous evening. He looked down at the plate he had just filled and paled.

"Perhaps," Henry said, "You should have stayed in bed a while. You do not seem quite ready for breakfast."

"I'm meeting Percy at ten," Freddy mumbled. "We're going to Tattersalls."

"Who is Percy?" Henry asked.

Marianne made a face. "Percy Bartlett. He and Freddy have become bosom friends."

"Sir Algernon Bartlett's son?" Henry asked, frowning.

Algie Bartlett had been two years above Henry at school and a perfectly nasty piece of work.

"That's him," Freddy said. "He's a jolly good fellow, actually. Been showing me around town."

"Been showing you around all the gambling hells, you mean," Marianne muttered disgustedly.

"Will you stop being so bloody interfering?" Freddy snapped. "It's no business of yours what I do."

"Freddy!" Henry said sharply.

Freddy's gaze swivelled to him. "Well, she started it!"

"And you're the one who's being insulting," Henry said. "Apologise for your rude behaviour."

Freddy had been worrying him for a while. He'd shown no interest in university and in the last year or so had been getting through his quarterly allowance within a fortnight of receiving it. Henry suspected he was gambling—so many young men did, falling into towering debt and ruining themselves. Two months ago, Henry had given Freddy a stern lecture about the need to live within his means, but the young man had only sat in sullen silence, saying nothing.

Just as he was doing now.

Henry opened his mouth to speak again, but Marianne beat him to it.

"Do you know, Freddy," she said. "Ever since you became friends with Percy Bartlett, all you do is talk about how gentlemen *ought* to behave, thinking yourself so wise. Well, if *this* how a gentleman behaves, I should rather invite a pig to my table!"

Freddy glared at her. "I don't recall asking for your opinion on my conduct."

Marianne's eyes flashed with temper. "And I don't recall asking for your permission to give my opinion in my own house."

Freddy stood up so abruptly his chair rocked. "Christ

almighty, Mari! For once in your life, can you just stay out of my business?"

"Watch you drink and gamble yourself to ruin, you mean?" Marianne snapped. "Because that's all you seem to do these days!"

"God in heaven, do you ever shut up, you *harridan*—"

Henry slammed his fist on the table and roared, "*Freddy!*"

Freddy startled and turned to face Henry, a flash of remorse touching his angry expression before he rallied and cried, "Well, she called me a pig, and a wastrel!"

"I did not," Marianne protested. "I merely said that I should prefer to invite a pig to my table, and pointed out that you've been drinking and gambling incessantly. Both of which are perfectly true!"

Freddy spluttered.

"And you might care to consider," Marianne continued implacably, "that I am your elder sister. A gentleman should treat both his elders *and* his sisters with the utmost respect, don't you agree, Jeremy?"

Marianne's husband, who had continued eating his breakfast with perfect equanimity throughout the spat, looked up and smiled at his wife. "Quite so, dearest."

"Well of course *Jeremy* agrees with you!" Freddy howled.

"Not so," Jeremy protested. "I only agree with Marianne when she's right. It's just that she's generally right about everything." He glanced Henry. "Vastly sensible woman, your daughter," he said in the manner of one bestowing a compliment.

Henry smiled at Jeremy, grateful to him for at least trying to take some of the heat out of the argument. Marianne and Freddy had always clashed.

Freddy stood abruptly. "I'm not hungry," he announced. "I'll get something to eat when I'm out."

"Before you go," Henry said. "Apologise to your sister, please." His tone was quiet but unmistakably firm.

"But—"

"And Marianne," Henry added, turning to his daughter. "You too. You are not blameless here."

Marianne's cheeks pinkened.

Henry merely waited, his gaze moving between them.

Freddy's nostrils flared with temper, but at length he turned to Marianne and said stiffly, "I apologise."

Marianne nodded, not meeting his eyes. "I do too."

"Thank you," Henry said. "Freddy, you may go now, but I wish to speak with you later, before dinner. Is that understood?"

Freddy nodded stiffly and strode out, closing the breakfast room door behind him sharply.

Into the silence, Marianne said, "He's becoming quite impossible, Papa."

Henry sighed. "It doesn't help when you scold him, you know. You're only a year and a half older. Of course he resents it."

Marianne flushed. "I'm sorry," she said stiffly, "But I don't want him to turn into a wastrel like that awful Percy Bartlett who—by the way, Papa—is at least five years older than Freddy."

"He needs occupation," Jeremy said quietly.

"I know," Henry said wearily. He'd looked into a career in the church for Freddy—a well-trodden path for second sons —but Freddy had rejected the idea out of hand when he'd raised it.

"Perhaps," Marianne said slowly, "you should consider buying him a commission."

Henry's gaze snapped to her and he said shortly, "What an absurd idea!"

Marianne met his look with a steady one of her own. "Papa, you know that's all he's ever wanted. His only ambition since he was a boy has been to have a military career."

"It's out of the question," Henry said flatly.

"But Papa—"

"No, Marianne," he said firmly. "My mind is made up."

She pressed her lips together, shaking her head irritably. "You should *un*make it, then," she said. "At least give it some proper thought."

But he *had* given it proper thought—far too much thought arguably. He'd lost a brother to the war, when Freddy was just a little boy. Philip had died in Portugal charging the French guns. A hero's death, they'd said.

When Henry thought of Freddy in a cavalry officer's uniform, his chest seized up with sheer terror.

"I'll speak with him," he said firmly. "And we will agree a way forward. I am sure."

To his surprise, Marianne's eyes filled with tears.

"Marianne!" he said, dismayed. "What's wrong?"

"I'm sorry I snapped at Freddy," she said. "This baby *has* made me a harridan, just like Freddy said."

Jeremy leaned forward and patted her arm. "Never a harridan," he said loyally.

Marianne made a strangled noise that was part laugh, part cry. "A watering pot then. And a whale, probably, by the time the baby arrives, given how many sweet things I keep eating."

Jeremy laughed softly. "Then you shall be the most beautiful whale in all England."

She snorted through her tears. "You wretch!"

Henry smiled to see their affection. The lot of a parent was to worry, and he did so daily: over the prospect of Marianne giving birth, and Freddy's nonsense, and George's quiet melancholy. But this at least, this marriage, brought him comfort. He'd been acutely aware that his daughter's happiness would depend on the character of her husband, and acutely relieved when she had selected Jeremy Fenwick. To see his daughter settled with a man who so obviously adored her was a blessing indeed.

Henry stood and walked round the table to where she sat, bending down to drop another kiss on top of her head, relishing the tiny gesture of affection even as he suppressed a pang of sadness at the knowledge she was growing further from him with each passing year.

"Don't worry about Freddy," he said gently.

She looked up at him then, her blue eyes very trusting, and he was reminded of when she was small and motherless and utterly dependent upon him.

A wave of love washed over him.

"Everything will be all right," he said.

He hoped it was true.

Mercier's was a pretty little place. When Henry and Marianne arrived, it was already bustling with custom.

A young woman in a black gown with a crisp white apron approached them, her hands folded at her waist.

"Good afternoon," Henry said. "Do you have a table free?"

"We have one left," the young woman replied, smiling. "If you don't mind sitting in the corner?"

"Not at all," Henry said. "Lead the way."

She led them to a table out of sight of the main door. Henry fussed over Marianne, getting her settled before taking his own chair.

They ordered tea and a plate of assorted cakes and pastries. Despite how busy the place was, everything arrived quite promptly, and Henry watched in amazement as Marianne worked her way through a *canelé*, a *conversation*, and a *Charlotte russe*.

"You didn't used to even like sweet things," he said in amazement.

"I know!" she exclaimed, blue eyes wide. "But ever since

the sickness wore off, I've been *gorging* on them." She sighed and took another spoonful of thick Bavarian cream, before adding, "Can we get some more tea?"

"Of course," Henry said, swivelling in his chair. He looked for the young woman who had seated them earlier, but instead an older man, scanning the tables with the air of a proprietor checking on his customers, caught his eye.

Henry's immediate impression was of a tidy, alert fellow with a pleasant expression. His next thought was that the man was oddly familiar. And then, as the man began to move towards their table, a polite smile on his face, Henry thought...

...*That's Jean-Jacques.*

Years before, this man had been a beautiful, lissom boy, all black hair and gleaming eyes and pouting lips—very popular at the Golden Lily, the brothel where Henry had met Christopher. Henry had been Christopher's protector then, and Jean-Jacques had been Christopher's closest friend.

Now Jean-Jacques must be around forty years old. He was still handsome, but the extravagant beauty of his youth had faded to something less eye-catching. Now he was a nice-looking, respectable sort of gentleman. Was he the proprietor of Mercier's, or the manager perhaps?

Actually... Mercier. Was that not Jean-Jacques's name? Jean-Jacques Mercier?

Henry saw the moment that Jean-Jacques recognised him in return, a brief flicker of shock, quickly veiled. The smoothing of his expression to blankness.

"Monsieur?" he said smoothly when he reached the table. "How may I help you?" Astonishingly, his accent was as thick as ever.

Somehow Henry managed to ask for more tea, and amazingly, the voice that came out of his mouth was calm and certain. But even as he placed the order, his mind was racing.

Was Jean-Jacques still friends with Christopher, he wondered? Might he have news of him?

Would Henry even want to know if he did?

Jean-Jacques glided away, and Henry watched him go, his heart thudding hard.

News of Christopher Redford was something that Henry had never permitted himself to seek out. Not on any of his rare visits to town, not by discreet inquiry, not by asking any former acquaintances who might happen to know.

After all, Christopher had signalled quite clearly his lack of interest in Henry.

Nevertheless, Henry had always wondered. And now, seeing Jean-Jacques here—well, it was tempting to take the opportunity to find out the answers to all the questions that had plagued Henry for so long. How had Christopher's life proceeded after Henry left? Was he well? Happy? Had he retired from his old profession, as Jean-Jacques appeared to have done?

Christopher would be forty—no, one-and-forty—now. So many years had passed that it was entirely possible Henry would walk past Christopher in the street without knowing him.

Perhaps he already had.

Yet he had known Jean-Jacques. Known him in an instant.

"Papa?"

Henry started at Marianne's voice. "Sorry," he said, dredging up a smile from somewhere. "I was miles away. What were you saying?"

She began talking again, imparting some family news from Mathilda that Henry nodded along to without quite taking it in. As hard as he tried to listen, his attention was fractured.

The tea, when it arrived, was brought by the same young woman who had shown them to their table before, and when

Henry discreetly glanced around, he saw no sign of Jean-Jacques.

Eventually Marianne set her cup down on the saucer. "As much as I should love to eat that last *canelé*, I shall resist. I am fit to burst." She sent him an accusing look. "You hardly ate a thing."

Henry glanced down at the barely touched *choux* pastry on his plate. "I wasn't very hungry."

Marianne sighed. "I see that."

Henry turned his head and caught the young woman's eye, signalling that they were finished. She nodded and turned away, then returned to their table with a neatly written receipt on a small silver tray. Henry paid their bill, adding an extra coin for the young woman, who smiled brightly in thanks.

"Everything was delicious," Marianne said. "Please do pass on my compliments to the kitchen—is the pastry cook French?"

"My mother is the pastry cook, ma'am," the young woman said, bobbing a small curtsey. "She and my father own Mercier's, and yes, they are both French, though they have lived in England many years now."

Henry glanced at her, noticing for the first time that she had the same dark hair and eyes as Jean-Jacques. The same fine features.

"Your father is the gentleman who was on the floor earlier?" he asked.

"Yes, sir. Monsieur Mercier himself," she replied, smiling. She lifted the silver tray. "Thank you for your custom."

They rose from their chairs and wove their way through the maze of tables to the front door. There was no sign at all of Jean-Jacques, and Henry's stomach knotted as he wondered if the man was avoiding him.

Perhaps Jean-Jacques was simply being discreet. That would be the sensible thing to do, after all.

Once outside, they made their way to the waiting carriage.

"The *conversations* were delicious," Marianne said wistfully. "I swear I could eat a half dozen for breakfast every day."

Henry chuckled. "Shall I buy you some more to take home?"

"Oh, yes," Marianne said, perking up. "Why didn't I think of that?"

Henry's heart began to race a little.

"Let's get you settled in the carriage," he said. "Then I'll go back and fetch some."

Marianne beamed at him. "Thank you, Papa."

In short order, Henry was entering the tea room again. The same young woman greeted him, and he placed the order with her, assuring her he was happy to wait a few minutes.

He opened his mouth then, to ask if he might speak to her father, when Jean-Jacques himself emerged from behind the counter, visibly startling at the sight of Henry.

Henry stepped toward Jean-Jacques. "Monsieur Mercier," he said. "I wonder if I might beg a word in private while I wait for the order I just placed."

Jean-Jacques scowled—actually *scowled*—but after a moment he gave a short nod. "Very well," he said succinctly. "Follow me, please."

He led Henry behind the counter and through a narrow corridor that Henry presumed ultimately led to the kitchens, given the mingled scents of caramel, caraway, ginger, and orange that drifted towards them.

Before they reached the kitchens, however, Jean-Jacques opened a door and led Henry into a small office. He closed the door behind them and turned to Henry, his expression cool.

"What do you want, your grace?"

"So, you did recognise me."

"Of course," Jean-Jacques said, giving a familiar Gallic

shrug that Henry recognised as a gesture of his from the old days. "Though why you wish to speak to me after twenty years, I can't imagine."

"Can't you?" Henry asked, somewhat taken aback by the man's faint hostility.

Jean-Jacques's expression tightened. "No."

Henry eyed him uncertainly for a moment, but he had to ask now, having come this far. "Do you—that is, are you still friends with Christopher Redford?"

Jean-Jacques's gaze hardened, and for a long, terrible moment, Henry wondered if he was about to tell Henry something awful. That something had happened to Christopher, perhaps. Henry's heart squeezed painfully in his chest.

But then, to his relief, Jean-Jacques said coolly, "Yes. We are still friends. Why do you ask?"

The relief was so huge that, for a moment, all Henry could do was exhale a long breath. "I thought you were going to tell me something had happened to him," he said.

Jean-Jacques seemed unmoved by this confession, standing silently as he waited for Henry to answer his last question.

"Can you tell me how he is?" Henry asked at last, shocked by how breathless he sounded.

Jean-Jacques frowned. "Forgive me, but I find the question very strange. It has been twenty years—"

"Eighteen," Henry interrupted.

Jean-Jacques eyed him curiously. "Close enough," he said, shrugging. "The point is, it is many years since you left Kit, and you did not ask after him then—and not in any of the years following. But you see me today, and suddenly you want to know?"

Henry swallowed hard. "I behaved rather shabbily, I know," he said. "I should have said goodbye to him in person, but in the circumstances, I thought he would understand." He broke off at the sight of Jean-Jacques's furious expression. "Why are you looking at me like that?"

Jean-Jacques turned away, giving Henry his back. "I don't know what you mean," he said roughly.

"You looked angry," Henry said. "Why?" A strange sense of foreboding was building in his chest.

Slowly, Jean-Jacques turned. His expression was back to being polite again, his gaze remote.

"Your grace," he said quietly, with the air of man who planned to bring the conversation to an end. "Kit is well and quite settled. I believe he has put the past behind him."

"Is he—?"

Jean-Jacques held up a hand. "That is all I can tell you. It is for Kit to decide what else to share with you after everything that happened."

Everything that happened?

"What do you mean?" Henry said faintly. "What happened? Other than my going back to Wiltshire?"

He caught another betraying flicker of emotion in Jean-Jacques's eyes.

Disgust.

Henry had known Jean-Jacques as a pert, provocative prostitute, given to sharp observations and sly humour. He had been outspoken in those days. Now he was reserved, careful. A respectable business proprietor with much to lose at the hands of a powerful aristocrat.

"There is nothing more I can say," he said. "You must speak to Kit if you want to know more."

And God, but *there was some story here*, Henry realised sickly. Something he did not know about from his own past.

"Can you give me his direction then?" Henry asked. Was that really his voice, asking for Kit's direction? Was he really considering doing something he had sworn he would never do?

Jean-Jacques stared at him for several moments, then he

shook his head. "I cannot do that, but I will pass on the message that you would like to meet, if you wish. Then it will be for Kit to decide."

Henry nodded, his heart racing. "I will come back on Thursday for his answer," he said. "If that suits?"

Jean-Jacques nodded. "Very well."

He conducted Henry back out into the tea room then immediately excused himself. After another minute, Jean-Jacques's daughter arrived with the pastries, all neatly tied up in paper and string. Henry paid and left, and returned to the carriage.

He smiled distractedly as Marianne chattered all the way back to Curzon Street, but the whole time he was thinking of Christopher.

Wondering what it was that Jean-Jacques would not tell him.

5

KIT

Kit did not like to rush his mornings. Since he was generally at the club till very late, he rarely rose before ten and would usually enjoy a leisurely breakfast and read the newspapers before he got to work.

And so it was that, when there was a rap at the dining room door at eleven o'clock on Wednesday morning, he was still wearing his favourite turquoise dressing gown as he sipped his fourth cup of tea and perused an article about the upcoming general election.

"Come in."

Tom, resplendent in his new footman garb, opened the door and announced, "*Mee-syoo-mer-see* to see you, sir."

Kit frowned, puzzled. "I beg your pardon?"

But already his guest—*Monsieur Mercier*, Kit saw—was strolling past Tom and setting two beautifully-wrapped boxes of cakes on the table while Tom bowed solemnly and withdrew.

"Jean-Jacques," Kit said, smiling warmly. "It's good to see you."

"And you," Jean-Jacques replied, tossing up the tails of his coat as he sat himself down. "The cakes are from Evie."

"Thank her for me."

"I will," Jean-Jacques assured him. "New footman, *mon amie*?"

"Yes," Kit said. He sighed. "Very new."

"Do you need such a fancy piece?" Jean-Jacques asked, one eyebrow raised. His French accent was still very thick, despite a quarter of a century in London. "Though I admit, I see the appeal—this one is handsome as a god. Are you...?" He trailed off with a suggestive look.

Kit rolled his eyes at the predictable response. Everyone who walked through his door panted after Tom.

"No," he said. "He was working at the club before this, but he doesn't lean that way. He wanted to get out of the game, so I agreed to let him come here and learn on the job, as it were. Clara's teaching him his letters and numbers in the evenings."

Six months from now, Tom would have choices. Choices were everything, but sometimes you needed someone to give you an opportunity, a way to get on the right path before life beat you down too much to change.

"A pity," Jean-Jacques observed. Then he waved his hand in an airy, dismissive gesture. "Well, never mind. Plenty more fish in the lake, yes?"

Kit sighed. "I'm not looking for a—fish."

"Everyone needs a fish," Jean-Jacques said kindly. "It is a fact of life. We are pairing creatures, like swans, or—"

"Jean-Jacques," Kit interrupted, reaching forward to pat his hand. "I don't know whether I'm a man or a fish or a bird at this point. But whatever I am, I can assure you I'm quite happy on my own. Now, tell me this: to what do I owe the pleasure of this visit?"

Jean-Jacques had been his usual merry self until Kit asked that question, but now a troubled expression crossed his face. He had a most expressive face, and Kit knew him very well. They'd met when they both worked at the Golden Lily and had become close friends. Like Kit, Jean-Jacques had had a careful eye to the future. He'd carefully saved generous parting gifts from several wealthy protectors to build up the funds he needed to marry his sweetheart, Evie, and set up his business. Now his life was good, his small family happy. Kit could not think what might have happened to make him look so worried.

"What's wrong?" Kit said, frowning. "Is it Evie? Or one of the girls?"

Jean-Jacques shook his head. "No, no, nothing like that. All is well with us, *mon amie*. It is just"—he broke off and took a deep breath—"someone came to Mercier's yesterday. A man I have not seen for many years. I think he was quite shocked to see me, but then... he asked after you, Kit, and wanted your address."

Kit's first thought was, *please not Lionel Skelton*, and his stomach began to roil with anxiety. He had only seen Skelton twice since that long-ago night when the man had beaten him senseless. But on each of those occasions, Skelton had looked at him with such hatred Kit had been worried for days afterwards.

"Who was it?" Kit managed, through stiff lips.

Jean-Jacques was silent for a moment, then he said gravely, "It was your duke."

"My *duke*?" Kit repeated, his tone disbelieving. "My— wait, you can't mean *Henry*? He would never—" Kit's head began to swim and his heart to thud in slow, slugging beats. He took a long, shuddering breath and let it out in a *whoosh*.

"Kit," Jean-Jacques said gently, worriedly. "Are you all right?"

"Yes, yes, of course," Kit said faintly. Then he added, "He's not my duke." It seemed vital to clarify that, for some reason. Perhaps to remind himself.

Henry Asquith had never been Kit's.

Jean-Jacques didn't answer, but his gaze was pitying.

The silence stretched, and still Kit's heart hammered. At last he said, his voice hoarse, "You say he was shocked. Didn't he know you owned Mercier's before he arrived?"

"No, I am quite certain of that. There was a woman with him. She was with child. I think he almost fell off the chair when he saw me."

Kit's mouth twisted. "He must have been horrified. I'm surprised he didn't run away with his tail between his legs." He tried to imagine the scene, Henry sitting in Mercier's with a pregnant lady, only for Jean-Jacques to hove into view. He wondered if Henry had flushed—he used to flush very easily, when he was embarrassed or felt uncomfortable.

Another thought occurred to him then—Kit had learned a few years ago that Caroline, the wife Henry had practically worshipped, had passed away. Henry must have married again. But that was to be expected, he supposed.

"I was surprised when he asked to speak to me," Jean-Jacques said. "At first, he pretended not to recognise me, and left with the lady—I thought that would be the end of it. But then he came back and asked for a word in private."

"What did he want?" Kit hated that he cared what the answer to that question was.

"News of you. I said I found it strange that he was asking. And he said—" Jean-Jacques broke off. He pressed his lips together and shook his head.

"What? What did he say?"

Jean-Jacques met his gaze. "That he behaved shabbily towards you by not saying goodbye in person—but he thought you would understand."

Kit hated how much that hurt. Enough time had passed, and enough had happened that such careless words shouldn't affect him in the least. But they did. Because Henry hadn't just *"behaved shabbily"*—he had broken their agreement entirely. Had effectively swindled Kit.

"Understand?" Kit said incredulously. "Understand what? Being cheated?"

Jean-Jacques gave a little shrug that was part mystified, part I-told-you-so.

"I was such an idiot," Kit groaned.

"I think I said so at the time," Jean-Jacques agreed.

Kit sighed. "Yes, I know. And so did Mabel and everyone else with half a brain, but I was stupid and stubborn and—"

"—in love," Jean-Jacques completed for him.

"Infatuated," Kit amended.

Jean-Jacques's gaze was sympathetic. "You thought he would come back, didn't you?"

Kit let his head fall back and stared at the ceiling. "I suppose I did," he admitted. "I hoped he'd wake up one day and realise he missed me." He scoffed at himself quietly. "I was a very foolish boy."

After a moment, he raised his head and met Jean-Jacques's steady gaze. "So how did you respond to him?"

Jean-Jacques shook his head unhappily. "I wanted to give him a part of my mind, but—how could I, Kit? The man is a duke, and I am just a—a man with a little bit of a business." He shook his head, his expression disgusted. "But I should have said something."

"No," Kit said firmly. "You did the right thing. Besides, Evie would have my spleen if you got into an argument with a duke over my head."

Jean-Jacques gave a dry laugh. "Very true."

"So," Kit said gently. "*Did* you tell him how I was?"

"Only that you were in good health and settled. I said there was no more I could share with him without your agreement. That was when he asked for your direction, and I said I could not give that either but I would ask you if you would agree to meet. I said I would let him have your answer tomorrow."

Kit gave an incredulous laugh.

"*Oui!*" Jean-Jacques exclaimed. "You could have knocked me down with a bird."

"Feather," Kit said absently.

Jean-Jacques gave a Gallic wave of dismissal.

"I can't believe he wants to meet me," Kit said at last. It was incredible. What had prompted such a notion? After all these years?

"Would you consider it?" Jean-Jacques asked curiously.

"It's been so long," Kit hedged.

"Eighteen years, your duke said."

Kit looked up, a little surprised. "That's right."

He tried to imagine what Henry might look like now, but all he could think of was Henry all those years ago, not quite thirty years old. He'd seemed so mature to Kit back then. Strange to think that if Kit met that Henry now, he would probably think of him as a mere boy.

Today's Henry was seven-and-forty. Only six years Kit's senior. Those six years had mattered a great deal when they had first known one another, but they meant very little now. The years between had equalised them in maturity, if nothing else.

Kit was a very different man now from the innocent Henry had once known. Well, perhaps "innocent" was a bit much. A boy who'd grown up in a brothel and serviced his first client at sixteen had no business calling himself an innocent—but in his way he had been quite naive.

When he looked back now at how he'd behaved after Henry had left him, he cringed to think what a foolish, idealistic boy he had been. It was not, even then, that he'd believed Henry had loved him—he had not been that stupid—but he *had* thought there might be a little affection there, enough to at least earn him the right to a farewell delivered in person.

Instead, he'd been given fifty pounds, his marching orders, and a single day to remove himself from the little house in Paddington Green. The news had been delivered not by Henry, but by his man of business, Silas Parkinson. And it hadn't been so much a farewell as a warning to stay away from Henry or risk losing the use of his legs.

Mabel—also known as Madame Georgette of the Golden Lily and the broker of his arrangement with Henry—had been furious at Henry's breach of the agreement. She had negotiated generous terms at the outset: Kit was to get the house and three hundred pounds as a parting gift, twenty per cent of which was due to her. She'd wanted to expose Henry for breaking the contract, but like an idiot, Kit had begged her not to do it, unable to bear the thought of bringing ruin to Henry, notwithstanding his shabby behaviour. And yes, perhaps hoping that Henry would have a change of heart.

Kit had given Mabel the fifty pounds Silas Parkinson had paid him. And then, after weeks had passed with no sign of Henry, and without consulting Mabel further, he'd foolishly leapt into the bloody awful disaster that had been his arrangement with Lionel Skelton. All to make sure he'd be able to pay up on his IOU to Mabel promptly and show her he could manage on his own.

Of course, the arrangement with Skelton had turned out to be a far, far worse mistake than any he'd made before. The misery of those four months had finally come to an end the night Skelton had beaten Kit half to death. By some miracle, Kit had survived the night he'd spent naked and unconscious on the bedchamber floor. When he'd awoken in the early hours, shivering and in agony, he'd realised he must get away if worse was not to befall him when Skelton returned. Somehow he'd managed to dress and had left the house by the servants' door, making his way back to the Lily to throw himself on Mabel's mercy.

He'd worried she'd tell him she'd washed her hands of him and send him away, but instead she'd *tsked* and taken him in, nursing him herself and personally negotiating the terms of the severance with Skelton.

And of course, she'd let him have a piece of her mind.

"You're a fool, Kit Redford," she'd told him sharply. "Lucky for you I was so fond of your mother."

Kit had been in a bad way for several weeks after Skelton's assault on him, recovering from broken ribs and fingers and whatever internal injuries had been inflicted that had him pissing blood and deaf in one ear. As he'd waited for his hurts to heal and his spectacular bruising to fade, he'd had plenty of time to dwell on the pain of Henry's betrayal—something he had assiduously avoided thinking about before then. But lying there in his sick bed, Kit had finally had to accept just how absurd and misplaced his feelings for Henry Asquith had been. Like a stray dog, Kit had fixed his affection and loyalty on a man who had neither asked for nor deserved such gifts.

The hearing in Kit's left ear never did return, but the other injuries had mended, in time. And life had gone on. After that, Kit followed Mabel's advice to the letter. An experience like the one he'd lived through with Skelton did not leave a man with even the dregs of romantic idiocy.

Unfortunately, by this time, it was being whispered in discreet circles that Kit had been thrown out summarily by his last two protectors and that there must be a reason for it. Rumours began circulating that he had thieved from them, or worse, and for a while it had seemed that no one else would touch him. But Mabel was nothing if not resourceful. She managed to secure a short contract for him with Phineas Warren, an elderly banker with a penchant for pretty young men in corsets. And they didn't come prettier than Kit.

Kit had had to swallow his pride for that one—not only had his price dropped humiliatingly low, he'd had to agree to Phin's desire to display him publicly however he wished. But in the end, it turned out well for him. Phin was no fool—a more sceptical, sharp-minded man one could not hope to meet—but his temperament was sweet and he'd grown very fond of Kit. He'd extended their arrangement to a year then renewed it twice more, each time with more generous terms.

The duration of their relationship and Kit's loyalty to Phin had restored Kit's reputation as a trustworthy man. What's more, Phin's final parting gift had provided Kit with everything he needed to open Redford's.

And so, finally, Kit had been able to put his mistakes behind him and get off the game. And in the years since then, he had not rented out his body to anyone—or rented anyone else's for his own pleasure for that matter. Now he restricted himself to his companionable suppers in Clapham with intelligent conversation, good food and wine, and unapologetic sex afterwards with likeminded men who treated him like an equal. Men who didn't mind him being forceful about what he wanted, instead of always expecting him to bend to their desires.

"Kit?"

Kit looked up to find Jean-Jacques regarding him with concern.

"I'm sorry," he said. "I got rather lost in my thoughts."

"I understand," Jean-Jacques said gently. "So, what is your message? Will you meet your duke? Or not?"

It was tempting. Tempting to see Henry and let him know exactly what Kit thought of him. Henry had probably thought that a contract with a whore wasn't worth the paper it was written on. Or perhaps he'd thought that, since Kit had not served out the whole year of their contract by the time Henry dropped him, he was not entitled to the severance terms. Whatever his excuse was, Kit would soon put him right. For a moment, he pictured Henry begging his forgiveness... and then he grimaced at his own idiocy. He was being absurd. Self-indulgent and, actually, downright pathetic. Why would Henry care that Kit had suffered? Had Kit learned *nothing*? Henry Asquith did not deserve a single moment of his time.

Firming his resolve, Kit said, "No, I am not going to meet him. There is no reason to after all these years."

Jean-Jacques nodded. "I think you are wise, *mon amie*. Is there any other message you wish me to give him?"

Kit considered that. The truth was, he wanted to take a swipe at Henry Asquith, and this was his last chance to do so. "Tell him that if he has something to say to me, to send Parkinson to do his dirty work instead of imposing on my friends."

When Jean-Jacques looked puzzled, Kit explained, "Parkinson's his man of business—that's who he sent to throw me out."

Jean-Jacques shook his head disgustedly.

Kit smiled crookedly. "I don't really expect you to deliver that message," he said. "I'm sorry you're getting dragged into this at all."

Jean-Jacques shrugged. "If I think I won't get into trouble over it, I will pass your message on." He quirked a half-smile. "And if I don't, I will bring you something nice from Evie to make up for it."

"If it's a choice between Evie's pastries or revenge," Kit said, smiling, "I'm willing to pass on the revenge."

6

HENRY

The two days between Henry visiting Mercier's the first time and going back dragged terribly. He occupied himself with business matters and unavoidable social calls, but he could not quite fasten his attention on anything.

On Thursday morning he rose early, breakfasted alone, and left the house before anyone else was up. He walked through town then spent some time in a coffee house reading —or rather staring unseeingly at—a newspaper. Eventually, at eleven o'clock, he made his way to Mercier's.

Once again, it was busy when he arrived. A group of older ladies occupied two of the larger tables while the smaller tables around them were taken by couples and families. Children tucked into their ices and pastries while young ladies giggled over the rims of their teacups.

The same young woman greeted him as last time.

"I'm afraid we don't have any tables just now, sir," she said apologetically.

"That's all right. I'm actually here to see Monsieur Mercier. Could you let him know? He's expecting me, I believe."

She looked puzzled. "Oh, I see. Who should I say is asking, sir?"

"The Duke of Avesbury."

Her eyes widened and she looked quite flustered. "Oh, I'm sorry! I had no idea, your—your—"

"Grace," he supplied gently. "But don't fret about it. It's quite all right."

She smiled gratefully and did an awkward bob of a curtsey. "If you don't mind waiting a moment, I'll just fetch him, your grace. Excuse me, please."

She hurried away, disappearing through the back of the shop.

A minute or two later, she reappeared with Jean-Jacques trailing behind her.

"Your grace," he said, his French accent very pronounced. "Please, come this way."

Without waiting for an answer, he turned on his heel and walked away, leaving Henry to follow and his daughter to stare after them, plainly astonished by her father's barely concealed rudeness, towards a duke no less.

Jean-Jacques showed Henry into the same small office as before, closing the door carefully behind them.

"So," he said. "You are back."

"I am. Have you seen Christopher?"

"Yes." Jean-Jacques's tone was very flat and somehow quite final.

Dread seeded in Henry's chest. He cleared his throat. "And what did he say?"

Jean-Jacques's lips tightened and he looked away. "I'm afraid Kit sees no point in meeting with you. So many years, you know."

Henry swallowed. "Did he have any message for me?"

Jean-Jacques met Henry's gaze again. For a long time he said nothing, his eyes searching Henry's face, then he sighed and said in a weary tone, "Kit said that you should send your servant, Mr. Parkinson, to do your dirty work instead of asking me."

Henry stared at Jean-Jacques, shocked. At last he said carefully, *"Parkinson?"*

Jean-Jacques's eyes glinted with anger. "Don't you remember? He's the servant you sent to throw Kit out."

"Throw him… what? Out of where?"

"Where he was living," Jean-Jacques snapped. "The house that you agreed to give him."

Henry stared at the man in disbelief. His mind couldn't seem to absorb the words, but his body was ahead of him, his heart suddenly racing and his palms sweating.

Parkinson.

Faintly he said, "I think you must be mistaken. The house you speak of belongs to Christopher, not to me. Or at least it did."

Jean-Jacques's expression, already unfriendly, darkened to anger.

"That is not the sort of thing a man makes a mistake over," he said harshly. "And I can assure you, I recall those events very well myself. Your servant threw Kit out on your orders, *your grace."* His nostrils flared with barely concealed fury. "At least have the decency to own your actions."

Henry closed his eyes for a long moment. He did not know what had happened—but *Parkinson* was involved.

Flatly, he said, "I never threw Kit out. I swear."

Jean-Jacques's expression was scornful, the veneer of politeness ripped away. "No? What would you call it?"

"How could I throw him out of his own house? It was his. I made it over to him after—" After he left for Wiltshire with Caroline, in those first awful weeks of the worst year of his life. He shook his head, dislodging the memory and turned his attention back to Jean-Jacques. "Please," he said. "Can't you tell me where Christopher is? I have to speak to him."

But the black eyes that met his own were hard and

unyielding. "I cannot," Jean-Jacques said. "Kit does not want to meet with you. And now, your grace, I think it is time you were on your way."

After leaving Mercier's, Henry stood on the street outside for several minutes, his mind racing. At length, he decided to call on Simon Reid, the solicitor who dealt with his personal business—and who had handled the chaos of the Parkinson debacle.

Reid's offices were at Serjeant's Inn, just off Fleet Street. Since it wasn't very far, and Henry needed to walk off some of his agitation, he dismissed his carriage and made his way by foot.

The walk did nothing to calm him, though. By the time he arrived, he had worked himself up even more. He barrelled into the office, barely pausing to glance at the two clerks sitting at their desks and strode past, making for Reid's office.

One of the clerks followed him.

"Excuse me, your grace, Mr. Reid is presently busy—"

"He won't mind me interrupting." Henry absently cast the words over his shoulder just as he thrust the door open.

"Reid," he said urgently. "I have to speak to you! I've discovered something that—" He broke off. Reid was not alone. He was standing by his desk with two men. One was tall and dark and somewhat familiar, though Henry could not place him. The other was red-haired and slender. "Oh," Henry said, brought up short. "I do beg your pardon."

Reid blinked, surprised, but quickly collected himself. "Your grace—" he began, then glanced at the two men with an apologetic expression.

The red-haired man smiled. "It's no trouble," he said in a pleasant Scottish burr. "We were just about to leave anyway." He glanced at the taller man who smiled his agreement, and they began to move towards the door. Henry stood aside to let them pass.

"I'll see you out," Reid said to the two men, then, glancing at Henry, added, "I'll be back momentarily."

Henry paced the rug in front of the fireplace till Reid returned, closing the door quietly behind him.

"Has something happened, your grace?" Reid asked worriedly. "You seem very anxious."

"I need you to check something for me," Henry said. "Right away—without delay—it's of the utmost importance."

Reid's brow wrinkled with concern, and he moved towards his desk. "Of course," he said. "Whatever you need. Won't you sit down?"

Henry felt some of the tension inside him ease. He could confide fully in Reid—Reid was not only Henry's solicitor, he shared Henry's inclinations and they had certain mutual acquaintances. Indeed, it was Henry's oldest and must trusted friend, Viscount Corbett, who had introduced them.

"Do you want a drink?" Reid asked now, frowning. "You look like you've had a shock."

Henry nodded, sinking into the chair on the other side of Reid's desk, while Reid fetched him a glass of brandy. He took a deep breath, rubbing the tense spot between his brows as he tried to collect himself.

When Reid set the brandy down in front of him, he immediately reached for it, taking a deep swallow and flinching at the burn in his throat.

"So," Reid said. "Tell me what you need me to help you with."

"I need you to check the title of a property I once owned in Paddington Green. I gifted it to someone a number of years ago—eighteen to be precise— but it seems it may not have reached the intended recipient."

Reid met Henry's gaze. "Given the timing, I have to wonder if this is another Parkinson matter."

Henry nodded miserably. "I think so. I'm hoping not, but I can't think of any other explanation, and his name's already been mentioned."

"I thought we'd got to the bottom of everything." Reid frowned, thinking, then looked up. "A missing house would be new though. It is not an easy thing to remove from a man's estate without him noticing."

"No," Henry agreed, "but if anyone had the sheer gall to try, it would be him."

Silas Parkinson had been Henry's father's man of business, and Henry had inherited him along with the dukedom. Having known the man since childhood, he had trusted him implicitly. Just as his father had done. Parkinson had simply... always been there. When Henry had sat at his father's elbow as a very young man, learning the business of the dukedom, Parkinson had always been with them, quietly noting and carrying out each and every instruction of his father without question. It didn't matter what it was: from the everyday carrying out of estate business, to the settling of gambling debts, to the arrangement of prostitutes for his father's entertainments at his hunting box. Parkinson hadn't blinked an eye at any of it.

"*He's an extremely reliable fellow,*" his father had once said to Henry. "*Utterly discreet and totally dedicated to protecting the family name — as well he might be, for the sums I pay him.*"

And it was true, in a way. Parkinson *had* been discreet, and he had protected the family name at all costs. And yes, when he was asked to do any task, he carried it out with admirable efficiency. But it was only when he had died, quite unexpectedly following a sudden heart seizure, eleven years ago now, that Henry had discovered the full extent of the rewards the man had been taking in exchange for his loyalty.

It was Harry Trimble, the man Henry had engaged to replace Parkinson, who had first alerted him to the discrepancies in the ledgers. Trimble had suggested a detailed examination of all the account books and records be undertaken to get to the bottom of the matter, and Henry, worried about what incriminating information might be found in those old papers, had gone to Corbett for help. That was when Corbett had introduced Henry to Simon Reid, vouchsafing that Reid was a man who could be trusted.

Reid had set about the matter with typical efficiency, sending his associate, Alun Jones, to Wiltshire to painstakingly go through the estate records. Jones had examined every entry in every ledger, and every single page in the voluminous boxes of papers pertaining to the estate. Quiet and unassuming, Jones had spent three long months at Avesbury House working his way through decades of documents. At the end of it, he had presented Henry with a file of evidence that showed the fraud Parkinson had committed, together with a box of papers relating to Henry's personal affairs that Henry had promptly locked away. The file had shown that Parkinson had been stealing from the ducal estate for years, long before Henry had inherited the title.

After that, Reid had spent a couple of years trying to track down the money Parkinson had embezzled, but most of it had been spent meeting the man's gambling debts. Eventually, Henry had given up on any further attempts at recovering the losses, and Reid had closed the case.

So far as Henry had been aware, Parkinson's fraud had been restricted to stealing money. But now he had to wonder. Christopher was supposed to get the property at Paddington Green when their contract ended. Parkinson had known that —he'd told Henry it was taken care of, and Henry had not questioned the matter.

Over those difficult first few weeks and months after leaving London, Parkinson had come to Avesbury House several times, on each occasion with a sheaf of documents to be signed by Henry. Documents that, Henry recalled, he had, uncharacteristically, signed without reading.

Had Parkinson seen an opportunity, and taken a chance?

Was it possible that he had stolen Christopher's rightful entitlement?

"What's the address of the property?" Reid asked, and Henry gave it to him, watching as the man wrote it on his blotter.

"And what is it you want to know about it?" Reid continued. "The current owner, I assume. Anything else?"

"As much as possible," Henry said. "Who owns it now, and anyone else who has owned it in the last eighteen years."

Reid eyed him curiously, but he nodded. "Very well."

"I need to know the position as soon as possible," Henry said. "Can you get to the bottom of the matter today?"

Reid looked doubtful. "Unlikely, but I'll see what I can do. If you wish, I can call by the house this evening on my way home to let you know what progress I've made?"

"Please do," Henry said. "I'm anxious to discover the truth as soon as possible."

7

KIT

By Thursday, Betty was feeling quite well and Clara was able to return to work, so Kit decided to leave Clara to deal with the club for the afternoon while he paid his fortnightly visit to Mabel Butcher.

Mabel had been known as *La Tigresse* at the height of her courtesan career. Later, she had become Madame Georgette, the presiding madam of the select Golden Lily brothel. But these days, almost ten years after her retirement, she preferred to use her rather more prosaic given name, and had adopted the persona of a respectable elderly widow.

Theirs was a strange relationship. Mabel had, after all, been the madam of the brothel where Kit had worked. She had procured patrons for his services. She had also left him to the not-so-tender mercies of Lionel Skelton, just because she had lost her temper with him for refusing to follow her advice about Henry Asquith. She had been hard-nosed and bad-tempered sometimes. But on other occasions, she had protected him fiercely, and she had nursed him when Skelton had beaten him, and looked after his money when he was being foolish. And when he wanted to get out of the game and build something of his own, she had given him endless help and advice.

She had never once in her life been soft with him, but she had looked after him, in her way.

She wouldn't have done those things for just anyone. She did them for Kit because of Minnie.

Minnie, Kit's mother, had died when he was not quite fifteen. She'd been a whore at the Golden Lily too. And she'd been something else to Mabel—even now, he wasn't sure precisely what.

The illness that had killed Minnie had come on quick and ended painfully. Mabel had never shown her soft side with Minnie before then—not that Kit had ever seen, at least—but that changed when Minnie was dying. In those last few weeks, Mabel had often sat with her through the night, dabbing her fevered face and neck with cool cloths, murmuring soft, soothing words, and spooning powerful medicine from a small blue bottle between her lips when the pain got too much.

Kit, young and terrified, had been grateful for her presence. She wasn't always there—sometimes Kit sat with his mother on his own—but she was there as often as she could be, and she was there when Kit had to eat or sleep.

She was there at the very end, on the night Minnie died.

It was late when it happened, in the early hours of the morning. Kit had been so weary, but he'd been afraid to leave his mother, feeling sure that if he did, she'd be gone when he woke.

He'd been curled up in an armchair, draped in a blanket and half asleep, while Mabel watched over his mother. There'd been almost no light in the chamber at all—only the dimmest glow from the fireplace—when his mother's breathing had begun to rattle strangely. The sound had roused him.

At the very moment he'd opened his eyes, his mother had rasped, "You got to look out for Kit, Mabel. Promise me."

"Course I will, Min," Mabel had said roughly. Her voice hadn't been like it normally was, all clipped and tight. Instead, it had been hoarse with emotion, and common as his mother's.

She'd been leaning over Minnie. To this day, that picture was burned in Kit's memory. It had been too dark to see her expression, but the defeated rounding of her shoulders in shadow had told its own story, as had her rumpled dress and disordered hair. He remembered her profile, hovering over Minnie's slight, still form.

That stillness.

Kit had understood—profoundly understood—in that moment that his mother's spirit had gone. He hadn't seen any evidence of it leaving her body—he hadn't been able to see anything of his mother at all in the shadowy room beyond the outline of her slender form. But he had known, somehow, the instant she was gone.

Mabel had made a sound, then, one that Kit had never heard before or since. It was a cracking, terrible sound that he felt sure was what a heart breaking sounded like.

She'd bent and kissed Minnie. Kissed her on the mouth. Kissed her with a passionate grief that Kit had never witnessed before. It had been so raw, so intimate, he'd had to look away.

Mabel had never explained to Kit why her grief had been so terrible or what Minnie had meant to her. Prior to his mother's last days, he had never seen them share any particular physical affection. Even then, other than that final kiss, he had only ever seen them hold hands occasionally, as friends sometimes did.

Perhaps that was all they were: friends. Although, in that case, to say they were *only* friends would be to miss the point entirely. Perhaps, for them, being friends was everything. Friends who loved one another. Friends who were *in* love.

Or perhaps they were more, and Kit had never seen it.

He doubted he'd ever know for sure.

As Kit strolled towards Covent Garden, where Mabel now lived, he wondered if she might talk about his mother today. Lately, she'd been mentioning Minnie more often. But it was always just little things—impressions of what she'd been like. No real clue as to what they had been to one another.

"She sang like a nightingale."

"She was the prettiest girl any of us ever saw."

"Well, of course, all the gentleman wanted her."

The door to Mabel's small but comfortable house was answered by her companion, Gracie, a quiet, faded woman of indeterminate years who had materialised out of nowhere one day and was sometimes vaguely referred to as a "distant cousin".

"Good afternoon, Mr. Redford," she said, smiling politely. "Mrs. Butcher will be pleased to see you."

"I brought cakes," Kit said, handing over one of the boxes Jean-Jacques had brought the day before.

"Lovely," Gracie said, taking it from him. "I'll fetch some tea. You go on into the parlour."

"Is that you, Kit?" Mabel called out before he even reached the parlour door.

"It is," he said as he walked inside. "How are you today?"

"Tolerable well," she said, beckoning him over to her chair and offering him a cheek to kiss—she was becoming down-right affectionate in her dotage.

"You look lovely," he said, brushing her dry cheek with his lips. She was always nicely dressed, was Mabel. Today she wore a blue-grey gown with a high-necked, ruffled collar, and an intricate paisley shawl of deep rose pink, ivory, and blue. A dark-blue velvet turban covered her hair, which had begun to thin quite badly over the last few years.

"Well, thank you, kind sir," she said, winking at him. "I does me best to please."

Kit glanced over at the domed cage in the corner of the room and was pleased to see that Nell Gwyn, Mabel's parrot, appeared to be asleep.

"Is Gracie making tea?" Mabel asked.

"Yes, I brought some of those of little cakes you liked last time. *Financiers*, they're called."

Mabel frowned, thinking. Then her brow cleared. "Oh, them little sponge cakes?" she said. "They was quite nice, I must admit."

Kit grinned—getting a compliment out of Mabel was like getting blood out of a stone. This was high praise from her.

"Jean-Jacques brought me them," he said. "Everything Evie makes is delicious."

"*Hmmm*," Mabel replied. She'd never quite forgiven Evie for luring Jean-Jacques away from her.

"Is that a new gown?" Kit asked, as he settled himself down on Mabel's too-hard horsehair sofa as best he could. "I don't think I've seen it before. It's not your usual style."

Mabel sighed. "My dressmaker persuaded me into it," she said. "I wanted to stick with the same pattern I usually have her make up for me, but she kept saying no one gets their gowns made up like that anymore." She made a face. "I'm not awful keen on these new fashions. Bloody great sleeves like legs of mutton."

Her own sleeves only featured a very small puff at the shoulders, but Kit didn't comment.

"In my day," Mabel went on, "there was such a wonderful *looseness* of dress. So freeing, it was!" She gave a happy a sigh, then met Kit's gaze. "I say *in my day*, but in fairness, when I was young, it was as bad as now, if not worse—all stays and petticoats and being laced up and having your hair piled up as high as a bloody tower with paste and gawd knows what in it." She made a face. "But *then*, when I got to be a bit older—when I was making good money, shacked up with my old marquess—oh, the clothes I had then, Kit! Us working girls would just put our stockings on, pull a muslin gown over the top, and call ourselves dressed!" She laughed immoderately. "Why, you could have your la-las right on show and no one blinked an eye!"

"*Woo!*"

The piercing shriek from the cage in the corner made Kit jump.

Nell Gwyn was awake.

"*Woot-hoo!*" The parrot whistled, then, sing-song-like, "*Show me yer la-las!*"

Kit shuddered discreetly. The parrot's voice was uncannily like Mabel's, whilst being oddly flat and strange. Coming out of that of unmoving beak, it was like some kind of horrible magic. Between the talking and the endless, demented whistling, Nell Gwyn made him feel horribly unsettled, but Mabel adored the creature.

"Are you awake again, my angel?" she said now. "Kit, let Nell Gwyn out, will you?"

Kit got up and went over to the cage, undoing the little latch on the door and opening it so the bird could hop out. She was mostly grey and white, with an odd flapping bit of orangey-pink tail that Kit always thought looked tacked on and that made her look quite comical.

Just then, Gracie came in with the tea tray.

"*Woo-hoot!*" the parrot shrieked from the back of the chair she was perched on. "*Show us yer la-las, Gracie!*"

Gracie just about dropped the tea tray, and Kit had to rush to her side to help her balance it.

"Thank you," she gasped as he helped her lower it onto the table.

The unapologetic bird flapped lazily over to Mabel, coming to land first on the arm of her chair, before hopping up on to her shoulder and rubbing her head against Mabel's turban.

"You're a lovely girl, aren't you, Nelly?" Mabel crooned affectionately, and the bird whistled back in that uncanny way that was somehow both tuneless and musical. Mabel fished down the side of her chair and pulled out a somewhat crumpled reticule. Digging her hand in, she brought out a walnut and offered it to the bird. Nell Gwyn took hold of it in one large claw and started in on it with her powerful beak, scattering tiny pieces of shell all over Mabel's lap.

Mabel, seeming unperturbed, returned her attention to Kit. "So, what about you, Kit? What's your news?" She accepted a cup of tea from Gracie with a quick smile and immediately began to nibble the delicate *financier* balanced on the saucer.

Kit paused. For a moment, he considered telling her he'd had Henry Asquith asking to see him, but he wasn't sure he was up to listening to what would inevitably follow. Even after all these years, she could still wax lyrical about Henry's failings for an inordinately long time.

"I've not much news," he said. "Jean-Jacques popped by yesterday."

"How is he?" Mabel asked. "Still married to that ugly cook, I see." She held up the last morsel of the *financier* before popping it into her mouth.

"Don't be unpleasant. Evie isn't the least bit ugly, and you know it," Kit said repressively.

"Well, she ain't pretty," Mabel said. "Not like you."

Kit half laughed, half sighed. "Firstly, I'm not pretty, and secondly, I have never at any point in my life had designs on Jean-Jacques, so you needn't talk like Evie and I are rivals. In fact, if it came down to it, and I had to choose between them, I'd pick her. Her baking's worth the loss of a friend."

Mabel shrugged unapologetically. "Just as well with a face

like hers." She turned to Nell Gwyn, handing over a second walnut. "You agree with me, don't you, angel?" she crooned.

"*Woo-hoot! Kit's a pretty boy!*" Nell Gwyn shrieked in reply.

Kit flinched and Gracie sent him a sympathetic look.

"Fine," Mabel said, "you don't fancy Jean-Jacques. So who *have* you got your eye on?"

Kit shook his head, smiling ruefully. "I don't have my eye on anyone. The last thing I need is a man."

"Oh, don't give me that," Mabel scoffed. "You're soft as butter, you. What you want, deep down, is someone on the other side of your fireplace."

Kit chuckled. "You must be getting me mixed up with someone else. I've never wanted anyone like that—never even looked. I'm perfectly happy on my own. I'm like a tom cat."

Mabel waved her hand dismissively. "I see you," she said. "And you ain't no tom cat, Kit Redford. Far from it."

"I'm no lad either," Kit said. "I'm one-and-forty."

She snorted at that too, but didn't dignify it with an answer.

"I'll tell you who *has* been hanging around me, though," Kit said, in a blatant effort to distract her attention.

She tilted her head to the side, interested now. It made her look disconcertingly like the parrot on her shoulder. "Who?"

"Jake Sharp," Kit divulged. "I told you he opened that new gambling den near the club, didn't I?"

"Lenny Sharp's boy?" Mabel's eyebrows rose. "Interested, is he?" Nell Gwyn began to nibble her ear, whistling softly. Absently, Mabel scratched the bird's head.

"He's interested in something," Kit said. "But I think it's the club rather than me."

"*Hmmm,*" Mabel said, digging absently into the reticule again and bringing out another walnut. "You may be right." When Kit laughed, she added, "Not that I don't think you're

worth being interested in for yourself, lovey, but the Sharps…
Well, the name says it all, don't it?"

"You're not wrong," Kit agreed.

"Mightn't be a bad idea to get rid of the club, though, you
know," Mabel added, looking away to offer the walnut to
Nell Gwyn. The bird took it gently.

"What do you mean?" Kit said.

"Well, you don't want to be running that place forever, do
you? You used to always say that you'd build it up, sell it,
and retire to the country."

Kit quirked a half-smile. "I did used to say that."

"Don't you want that anymore?" Mabel asked curiously.

Kit sighed. "Oh, I don't know. I used to imagine myself
setting up as a gentleman farmer or some such thing. But now
I realise—well, I wouldn't have the first idea what to do. I'm
more of an alley cat than a farmyard one."

"*Pah!* If you've got money you'll be fine. You can always
buy expertise. But whatever you decide to do, my advice
would be to consider selling up sooner rather than later. I
wish I'd stopped earlier—if I'd got out five years before I did,
I'd've avoided that business with Jem Bailey and been able to
sell out for twice or three times as much."

Mabel had hired Jem Bailey as a doorman for the Lily.
He'd been a hot-headed sort. After deciding he was in love
with one of the girls, he'd assaulted a wealthy customer
who'd been enjoying her favours on the premises. The incident had brought all sorts of trouble to Mabel's door, and
she'd ended up selling the Lily for a sum she'd always
insisted was considerably less than its true worth.

"Look at it this way," Mabel said. "The value of your club
ain't going up any more. You can't go bigger without losing
members—it's the fact that it's discreet that they like. You
should get out now, while the going's good." She shrugged
and the sudden movement made Nell Gwyn flap and squawk
for a few moments before settling down again. "I reckon

you'll do nicely if you're smart about it, but I'd be quick if I were you. Especially now there's a Sharp hanging about. From what I remember of old Lenny Sharp, if you didn't *give* him what he wanted when he asked, he wouldn't wait too long before taking it without your blessing."

"I'll think about it," Kit promised.

"You do that," Mabel replied. "Now, tell me what all the gossip is, and don't hold back."

8

HENRY

On Thursday evening Reid called in at Curzon Street as promised.

"Well, your grace," he said, once they'd greeted one another and sat down, "I have some information for you, if not the whole answer quite yet."

"That's good," Henry said. "You did not seem hopeful of that earlier."

"There are some things that can be quite quickly established."

"Such as?"

"Such as the fact that the owner of the house has not changed in twenty years."

Henry stared at him. "I beg your pardon?"

"The house is yours," Reid said calmly. "It never left your estate."

Henry blinked. Of all the possibilities he'd entertained, this was not one of them. He'd been prepared to purchase the house back from its current owner, no matter what it might cost, just so he could give it to Christopher. To learn it was still his was unexpected.

"I don't understand."

"The title remains in your name. It has been so since you bought it. There's a tenant in occupation who I spoke with this afternoon—he tells me he's lived there these last thirteen years, and before him there was another tenant."

"Thirteen years!"

"Yes. And the lease is with none other than your good self."

Henry frowned. "He pays rent, this tenant? I am quite sure there was no income that we missed."

"Quite so," Reid agreed. "The rent did not appear anywhere in your accounts. According to the tenant, he's paid up every quarter without interruption during the whole period of the lease—but the payments have been made to a firm of solicitors in Lambeth called Davies & Gillingham. Has your family used that firm before?"

"Not to my knowledge."

Reid nodded. "I'll look into that further and report back once I know more."

"It's unfortunate there's a tenant," Henry said. "I can hardly throw him out on his ear after so long. Do you think he might agree to leave, in return for a compensatory payment? Or perhaps I could sell the property with the tenant in place and give Christopher the proceeds..." He trailed off, only then becoming aware of Reid's penetrating gaze.

"Christopher?" Reid said. "Was he the intended recipient of this gift?"

Henry nodded.

"A family member?"

Henry flushed and shook his head.

Reid said softly, "I can't think of many reasons a wealthy man might gift someone with something as substantial as a house." He paused, then added, "Is opening this up wise, your grace? You've always been so... careful about these things."

"I used to be less careful," Henry admitted. "I knew

Christopher when I lived in London, when the children were very young and Caroline"—he broke off—"well, she was content for me to suit myself."

"And you were... less careful with this Christopher?"

Henry ran his hands over his face, unable to meet Reid's gaze. "Yes. I met him at a rather scandalous party that a friend took me to. It was at a very discreet, very exclusive brothel called the Golden Lily. I wanted Christopher from the moment I set eyes on him." He gave a hopeless laugh. "Hell, I completely lost my head over him. I told the madam I wanted to become his protector that very night." He sighed. "I'd never done anything like that before."

Reid's eyebrows rose. "So, you set him up like a mistress?"

Henry looked up at that and snorted. "Aside from the one obvious difference, yes."

Reid's mouth quirked. "And what was the arrangement you fixed upon?"

"I purchased the house for him—furnished, of course—and staffed it, and he received a monthly stipend besides. When we parted ways, there was to be a severance payment and the house was to be made over to him."

"And part ways you did."

Henry nodded. "Before the end of our contract. Caroline had fallen ill by then. She wanted me to give up Christopher and take her back to Wiltshire so we could spend her last months together. I couldn't refuse her."

Reid's gaze was sympathetic. "And how did your Christopher react?"

Shame drenched Henry. "In all honesty, I don't know. It was all very sudden. Caroline insisted we leave town immediately and I'd made her a promise..." He trailed off, his gut twisting unpleasantly. "In short, I wrote Christopher a letter giving him the news and gave it to Parkinson to deliver in person, along with instructions to have the house made over and the money paid."

"Ah," Reid said, heavily. "And now you have discovered that Parkinson didn't carry out your instructions."

Henry closed his eyes. "It would seem not. Well, at least not in relation to the house. I'm hoping he at least honoured the severance payment."

And delivered the letter.

"How much was that payment to be?"

Henry raised his head and met Reid's curious gaze. "Three hundred pounds."

Reid's eyes widened and he whistled, low. "*And* the house? You did lose your head."

I lost my heart, Henry thought.

But he didn't say that aloud.

Reid looked thoughtful. "It seems to me more likely than not that the severance payment was made. If you'd broken the agreement entirely, surely Christopher or the madam would have kicked up a stink?"

"That's what I thought," Henry said. "After I went to Wiltshire I heard nothing more from Christopher. Not a thing. But then, why not make a stink about the house? That was part of the agreement too."

Reid frowned. "Without knowing what Parkinson said to this Christopher, I don't think you can make any assumptions. Perhaps Parkinson offered him more money instead? Have you asked Christopher?"

Henry shifted uncomfortably in his seat. "He has refused to meet with me. I only learned he had not received the house through a chance meeting with a mutual acquaintance. Otherwise I would never have known."

"So, what will you do now?"

"Try to find Christopher for myself," Henry said. "I was hoping you might assist me with that."

"Of course." Reid nodded. "What's his full name? I can make enquiries."

"Christopher Redford."

"*Redford?*" Reid's gaze was sharp, almost disbelieving. "Not *Kit* Redford?"

Slowly, Henry said, "Do you know him?"

"Not well, but I know *of* him," Reid replied. "Your Christopher is the owner of an exclusive club for gentlemen of our persuasion. Redford's on Palfrey Terrace."

Henry gawked at him.

Reid said, almost apologetically, "I'm a member myself."

"Does he live there? At Palfrey Terrace?" Henry asked.

"I'm not sure, but that's something I can soon find out. Let me look into it and I'll send a note over in the morning." He paused, then added quietly, "If you're sure that's what you want."

"I'm sure," Henry said quickly.

Reid's gaze was sympathetic. "It's worth giving some thought to," he said gently. "These events took place a very long time ago, and in all the years that have followed, no trouble has come your way. Is it prudent to stir this up now?"

"You think I should let sleeping dogs lie?"

Reid's gaze was steady. "It's worth considering. Redford probably won't be how you remember him. Only think how much *you* have changed in the last two decades. I know I'm a different man from who I was twenty years ago."

It occurred to Henry then, for the first time, that he may not like the new Christopher—and that the new Christopher may not like him. That they might find each other sadly lacking in comparison to the memories they had of the young men they had once been.

Memories were such crude and unreliable things.

Henry shook his head. That didn't matter. This wasn't about satisfying his curiosity about Christopher—thought he was, of course, curious. It was about righting a wrong that he was responsible for. He wouldn't shirk from that. If he had breached his agreement with Christopher—even inadvertently—it was up to him to make good the deficit.

He met Reid's eyes and said quietly, "I'm quite sure."

Soon after that, Reid took his leave, promising to return with Christopher's direction as soon as possible.

Henry spent the rest of evening brooding over his memories of Christopher, and trying to envisage what he would be like now.

Ever since his last interview with Jean-Jacques, he'd been tormented by the thought of Christopher being thrown out of the little house in Paddington Green. They had been so happy there, in the limited time they had spent together.

Well, Henry had been happy.

Perhaps that was all it had ever been. Perhaps Christopher had only ever been performing his duties. Tolerating the attentions of the man who put a roof over his head, paid his bills, and put money in his pocket.

It was a depressing thought, but it was one that Henry could not shake as he stared into the fire and made his way through more of the brandy bottle than was wise.

9

KIT

On Friday afternoon, Kit was writing a letter in his private sitting room, when Tom burst into the room, his eyes wide.

"Kit, you'll never guess who's here!" he gasped.

Kit looked up from his writing slope. "Tom," he said wearily. "Footmen do not enter rooms without knocking. Nor do they—"

He got no further as Tom blurted out, "There's only a bleeding duke here to see you!"

Kit's mouth dropped open. *Not Henry? Not here?*

"Sorry," Tom said hurriedly, straightening himself up. In a more dignified tone, he added, "His grace, the Duke of Avesbury is here to see you, sir."

For several long moments, Kit could only stare at Tom, his heart racing, and when his voice came out it was shaky. "I beg your pardon?"

"His grace, the duke—"

"Sorry, no, I heard you—I'm just—just rather shocked." Kit forced himself to take a deep breath, hating the audible shudder in his exhalation that Tom could not fail to notice.

"Did you show him into the drawing room?" he asked.

"Yes, and I asked if he'd like some tea, but he said no."

Tom paused and bit his lip. "Is that all right? Did I do the wrong thing? He swore he knew you. If he's a fake, I'll chuck him out, you just say the word." Tom didn't look quite as confident as his words suggested. Tom was a big fellow but Henry was bigger... wasn't he?

Kit frowned. It had been so long, he wasn't sure how reliable his memories were.

"Kit?" Tom said uncertainly. "Do you—do you want me to ask this cove to leave?"

"No, no," he said. "I'll see him." He offered Tom a reassuring smile. "It's fine. I know Avesbury—or at least I did, a long time ago. I'm just surprised he came here, that's all."

Tom's expression was pure relief.

"Tell him I'll be along in just a few minutes, once I'm properly attired." Kit was wearing a pale-yellow silk banyan, embroidered with tiny blue flowers, and he would *not* be receiving Henry in it, thank you very much. If the man was prepared to call on him after eighteen years without so much as sending a note, he could kick his heels for a few minutes while Kit made himself halfway presentable.

Tom nodded and left to deliver the message.

Kit shook his head, remembering how eager he used to be to see Henry. Back then, he'd have run down the stairs in naught but his drawers to have a few more moments with the man.

He shook his head at his own past foolishness. God, he'd thought himself so desperately in love.

Realising his heart was racing, Kit took a deep breath and forced himself to calmly put away his writing slope, before making his way back to his bedchamber to dress.

He selected a cream-and-maroon striped waistcoat and a beautifully tailored coat, tying his neckcloth with great care. He put a little pomade in his hair, used a little of his favourite cologne—a blend of bergamot, orange blossom, and rosemary

—and pushed a large topaz and gold ring on his right index finger

He examined himself in the looking glass.

His stomach was in knots, his palms damp.

God damn but he was as nervous as a kitten and he *hated* that. He didn't want to be nervous. He wanted to be cool and in control. Reserved and unaffected.

He said aloud, "Henry. To what do I owe this pleasure."

He groaned. His voice was thin and tense, and "*Henry*"? "*Pleasure*"? No!

He took a deep breath, then another.

"Your grace. How may I help you?"

Christ, no.

"Your grace. This is unexpected."

Yes.

He took another breath, in and out, and said it again, his voice a little deeper this time.

"Your grace. Well, this *is* unexpected."

No, he sounded arch now. He went back to first version.

"Your grace. This is unexpected."

Now he sounded defensive.

"Your grace—" He broke off, groaning.

Perhaps he should have told Tom to send Henry away.

Henry.

"Henry," he said. "This is unexpected."

The lump in his throat was unexpected.

He used to think that "*Henry*" was the dearest name in all the world. The most perfect two syllables created.

Strange, how one's reaction to a mere word could change so fundamentally.

He turned away from the looking glass and strode to the door, trying to take big, even breaths, to consciously manage his own racing nerves.

When he got to the bottom of the stairs, he saw Tom.

"Come on," he said. "You can announce me. It'll be good practice."

Tom grinned and straightened his coat. "Right-o!" he said, and started down the corridor at a clip, Kit following in his wake.

Kit's heart thundered in his chest as he followed Tom, an odd mix of nerves and long-suppressed, slowly-building anger filling him. And something else too, mortifyingly. A touch of the old excitement he used to feel, on the nights he knew Henry was coming. He was honest enough to admit that, and had enough pride to hate himself for it.

When Tom reached the drawing room, he opened the door with sweeping formality, as if Kit was the duke in this tableau.

Just before he stepped inside, Kit wondered what Henry would make of this grand entrance. Perhaps he'd think Kit was putting on airs? That he'd got above himself over these last eighteen years?

Well, what if he did think that?

Fuck him.

Fuck Henry Asquith, Duke of Avesbury.

Kit lifted his chin and stepped inside.

1 0

HENRY

Henry stood at the window of Christopher's drawing room, looking down at the street below. The street where Christopher now lived. This was a quiet corner of London. Not fashionable but reasonably well-to-do, and the house was much larger than the one he'd bought for Christopher in Paddington Green.

He hadn't been sure if Christopher, would agree to see him. The footman who greeted him had been wide-eyed from the moment Henry gave his name. He'd respectfully—and rather too trustingly, in Henry's opinion—shown him into what looked to be the best room of the house, before offering to have tea sent up without even checking with his master.

When the same footman had opened the door again less than ten minutes later, Henry had half-expected to be asked to leave, but the man had merely said that Mr. Redford would be down in a few minutes, if he would care to wait.

And that was what Henry was now doing. Waiting nervously. Staring unseeingly out of the window at the street below as his mind whirred with thoughts.

When the drawing room door finally opened again, he spun on his heel.

The footman was holding open the door, and the man who was stepping forward, into the room, was, quite possibly the most elegantly dressed man Henry had ever seen. His clothes were beautifully tailored, his hair perfectly coiffed. His face—

It was the same face.

"Christopher—" The name escaped him on a shaky breath.

Christopher Redford was just as he had been nearly twenty years ago—and he was so very different.

For several long moments, they stared at one another. Henry couldn't have moved or spoken to save his life. His gaze moved over Christopher hungrily, absorbing every fascinating detail. His hair was a more seasoned, darker gold than before, but otherwise he wasn't much changed. Still slim, still fine-featured, unmistakably the same man, only older.

The same; and different.

He was still beautiful, Henry thought, but there was a slight reserve—a coolness even— in the green eyes. And there were lines of character etched in his face that hadn't been there before. Henry found he wanted to study him, to step close and explore all the minute changes time had wrought.

Perhaps he would have done so, if Christopher hadn't given a wintry smile, inclined his head almost mockingly, and said with devastating and chilly politeness, "Well. This is rather unexpected, I must say."

Henry's heart plummeted.

In that instant, he saw that Christopher was miles distant, holding himself back behind a politely inquiring mask. Beneath the mask, Henry detected traces of wariness and anger. He saw it in the tension in Christopher's jaw. In the slight glitter in his eyes.

"I'm afraid Kit sees no point in meeting with you. So many years, you know."

Henry swallowed, hard. "Christopher, I—"

"Please," Christopher interrupted, his smile a little savage. "My friends call me Kit." He threw the name at Henry like a dart, the 't' very precise and sharp. "Though you may address me as Mr. Redford."

Henry blinked at him. Although it had been plain from his conversations with Jean-Jacques that Christopher did not remember him fondly, the sheer hostility the man was giving off shocked Henry. The last time he had seen Christopher, they had been lovers.

And now this.

Evidently, Henry was not considered a friend. In fact, by the look on Christopher's face, he was very much the enemy.

Henry cleared his throat. "Thank you for agreeing to speak with me," he tried again, moving forward a step. Christopher immediately stepped back, keeping the distance between them the same as before.

Henry stilled. He tried again. "I recently met Jean-Jacques —I believe he mentioned to you that he'd seen me?"

"He said he saw you in Mercier's, with your wife," Christopher said tightly. His lips twisted into a mockery of a smile. "I understand congratulations are in order. Again."

Henry gave an uncomfortable laugh. "Oh, no, not at all. Unless you mean to congratulate me on my first grandchild. The lady I was with was not my wife, you see. Marianne is my daughter."

Christopher's eyes widened at that, and his cheeks flushed pink. "Oh," he said, seeming entirely discombobulated. After a moment he added, a little shakily, "Well, it seems I'm even older than I thought."

Henry let out an undignified snort of laughter at that, making Christopher glance at him in surprise, then rub his left ear in an uncomfortable gesture that was somehow endearing.

Henry said lightly, "You are not the one who is about to be a grandfather. Imagine how *I* feel."

Christopher stared at Henry for long moments, his gaze unwavering. At last, he sighed and said, wearily, "Why are you here, Henry? Really, I mean."

"Didn't Jean-Jacques tell you?"

Christopher shrugged one slim shoulder. "He said you felt bad about the events of the past—I can't imagine why you should suddenly feel that way after all this time. It was a thousand years ago. We are past all that now, don't you think? And it's not as though we move in the same social circles." He gave a derisive laugh. "Unless you're angling for a membership to my club. Is that it?"

Henry flushed. Was that what Christopher thought of him? That he'd presume on their past friendship to gain entry to his club?

"I'm not angling for anything," he said. "I came because I have just learned that you may not have received what you were entitled to when our arrangement came to an end, all those years ago."

Christopher's unimpressed gaze did not alter.

Henry stepped forward, meeting Christopher's sceptical look with an open one of his own, one that let all his regret show. "I swear to you, it was only a few days ago that I first learned anything of it—I still don't know the whole story. I was horrified to learn that you were led to believe I broke our agreement."

Christopher bristled at that. "You *did* break it."

Henry flinched at the man's sharp tone. Then he nodded. "Yes. Unintentionally, I did. I entrusted my man of business to carry out certain instructions, and I have only now, in the last few days, learned that he did not do so. Instead of conveying the house to you as he was supposed to, he let the property to a tenant I knew nothing about and diverted the rent payments to himself. My solicitor is looking into the matter now."

Christopher gave him a disbelieving look. "*Really*, Henry?

That is your story? Were you really so careless with your personal affairs?"

The pang of hurt that comment caused was profound. The last time he'd seen Christopher, the man had looked at him with frank adoration—as though he'd hung the moon in the sky. Now Henry had fallen so far in his estimation that Christopher all but called him liar to his face.

Henry, hoping his distress did not show, tried to keep his voice steady and calm. "I am generally reasonably diligent about my affairs, but I had no reason to doubt Parkinson's loyalty. He had been my father's private secretary for many years, and I trusted him implicitly. Besides, at the time I was preoccupied with Caroline."

"Caroline?" Christopher's frown made Henry's stomach sink. "Why were you preoccupied with Caroline?"

"You don't know?" Henry asked faintly.

"Know what?"

This was what he had feared.

"Did Parkinson give you my letter?" Henry said hoarsely.

Christopher's blank look was all the answer he needed. A wrenching ache near split his heart into two, and for the first time ever, Henry wished Parkinson was alive again, just so he could punish him for his reckless, selfish actions.

Christopher had been so young and trusting back then, despite his worldly ways—it was unbearable to imagine how he must have felt when Parkinson had arrived at the little house to turn him out. Without so much as even a note from Henry.

Henry said huskily, "I had to leave London with Caroline and the children quite suddenly. Caroline was very ill— cancer of the breast." He rubbed at his chest with the heel of his hand. "I got home early one morning—after our last night together—and she was waiting for me with the news. She asked me to take her back to Wiltshire straightaway." He paused, swallowing hard before he added, "And she asked me to give you up."

He glanced back at Christopher who was staring at him with a stunned expression.

"I had no idea," Christopher said faintly. "I heard she'd passed away a few years ago, but I had no notion it was so soon after you left town."

"She died only a few months after we returned to Wiltshire. I've never come back to town to live since then. I only visit from time to time."

Christopher looked stricken. "Christ, Henry. That must have been awful."

Henry blinked, unsure how to respond. "It was... sudden," he said. "She found the tumour in her breast, and it grew very quickly. We knew how things would likely go. Her mother had died of the same disease." He came to a halt, a shard of old grief piercing his heart.

"I'm sorry," Christopher said, his eyes soft with sympathy. "I know how much you loved her."

He *had* loved her, but somehow, those words from Christopher's lips filled him with another old pain. An old pain that threw up memories of Christopher; how he used to look when Henry arrived at the little house in Paddington Green, eyes shining with happiness and anticipation. The old pain of losing that. Of losing Christopher.

The pain of Caroline asking him to give Christopher up.

"It is time to put your toys away. We must think of the children now."

In the months—hell, the years—that followed, Henry had felt like a selfish cur every time he'd thought of Christopher. Every time he'd missed him. Every time he'd longed for him.

"Take lovers by all means—but don't lose your head over them, Henry."

Love was only for his family. For his wife and children.

But the truth was, he had loved Christopher too. And

what did that say about him? What did it say about him that he'd still longed for Christopher, when his wife and children needed him so?

He hadn't even had the decency to walk away without looking back. He'd written that letter for Parkinson to deliver, practically begging Christopher not to forget him. Even as he'd promised Caroline to leave his lover behind, he'd still wanted to keep some tiny flame of hope alive for himself.

And now it turned out that Christopher had never received the letter. That he'd never even known how grieved Henry was over leaving him.

"So," Christopher said into the silence. "Caroline asked you to give me up?"

"Yes," Henry said, his voice raw now. "I'd promised her I would, you see, if she asked."

Christopher didn't say anything, only watched Henry with his clear, green gaze.

Henry continued, "I told Parkinson to make the house over to you and pass you a bank draft for three hundred pounds, just as we'd agreed. And—I gave him a letter for you." He took a deep breath. "I always thought, until I spoke to Jean-Jacques a few days ago, that you had got everything that was due to you." He gazed at Christopher. "Did you at least get the bank draft?"

Christopher met his gaze. Slowly he shook his head.

Henry groaned and closed his eyes. "God *damn* him."

Christopher was silent.

When at last Henry opened his eyes again, he forced himself to meet Christopher's gaze. The man's face was quite unreadable. He'd changed in that respect, Henry thought. He used to wear his heart on his sleeve.

"What did Parkinson say to you?" he asked.

"Not much," Christopher admitted. "He gave me fifty pounds and told me I had to get out by the next day."

"*What?*" Despite everything, Henry was still shocked to hear that.

"He wasn't unpleasant about it. Simply factual. He said you were finished with me, and I was to leave." He tilted his head, eyes narrowing as he tried to remember the long-ago conversation. "I think I said, '*But we have a contract.*' He laughed at that part. As though I'd lost my mind. And then he said—and this part I do remember quite well—'*People like you do not have contracts with dukes.*'"

Henry stared at him in horrified disbelief. "But we *did*," he breathed. "And he knew that I fully intended to honour that agreement. Back then, he knew all my business."

"Back then?" Kit echoed. "Doesn't he work for you anymore?"

"He died years ago," Henry replied. "Soon after it was discovered that he'd been stealing money from me, and from my father before me. My father had taught me to trust him, and Parkinson himself had never given me any reason to doubt him." He paused, then added, "I'm only surprised you took no action against me. Isn't that how these things normally work?"

Christopher flushed and turned away. He muttered, "I was a fool back then. I wouldn't let Mabel—Madame Georgette, that is—do anything to you. The money from Parkinson was enough to pay her most of her cut, so she agreed to leave you be."

Henry's gut clenched. "You gave her the fifty pounds?"

Christopher sighed. "Yes. Like I said, I was an idiot. Later I wished I hadn't been so stupid, but at the time I was convinced it was the right thing to do."

Henry was almost afraid to ask the next question, but he made himself do it. "And what did you do after that? How did you manage?"

Christopher shook his head.

"Please tell me," Henry pleaded. His voice was hoarse.

Christopher's face, when he turned back to face Henry, was furious. "I was a whore! What do you *think* I did?" He shook his head. "Anyway, what do you care, Henry? You left. You had no intention of returning and you *didn't* return. You never checked up on me once, till now, or likely gave me a second thought. It's all water under the bridge."

"I *did* think about you," Henry said in a low, driven tone. "Too often, in truth, when I ought to have been thinking of others."

"I understand," Christopher interrupted tersely. "You had to put your family first. It's not as though I didn't always know that was the case. What eludes me is why you are here now, all these years later, when, to be frank, it's too late for apologies."

"I want to make it up to you." Henry reached into his coat and drew out the papers Reid had drawn up for him. "Here," he said, thrusting them into Christopher's hands.

Christopher opened up the folded pages and stared down at the lines written there, his brows pleated in confusion. "What's this?"

"My solicitor wrote it up. It explains that I'll either transfer the Paddington Green house over to you with the sitting tenant so you can collect the rent, or pay you the equivalent value. You've only to decide which you prefer. And of course, I'll pay you the three hundred pounds you ought to have had, and the back rent you've missed."

Christopher thrust the letter back towards Henry, the neatly written pages shaking in his grip. "I don't want that," he said angrily. "Not any of it!"

For a moment, Henry could only stare at Christopher, shocked. Then, slowly, quietly, he said, "We made an agreement. You must allow me to honour it, Christopher, I shall be wretched if you don't."

Christopher stared at him in astonishment. "I must allow you to"—he broke off, giving a harsh laugh—"I think you'll find that I can do whatever I please, Henry! You didn't give two hoots what happened to me eighteen years ago, but now your honour can't bear it if I won't let you pay up late?" He snorted disgustedly. "Well, here's the thing, Henry: I've made my own way in this world without your money, thank you very much. I neither need nor want it now!"

"Christopher, please," Henry said. "It's not about need, or even want—it's about what's fair. It's only just for me to make amends to you, and I—"

"Don't give me that!" Christopher said sharply. "This isn't about fairness, or justice. Or you making amends. It's about you trying to buy off your guilt. But you can't do that, Henry. You owed me that house and that money, *eighteen years ago*. *That* was when I needed it. *That* was when I suffered the consequences of not having it. You can't balance the ledger between us simply by giving me that sum now, when I no longer need it—not even if you add compound interest— because there's no cost to you. Not really. You're so wealthy you could give me that money ten times over and still not notice its loss. So how does that—that *transaction*—make amends for what you did?"

Henry stared at him, horrified. Horrified... and mortified, because there was something in what Christopher said, wasn't there? Henry *was* trying to buy his way out of the guilt that had been dogging him since the day he'd sent Parkinson to Christopher's door. Oh, he'd dressed it up in the fine clothes of principle and honour and fairness, but was he more driven by the desire to have his own sins forgiven, his own slate wiped clean, than by an honest desire to do right by Christopher? Was he even thinking about what that would entail?

"I'm sorry," Henry said desperately. "I do want to make amends to you, just tell me what you want and I will see it done."

Christopher's expression was all bitter fury. He gave a

harsh laugh. "What could I possibly want from you now? Wait, I know—perhaps you should earn the money you owe me the way *I* had to earn it? On your knees, and on your back, taking my cock like a whore."

Henry blinked, stunned—and, mortifyingly, aroused—by the filthy, furious words. He was suddenly aware of his cock pressing against the placket of his buckskin breeches, and when Christopher's gaze dropped to his groin, his eyebrows slowly rising, Henry's cheeks burned.

"Well, would you look at that," he said bitingly. "It seems you *like* that idea."

They stared at one another, the silence between them oddly charged.

Christopher stepped closer to Henry. He was still a very beautiful man, but his face did not have the uncomplicated comeliness it had once had—it had more character now. More grit. There were faint lines of experience etched onto it. Creases at the corners of his eyes that—despite his current fury—suggested he smiled often.

"Perhaps it *would* be interesting," he said now, "to invert our transaction." His gaze on Henry was curious. "I'm not sure you'd be up to the challenge though."

"What makes you say that?" Henry managed, his mouth very dry.

"You're a *duke*," Christopher said, his tone making the title sound like an insult. "You're used to being in charge, used to having your desires indulged, used to being the user—rather than the provider—of services."

Services.

Henry did not want to let that pass.

"I realise that is how you see our arrangement now," he said. "As some hard-nosed exchange of services for money— and perhaps it was like that, at the beginning. But later... well it was not like that for me." Heat stole into his face as he made himself admit the truth aloud. "Maybe I am being very naive, but… I felt that we were making love together."

For just a moment, Christopher looked wrecked, but then he gave a derisive snort. "Pathetically enough, I would probably have agreed with you once, but then I did used to be a perfect idiot."

"Don't say that," Henry breathed. His heart felt raw and bleeding, but he felt oddly alive too, for the first time in a very, very long time. Christopher might hate him, but he was looking at him, reacting to him. Reacting to Henry, as a person in his own right.

In this moment, Henry wasn't the Duke of Avesbury, or the father of the Asquith children.

He was just… Henry.

Christopher said flatly, "Before you get carried away, Henry, consider this aspect of our arrangement: I was always the one on my knees—or my back—and you were always the one shoving your cock in a hole."

Henry's blush had faded, but now it returned, heating his cheeks.

Christopher laughed, not particularly kindly. "Providing services, you see. Holes to be filled, just as often as you'd like."

"Christopher—"

The man smiled brightly. "Would you like to give it a try? Earn back the money you owe me by letting me use *your* holes?"

"Christopher, please," Henry said weakly.

Christopher laughed again, and this time a bitter edge crept in. "Oh, don't worry," he said. "I'm not really going to ask you to service my cock, Henry. But it was worth saying out loud, just to see your face." A strange smile twisted his lovely mouth. "And now I think it's time you left, *your grace*. I do believe I've had enough reminiscing for one day—for one lifetime actually.

So, let us leave it at this: you have made your apology, and I have accepted it." Christopher moved towards the bell rope, stretching his arm out to pull it and summon the footman.

To see Henry out of his life, once and for all.

Henry didn't want that. He found himself stepping forward, taking hold of Christopher's reaching arm and saying roughly, "Wait. Please."

Christopher turned, his expression mingled confusion and irritation.

"I'll do it," Henry said. "I'll do whatever you want."

Christopher's eyes went wide. Henry had surprised him, it seemed. His expression flickered between disbelief, intrigue, suspicion... and yes, *lust*. It was that last that lit a fire in Henry's belly and made him feel that strange sense again, of being fully alive for the first time in a long time.

At last Christopher said, with almost eerie calm, "You really want to do this? To make amends to me?"

"Yes."

"Not for your own gratification?"

"No," Henry said. "Though I can't promise not to enjoy it. You seemed to do so, all those years ago."

Something flared in Christopher's green eyes, then subsided.

"If you are making amends," Christopher said, "it has to cost you something. It cannot be some game for your own titillation."

Henry's gaze was steady. "I understand."

Christopher gaze hardened and his light voice grew challenging. "Fine. We do it at Redford's then. In the back room, where anyone can see. You, on your knees for me. Sucking me off in front of everyone."

The jolt of alarm in Henry's chest at those words was profound, and he saw that Christopher noticed his reaction— a thin smile stretched his mouth and his hostile gaze was fiercely disbelieving. He was waiting for Henry to back down —certain of it, in fact.

"All right," Henry said faintly. "I'll be there. When?"

For the second time, Christopher's eyes widened with surprise, but a moment later, he had himself back under control. "Tonight," he said tightly. "I'll tell my doormen to let you in. Come any time after nine o'clock."

"Very well," Henry said. "Until this evening, then."

He bowed then, very properly. As though to a lady he had called upon after a ball.

When he straightened, Christopher was looking at him strangely, suspicion and disbelief in his cool green gaze. And something else. Something vulnerable.

In that moment, Henry made his decision.

As terrifying as the prospect was, he was going to Redford's tonight.

Come what may, he would be there.

1 1

KIT

After Henry left, Kit didn't know what to do with himself. He tried to go back to his letter, but he could not concentrate. He kept returning to his conversation with Henry.

He was astonished at himself—where had that deep-rooted anger come from? Until today, he would have sworn that he had largely put his history with Henry Asquith behind him, but faced with the man, he had been blindly, violently furious.

His old hurts and resentments had flowed out of him like lava, scorching the ground between them.

Where had his absurd idea of being serviced by Henry in public come from? What had he been thinking to suggest such a thing? What had *Henry* been thinking to agree to it?

And Christ, he was coming to Redford's tonight!

Except, no. Of course he wasn't. He would not. He would go away and think better of this madness.

Surely he would think better of it?

Kit was still brooding over an hour later when the quiet of the house was interrupted by a very loud knocking at the front door. Curious, Kit went to his front window and peered down. To his surprise, one of the two figures standing there was Clara—he recognised her pale-blue bonnet and shawl. She was leaning on the arm of an unfamiliar man wearing a high-crowned hat.

What on earth?

Kit turned on his heel and left his sitting room, heading for the stairs.

By the time he had descended, Tom had already opened the front door and Clara and the strange gentleman were standing there, with Tom glaring at the young man.

It was only then that Kit noticed Clara was distinctly dishevelled. Her bonnet was crumpled on one side and her gown was mud-stained. When she turned her head towards Kit, he saw her cheek was red and grazed.

"Clara!" Kit exclaimed. "My God! What happened?"

"Oh, Kit!" she sobbed, and threw herself into his arms.

Kit pulled her close. She was shaking and giving awful, strangled sobs, but somehow Kit managed to turn and meet the gaze of the strange gentleman she had arrived with.

He was a very young gentleman, and quite handsome. His clothes were fashionable, his high collar points forcing his chin into a slightly raised position that gave him a haughty look. He was saved, however, from appearing entirely arrogant by the anxious look in his eyes.

"My apologies for intruding," he began, "I escorted your sister home after she was attacked in the park—"

"*Attacked?*" Kit said, alarmed.

"Yes, I caught sight of her being set upon and began to run towards her. Unfortunately, her attacker saw me coming and made off before I could apprehend him."

Kit stared at him, shocked. Who would attack Clara? On the heels of that thought came another: it seemed Clara had not been imagining things when she thought she was being followed.

"I wish I could tell you more," the young gentleman said unhappily, "but I saw very little of the man. I was some way off when I noticed them struggling, and he was long gone by the time I reached your sister." He shook his head. "Perhaps she will be able to tell you more when she has calmed."

Kit nodded at him. "Thank you for helping her home, sir. We are indebted to you."

"Not at all," the young gentleman said. "I'm glad I could be of service."

Clara had gone still in his arms now, which was somehow worse than the shaking. Concerned, he said, "I'm sorry to be rude, but if you'll excuse us, I think my sister needs to lie down."

"Of course," the young gentleman said promptly. Then, addressing himself to Clara, he added gently, "I hope you feel better soon, ma'am."

"Thank you for helping me," Clara managed to whisper.

Kit nodded at the young man, then turned to help Clara upstairs, leaving Tom to see him out.

When they were nearly at the top of the stairs, Clara said in a strangled tone, "Is Peter in the kitchen with Mrs. Saunders still?"

"Yes."

"Don't tell him I'm back yet," she said quickly. "And can you ask Mrs. Saunders to keep him down there until I've washed and made myself presentable? I don't want him to see—" She broke off, pressing her hand to her mouth.

"Don't worry, my dear," Kit said gently. "Go and fetch fresh clothes from your chamber. You can bathe and change in my rooms—Peter won't even know you're home until you're ready to face him. I'll go and speak to Mrs. Saunders and get hot water sent up. And then we'll eat and talk. Does that sound all right?"

She lowered her hand and took a shaky breath. "Yes. Thank you, Kit."

An hour later, Kit and Clara were ensconced in his small sitting room. She'd bathed and dressed in clean clothes, and they'd eaten a light luncheon. Now Clara was lying back on the chaise longue with a vinegar poultice on her cheek to take out the bruising and swelling that was coming up.

"So," Kit said mildly. "Are you going to tell me what happened?"

Clara didn't move her gaze from the ceiling. "I've been a fool," she said bitterly, and her eyes brightened with sudden tears for a moment before she screwed them tightly closed. A tear slid from the outer corner of her eye, down her temple and into her hair.

Kit waited, silent, for her to speak.

At last, she let out a shuddering breath and said shakily, "A few weeks ago, I went to see Percy Bartlett. I asked him for money. I told him I wanted it to help with Peter's upbringing, and if he didn't give me it, I was going to see Sir Algernon." Holding the poultice in place with one hand, she turned her head to meet Kit's gaze, her own defiant—she knew already what Kit's view would be.

Percy Bartlett was Peter's father—and Peter was not a love child. Clara had been a servant in Sir Algernon Bartlett's house, governess to Percy's younger sisters. A very pretty, very appealing young governess, with no one to protect her from the rapacious son of the house.

Kit sighed. "Oh, Clara."

"I know what you're thinking," she gritted out. "You're wondering why I did such a stupid thing?"

Kit eyed her for a moment. "Why did you?" he asked gently. "And why didn't you just come to me if you need money?"

Still holding the poultice, she shook her head minutely, her expression tight and angry. "Why should he get away without contributing anything to the cost of raising the son he forced upon me?" she demanded. "It's only right he pay something towards Peter's upkeep!"

"How much did you ask for?"

Her jaw tightened. "Five hundred pounds."

Kit considered that. On the one hand, it was not an unreasonable sum to request from a man of Bartlett's standing, who would one day inherit his father's sizeable wealth. On the other hand, Bartlett was known to be a wastrel who gambled away every penny he was given, and whose father kept him on a very tight leash. If he had a tenth of that sum to hand, Kit would be astonished.

"And what did he say?" Kit asked.

Clara returned her gaze to the ceiling. A muscle in her jaw worked. "He was furious. He told me he'd not give me a penny and if I didn't promise to stay quiet, he'd make me sorry."

Kit nodded. "I suppose it's too much to hope that you agreed?"

Clara shook her head minutely. "I told him if he hadn't paid me by the end of the month, I would be going to see his father."

"And since then, you've been followed in the street at least once—and now attacked in the park?"

Clara was silent. She stared miserably at the ceiling.

"You don't need his money, Clara," Kit said gently. "Peter is my godson, and if I've not made it clear to you already, then know this: I regard him as my personal responsibility. I may not have Sir Algernon Bartlett's wealth, but I'm comfortably off and will make provision for Peter's future. You have no need to worry about him."

"Kit," she said, her voice breaking, "You don't understand —I wanted the money so I could—so I could—" She gave a sob and covered her mouth with her free hand.

"So you could what?"

"So I could leave London," she whispered.

Kit stared at her, unsure what to say. His heart twisted at the thought of her and Peter leaving. It just being him, alone in this big house.

"I'm sorry," she whispered. "I don't want to go, but it's Peter's chest. I took him to a doctor two months ago. He says I have to get him out of London. There's no choice." She pressed her lips together for a moment before she went on. "His cough's getting worse. It plagues him at night. I can't—" She broke off, shaking her head helplessly.

"It's all right," Kit said. "I just wish you'd come to me, Clara. Don't you know I'd do anything to help you? Did you think I'd cut you off because of this? Leave you without an income? When you and Peter have lived with me these last five years?" He could hear the hurt in his own voice, and Clara heard it too. She fumbled blindly for his hand with her own, taking his fingers and squeezing them.

"You're too good to me," she whispered. "I don't deserve you, Kit."

He patted her hand. "Yes," he said. "You do. And the sooner you realise it, the better."

For a few moments, they sat quietly, then Clara whispered, "There's something else."

"And what is that?"

She swallowed. "I'm not sure I can get Bartlett to leave me alone now."

Kit was silent, waiting for the explanation that was surely coming. Another tear made its slow way down her temple and into her hair. "He's a monster, Kit," she whispered. "If he goes after Peter, I'll never forgive myself."

"Perhaps if you withdraw the threat to speak to his father?" Kit prompted gently.

That was when she began to sob in earnest.

"What's wrong?" Kit asked anxiously. "Clara?"

After a minute, when her sobs had subsided and Kit was nearly beside himself with worry, she said in a wobbly voice,

"I—I already tried. I went to see him again, to call my threats off, and he just *laughed* at me—so nastily, Kit—he saw how frightened I was, and I could see he liked it. And now I don't know what to do!"

"You should have told me before," he chided gently, before adding more firmly, "Bartlett may be a nobleman but I am not without resources."

"I know," she sobbed, turning her head to him. "But why should you be put to trouble over my idiocy? It's unfair on you."

"Friends put themselves to trouble for each other," he said reassuringly. "And I am very capable of dealing with a bully like Bartlett."

"How?" she asked.

Kit gave it some thought. After a moment he said, "A public confrontation, I think. Something that exposes his behaviour to his peers. We will aim to shine a light on that cockroach and see if we can send him scurrying back under his rock."

"Kit," she whispered. "Don't put yourself at risk for me."

"I won't," Kit said with more confidence than he truly felt. "In fact, I intend to seek assistance from someone Bartlett would not dare to cross."

12

HENRY

"I'll tell my doormen to let you in. Come any time after nine o'clock."

After Henry took his leave of Christopher, the man's final words continued to echo in his mind.

Did Christopher actually *want* to see Henry tonight? He'd seemed surprised when Henry had agreed. Maybe even disappointed, as though he'd only wanted to offend him, not to have him comply.

It was a thought that troubled Henry as he turned in the direction of home and began walking.

"If you are making amends, it has to cost you something."

Christopher had plainly been angry and resentful about the events of the past—and Henry could hardly blame him.

As he strode back towards Curzon Street, his mind teemed with an undisciplined mix of thoughts. His memories of Christopher as he had been all those years ago. How he had appeared today. Henry's fears as to how matters might unfold at Redford's that night.

"You, on your knees for me. Sucking me off in front of everyone."

Henry bit the inside of his cheek as he remembered those words, only easing up when he tasted blood.

"In the back room, where anyone can see."

Henry's heart thudded so hard at that thought, he felt it might burst out of his chest.

Could he really do that? Get down on his knees in Christopher's club, in front of whoever might be there, and suck a man's cock?

Christopher's cock.

Well, he had to, didn't he? He simply had to. He had begged Christopher to allow him to make amends after all.

And hadn't Henry once asked the same of Christopher? Their first encounters, all those years ago, had taken place in the heady atmosphere of the Golden Lily, several of them in front of other patrons.

It had felt like the most debauched of sins. Settling himself down on one of those low velvet divans that were scattered about the place and just watching as Christopher Redford— the most beautiful creature Henry had ever seen—crawled gracefully between his legs and took Henry's cock into his lovely mouth.

He remembered all those envious, hungry gazes, watching them. They probably thought he felt like an emperor being catered to, but that wasn't it at all. He felt more like a prisoner, held fast and helpless by the skills of the alluring young man who was playing with him in front of everyone else. Making him spend into his mouth.

He'd felt helpless, a little humiliated.

And he'd loved it.

He'd never admitted that to anyone, not even Christopher himself. After they'd entered into their arrangement properly, he'd brought those encounters to an end, telling Christopher he wanted him all to himself—which was not untrue. But nor was it the whole truth.

All in all, he'd taken a great deal from Christopher during

their time together, and what had he given in return? Christ, he hadn't even met the most basic terms of their agreement. That thought made his stomach twist with shame.

So, if Christopher wanted to humiliate Henry—to give him taste of his own medicine as Christopher would see it— was that really such a surprise?

Pathetically, part of Henry just wanted *something* with Christopher, no matter what he had to do to make that happen. Even if it meant getting down on his knees and begging for the privilege.

When he'd walked into Christopher's drawing room earlier this afternoon, and seen him for the first time in near enough two decades, his heart had quickened in his chest like it was stuttering into rude and painful life for the first time in years and years.

He had felt—not so much young, as *alive*—as though new blood filled his veins.

A terrifying and wonderful feeling.

When Henry returned to the townhouse, he found Marianne and Jeremy in the drawing room, both reading. Henry smiled to see their easy companionship. They were a very well-suited pair.

"Papa," Marianne said, looking up. "Did you have a good day?"

He smiled, joining her on the small sofa. "I suppose so," he said. "I met with my solicitor and... dealt with some other business." His smile felt strained. "What about you?"

"Oh, I've been perfectly idle," Marianne said happily. "I stayed in bed all morning and spent all afternoon reading. It's glorious having an excuse not to pay calls—or accept callers for that matter."

Henry laughed. "I thought that was why you liked living

in town!"

"It is," Marianne said. "Only not so much now that I'm size of a house."

"Don't be silly," Jeremy said. "You'd barely make a gazebo!"

She laughed. "Wretch!"

"Only a dainty, charming little gazebo," Jeremy said. "Barely big enough for one, standing!"

"You are an absurd person," Marianne told him, blue eyes twinkling and lips twitching with humour. "Isn't he, Papa?"

Before Henry could reply, she exclaimed, "Oh, I almost forgot! I had a letter from George today. I'll let you read it later—it's in my bedchamber."

"How is he?" Henry asked.

"He sounded in reasonably good spirits," Marianne replied. "But you know George—he's not exactly one for those sorts of confidences."

That was certainly true. Marianne shared her every thought with everyone, but George was quite the opposite.

"It sounds as if he's been going round the estate with Mr. Holland quite a bit," Marianne said. "And reading lots of his old Greek stuff." She rolled her eyes.

"Different people enjoy different things, Marianne," Henry said mildly.

Just then the door opened and Freddy entered.

"I'm starved," he announced, flopping into a chair. "Can you ring for some tea and cake, Mari?"

"We'll be having dinner soon. Can't you wait?" she replied irritably.

"I'll eat both, easily enough," Freddy replied. "I missed luncheon, on account of my adventure."

"Adventure?" Marianne echoed, interested now.

"A small one," Freddy said, shrugging. "I had to rescue a lady in the park."

Marianne gasped. She closed her book and set it aside, leaning forward. "What happened?"

Freddy proceeded to tell them that he'd been walking through Hyde Park when he'd spotted a man attacking a woman from afar. When he'd shouted and begun running towards them, the man had taken off, leaving the lady lying on the ground.

"Was she badly hurt?" Marianne asked worriedly.

"Thankfully, no," Freddy said, "but she was terribly shaken. I escorted her home—she's a widow who lives with her brother."

"She was an elderly lady?"

"Not at all, perhaps only four- or five-and-twenty, though her brother was older."

Pride warmed Henry's heart. "Well, I think you're a veritable Sir Galahad," he said. "I daresay she was very relieved you came along. Her brother too."

Freddy flushed a little, ducking his head. "It was nothing. Just what anyone else would have done. But I admit, I'm glad I was there. Goodness knows what would have happened if I had not been."

"Do you have any engagements this evening?" Marianne asked, changing the subject.

"Percy and I are going to Sharp's."

Marianne frowned. "That's a gambling hell, isn't it?"

Freddy rolled his eyes. "It's not a *hell*," he said. "It's a very respectable club."

Marianne carried on doggedly, "So, you won't be playing cards then? Or gambling at all?"

Freddy rolled his eyes at that. "I don't plan to. Percy's been asked to make up a table with Skelton, Tavestock, and someone else. I shall probably just watch."

Henry frowned. "Skelton?" he said sharply. "Not *Lionel* Skelton?"

Freddy visibly bristled at the disapproval in Henry's voice. "What's wrong with Lionel Skelton?"

"He's a scoundrel," Henry said flatly. "His reputation is appalling, and Nigel Tavestock's isn't much better. I suggest you stay away from them, Freddy."

Freddy blinked. "I beg your pardon?" he said. He sounded disbelieving and his cheeks had reddened.

"My advice to you is to stay away from Skelton and Tavestock," Henry said firmly. "I can assure you that if they are being friendly to you and your friend, it will only be with a view to fleecing you."

"I'm not a child," Freddy said, getting to his feet. "I'm perfectly able to make my own judgments on the people I come across."

"Whilst I would like to think that's true," Henry said, "your choice of companions lately rather suggests otherwise."

Freddy opened his mouth to say something, then closed it again, but his expression told Henry everything he needed to know about his state of mind—there was resentment in his gaze, and his jaw had a stubborn thrust to it.

"I'm going to change for dinner," he said flatly, and left the room, shutting the door sharply behind him.

For a few moments, the rest of them were silent, then Henry sighed. "Well, that went well."

"It's not your fault, Papa. He's so bad-tempered these days," Marianne said.

"*Hmmm*," Henry replied, not quite agreeing. Freddy had always had a bit of a temper, even as a little boy, but it stemmed from that boundless energy of his. With direction, he would be a formidable young man. His actions today— rushing to the rescue of that young woman without hesitation —demonstrated as much. But without direction or purpose, he had a tendency to become easily bored.

Marianne said, "I don't think he's going to take your advice, Papa."

Henry agreed. And though it would prevent him getting to Redford's promptly, he knew what he had to do.

"Well, I think I'll call in at this gaming club he's going to," Henry said. "And see for myself what he chooses to do. Besides," he added. "I'd like to get a look at this new friend of his. Percy Bartlett."

By ten that evening, Henry was near grinding his teeth in frustration.

He'd told Christopher—*Kit*—that he would arrive at Redford's at some point after nine o'clock, but now he had to stop by Sharp's first. Freddy had only left half an hour ago, and Henry had decided to wait a full hour before venturing to Sharp's for himself. No point arriving before Freddy had so much as sat down.

The delay was giving him far too much time to brood over what might happen—or what might *not* happen—at Redford's.

He tried to read a book to pass the time, but could not concentrate, and found himself staring endlessly at the same page.

Getting to his feet, he paced the room, finally halting in front of the looking-glass above the mantel. He sighed. Sometimes it was startling to look at one's reflection and recall how old one was.

He was seven-and-forty.

When last he'd seen Christopher, he had been nine-and-twenty.

Not so *very* much older than Freddy was now.

He sighed, remembering his argument with Freddy earlier.

"I'm not a child! I'm perfectly able to make my own judgments on the people I come across."

It was really quite galling, Henry reflected, how he had gone, in his children's eyes, from being a godlike creature whose sage advice was sought on the smallest matters to being someone whose every word was apparently quite superfluous and unnecessary. George barely confided in him at all these days, and if Henry gave Marianne enough rope, she'd manage him as though she were the parent and he were the child.

Henry sighed again and turned his head to examine more closely the streaks of grey at his temples.

Silver threads amongst the gold, as his mother used to say— or amongst the chestnut-brown in his case.

He ran his hands down his torso, frowning at the slight softness to his once-flat belly. He was fortunate enough to still be reasonably fit, thanks to his daily rides in Wiltshire, but he was beginning to notice that the years were taking their toll. His left knee had begun to ache when it rained—the niggling remnants of a twisting sprain he'd suffered after catching eleven-year-old George jumping down from a tree he'd got stuck in.

It made him feel old.

He thought back to when he'd first met Christopher. He'd had no conception then of how handsome and healthy he had been.

Perhaps no one realised how fortunate they were at that age.

Perhaps it was only later, as one witnessed the gradual, unrelenting loss of those attributes, that one began to truly understand what one had once had.

The clock in the corner chimed the half hour.

Time to go.

Henry carefully adjusted his neckcloth, minutely rearranging the folds, then made his way downstairs, to where the carriage would be waiting.

When he arrived at Sharp's, Henry stayed inside the carriage, sending his groom to tell the doorman that the Duke of Avesbury sought to be admitted. Though not a member, his title and fortune would undoubtedly grant him entry. Sure enough, only a few minutes later, a well-dressed man emerged. Henry watched from the carriage window as the man took in the elegant equipage, and the ducal crest painted on the door.

"Your grace," the man said as he approached the carriage window. He executed a creditable bow. "William Tait, at your service. Do I take it you will be honouring us with your presence this evening?"

"I thought I might," Henry replied, offering a remote, polite smile. It never did to appear too keen.

"Ordinarily, we require our patrons to apply for membership in advance," the man told Henry, "but in your case we would be very happy to make an exception."

Henry nodded at the groom to open the door and stepped out of the carriage. He followed Tait to the front door, and the doorman stood aside to let them pass.

Inside, Sharp's was gleaming and new-looking. The main gaming room was all dark green and gold. Gold-striped wall hangings and heavy, bottle-green velvet curtains. Dark-green leather upholstered armchairs and baize-topped walnut card tables.

Most of the chairs were occupied, and the play looked to be serious. The conversation was relatively muted, and there were no lightskirts patrolling in search of customers.

"Do you wish me to have a new table set up for you, your grace?" Tait asked.

"Let me do a circuit of the room first, to see if there is anyone I know here whose table I might join."

"Very good, your grace. Would you care for some refreshment? Some champagne, perhaps?"

"That would do very well," Henry agreed. "Thank you."

The man nodded and disappeared, and Henry began to slowly make his way around the room.

He recognised almost no one. Having been gone from town nearly two decades, he had relatively few acquaintances in society circles. There were a few faces he thought he recognised, but only one he could positively identify: the elderly Viscount Linton. Linton had been ancient when Henry was a boy and appeared not to have changed so much as a hair in the last eighteen years. He frowned in Henry's direction as though trying to work out who he was.

The other men in the room glanced at Henry less obviously, mildly curious but mostly hiding their interest. As for Henry, he smoothly wove his way between the tables, stopping every now and again to watch play for a while before moving on.

He finally found Freddy in a small, private room off the main chamber. There was no croupier dealing the cards or observing the play in here. Just the players at the table.

Henry stood, unnoticed, in the doorway for a few moments. Despite having claimed he would be taking no part in the game, Freddy was indeed one of players.

Henry glanced around the table. He immediately recognised Lionel Skelton, who was around the same age as Henry. The younger son of some minor baron, Skelton had been a wastrel when Henry had first known him, and Henry could see that nothing had changed. Back then, Skelton had been a big, strapping fellow, but he had not aged well. Now his face was bloated from drink, his features coarse, his small eyes bleary.

Henry took a little longer to recognise the man sitting beside Skelton, but finally placed him: Nigel Tavestock. Eighteen years ago, Tavestock had been an unremarkable, quiet young man with mousy hair, always in the shadow of the larger, more assertive Skelton. Now, Tavestock was bald as a coot, thick in the waist, and had a florid complexion that made him look rather flustered, an impression that was not improved by his dishevelled cravat and wrongly buttoned waistcoat.

Beside Tavestock was another of Skelton's old cronies, Cecil Hammond. Where Skelton and Tavestock had swollen with age, Hammond had shrunk. He was a weedy, thin-mouthed fellow with a weak chin and watery eyes.

It seemed these three birds still flocked together... and were still seeking to take advantage of pigeons. Pigeons like Freddy, who was not—as he had suggested earlier this evening—merely watching the game but was fully engaged in it, and was presently studying his cards in complete igno-rance of Henry's arrival.

Henry felt an odd combination of helpless love and frus-trated anger as he watched Freddy. He may be two-and-twenty, but Henry would always see the little boy in him. The sturdy, adventurous little boy, who used to lead his more careful elder siblings into scrapes that Henry would inevitably have to rescue them from—like George from that tree.

Just then, Freddy looked up, as though sensing Henry's attention, and his eyes widened with horror. "Father," he said. "What are you doing here?"

The other men around the table all looked up at that.

"*Avesbury?*" Tavestock said, sounding surprised.

Henry nodded. "Good evening, Tavestock," he said. "You don't mind if I join you." It wasn't a question—he pulled out an unoccupied chair and sat down. Tavestock blinked and shot a panicked glance at Skelton, who pressed his lips tightly together but voiced no objection.

Hammond kept his cool a little better, merely nodding at Henry, who returned the gesture politely.

The final member of the party, who looked to be a few years older than Freddy but considerably younger than the others—perhaps in his late twenties—had to be Percy Bartlett. He was certainly dressed like a dandy, just as Marianne had described, with absurdly high shirt points and a complicated-looking cravat arrangement. His brown hair was carefully curled and arranged to look romantically tumbled.

He was almost handsome, but not quite. There was something about his pale eyes that Henry didn't like. They were slightly bulbous and a little too far apart, giving him a vaguely froggy appearance, and his upper lip looked as though it had a tendency to curl in a sneer.

"Your grace," the man said, inclining his head.

Henry smiled coolly. "Mr. Bartlett, I collect?"

Bartlett nodded and smiled, seeming gratified at being acknowledged by a duke.

"Yes, your grace, I am pleased to make your acquaintance."

"Likewise," Henry said with cool politeness. "Any friend of Freddy's."

Freddy's face was pink and his mouth was pinched. Plainly, he was mortified by Henry's turning up here.

"Checking up on me, Father?" he asked tightly.

"I thought I'd call in and see what Sharp's is like," Henry replied mildly. "I won't stay long. I've an engagement elsewhere."

"You'll stay for a hand at least, your grace?" Bartlett said.

Henry noted Skelton's flinch at that comment. It was a small, involuntary movement, so much so that Henry almost discounted it.

Almost.

But he knew Skelton of old.

"Why not," he said, smiling in Bartlett's direction. "Once you finish this game."

While the other gentleman played on, a servant arrived with champagne for Henry. He ordered more for the table and sat back to watch the remainder of their play.

Skelton quietly dominated the game and at the close of play collected a good deal of money from the other players, including Freddy, who squirmed under Henry's calm gaze.

"Are you playing this hand, your grace?" Skelton asked when it was time to deal the cards again.

Henry nodded, watching Skelton closely. He did not react but proceeded to deal out the cards methodically.

Henry waited till he was almost finished to observe, "These are not the house cards, I see."

Skelton paused, just an instant, before he said quietly, "I beg your pardon?"

Henry began to sort through his hand. "I noticed on my way in that the house cards are green with gold edges. These are different."

"Ah, yes," Skelton said. He cleared his throat. "They are mine. This is a private game, you see."

Henry looked up and met Skelton's gaze, which was quite blank. Beside him, Tavestock was fiddling with his cravat.

Henry shrugged. "Unusual," he said succinctly, then turned his attention to his cards again. He examined the faces of the cards with his eyes and, delicately, unobtrusively, the surfaces with his fingertips.

He was unsurprised to find that one appeared to be marked, two tiny, almost indiscernible pin pricks close to the edge of the Queen of Spades.

Retaining that card, he allowed play to proceed through several rounds, picking up and setting down other cards, till he had several marked ones.

How very tedious this was going to be, he thought. Freddy was not going to be happy with him at all, but then, he was going to learn a lesson this evening that should do him some good in the long run.

He set down his hand, and the other players all looked up.

"Are you folding, your grace?" Bartlett asked. He was half-foxed already, and his words were very slightly slurred. Henry decided that he agreed with Marianne—he did not like Percy Bartlett.

"I'm afraid not," Henry said. "I'm calling an end to the game entirely." He looked directly at Skelton and said flatly, "The cards are marked."

"*What?*" Bartlett shrieked.

Henry ignored him. He kept his gaze on Skelton, who visibly paled, then hissed, "That's impossible."

Tavestock shrunk back into his seat. Hammond toyed with his wine glass.

Freddy said, his tone agonised, "*Father—*"

Henry lifted his cards and slowly laid them out in a line. "There are pin pricks on these cards," he said calmly. "Here, and here"—he touched the edges of the cards, showing where the marks were—"and here."

No one moved or said anything.

Skelton's nostrils flared, and twin spots of colour blazed on his cheeks. Henry had not—as yet—outright called him a cheat, but the word hung in the air. Idly, Henry wondered if Skelton would call him out if he said it. He suspected he would not. Twenty years ago, Skelton had been considered a decent shot, but Henry—who had been something of a sportsman in his youth, excelling at horsemanship, swords, shooting, and pugilism—would certainly have bested him.

And Skelton wasn't to know he'd let most of those skills lapse.

Henry glanced at Freddy, who was staring miserably at the green baize, utterly mortified. How he would hate any further escalation of this already unpleasant scene.

It was that thought that made Henry decide to be merciful.

Calmly, he said, "Mr. Skelton, I believe you've been given a bad set of cards. It's most unfortunate, but I'm sure if you return your winnings from the earlier games, the matter can be forgotten."

It was a generous concession to make, Henry thought, and both Tavestock and Hammond looked relieved. Skelton, though, plainly burned with resentment—though not so much that he'd ignore the lifeline he'd been thrown.

"I was quite unaware of the markings," he bit out, "but as a gentleman, I will of course return my winnings, though they were fairly won." He turned to the pile of guineas and vowels at his elbow and began to sort them into piles.

"I don't—" Freddy said desperately, as Skelton shoved a pile of guineas and a paper at him, but Bartlett interrupted him.

"A handsome gesture, Skelton," he said, scooping his own, much larger pile towards him. "Shall we call for fresh cards and continue the game?"

Henry saw the flicker of amusement in Hammond's eyes at that fatuous response. Christ, could Bartlett not see what he was dealing with?

Henry pushed his chair back and stood. He looked at Freddy.

"I have the carriage," he said. He left the question unsaid.

Freddy. Poor Freddy; he looked utterly mortified. But hopefully, he was no Bartlett—too dim to see what sort of men he was playing with.

Several long, agonising moments passed, and then Freddy slowly rose.

"I think—I am done for the night." He turned to Bartlett and offered a tight smile. "Tattersall's tomorrow, Perce?"

Bartlett scowled. "Don't be a spoilsport, Asquith!" His

pale gaze shifted between Henry and Freddy, though he made no other comment.

Freddy gave a short laugh. "I'm tired," he said. "Too many nights on the town. I'll see you tomorrow." And with that he turned away and walked towards Henry, who was already standing in the doorway.

Henry smiled at him reassuringly—Freddy did not return the smile.

"The carriage is outside," Henry murmured as Freddy passed him. "I'll be out in a moment. Need to use the convenience."

Freddy nodded and left the room.

Henry caught Skelton's eye and gestured with his head, letting him know he wanted to speak to him. Skelton's mouth tightened, but he gave a slight nod. Tavestock and Hammond noticed the exchange, but Bartlett, who was draining his champagne glass, was entirely oblivious.

Henry strolled out of the room and waited in the corridor. A few moments later, Skelton joined him, closing the door softly behind him.

Henry smiled. He said gently, "Don't come anywhere near my son again. Do you understand?"

Skelton's face purpled with anger, but he nodded, saying nothing. Henry turned and began to walk away.

"Avesbury—"

Henry turned back. Skelton's gaze was calculating now, his upper lip sneering.

"Do you remember Kit Redford?"

Henry flinched at the shock of that name on Skelton's lips. It shouldn't have been a shock—Skelton had also been an occasional patron of the Golden Lily—but there was an unwritten rule among men like them that such things were not mentioned.

Henry said nothing, only stood, waiting.

Skelton took two steps forward. In a confidential tone, he

said, "After you dropped him, no one would touch him with a bargepole—except me. I took him on, and my, he was an eager little bitch." He laughed nastily, then whispered, "I used to make him beg for my cock like a dog."

Henry's gut twisted sharply as the pictures Skelton's words painted flowered in his mind, in all their graphic horror.

Christopher on his knees before this monster.

"After you dropped him..."

Henry felt like he might throw up, but he would not let his feelings show to the man standing before him. The man who was only saying this as revenge for what had just happened.

Without emotion, Henry said, "Stay away from my son. If you don't, I'll destroy you."

He was only a little gratified to see Skelton pale before he turned away and stalked back to the gaming room.

———

Freddy was waiting in the carriage. He didn't say anything when Henry climbed in, keeping his face turned towards the window.

"As I mentioned," Henry said as he settled onto the opposite bench, "I have an engagement this evening, but I'll take you back to Curzon Street first."

"Fine," Freddy said. His tone was flat and uninviting.

Henry suppressed a sigh and stuck his head out of the window to call out instructions to the coachman.

Once they were on their way, he watched Freddy's shadowy profile. Freddy had to be aware of his scrutiny, but he said nothing, his jaw tight, lips pressed together.

At last, unable to bear the silence any longer, Henry said, "Skelton is scoundrel. You do see that?"

"Yes," Freddy muttered.

"Good," Henry said, "because your friend, Bartlett, doesn't seem to have cottoned on."

"He's just foxed," Freddy said shortly. "I'll put him right on it tomorrow. There was no talking to him tonight."

"If he's the sort of man who won't listen to reason, perhaps you should consider whether you want to have him as a friend," Henry said.

Freddy turned and glared at him, the angry gleam in his eyes unmistakable.

"Who would you rather I spend my time with, Father? Edgar, perhaps?"

Edgar Maitland, Freddy's best friend at school, was an exceedingly likeable young man. He and Freddy had got along famously, since they were both energetic and adventurous, though their escapades had given Henry more than a few grey hairs over the years.

"Freddy—" Henry began wearily, knowing what was coming.

"I could have," Freddy said, bitterly, "If you'd agreed to buy my colours."

Henry made a sound of frustration. "I'm sorry, but I don't want you to join the army—"

"Cavalry," Freddy interrupted.

"Army, cavalry, navy—it's all the same," Henry said flatly. "You'd be signing your life away."

"It's a good career!" Freddy exclaimed. "Most fathers would be proud at the idea of their son taking a position as a cavalry officer."

"It's dangerous."

"Just because Uncle Arthur died, doesn't mean—"

"*Frederick—*"

Freddy fell silent, just as the carriage began to slow. They were home.

"I'll let you get to your engagement then," Freddy said stiffly, opening the door.

And then he was gone, and the carriage door slammed shut.

Henry sighed.

He checked his watch—nearly midnight. He wondered if Christopher would be annoyed by his late appearance. If he would even admit Henry now.

He stuck his head out of the window again.

"Take me to Palfrey Terrace."

13

KIT

Kit had made it his business some time ago to find out as much as he could about Peter's natural father, Mr. Percival Bartlett.

Bartlett was a typical idle gentleman of the ton. He liked clothes, gambling, and drinking. He disliked work. Or, more accurately, he considered work to be something that did not fall within the purview of a man of his class. Work was contemptible. But apparently, to be work-shy, to sponge off of others, and to neglect to pay his bills was the height of good taste.

And on top of all that, the man was a rapist and a bully.

Despite his father's considerable wealth, Bartlett was nearly always strapped for money. His allowance was generous, but he gambled whatever he had away within days of receiving it, and for the next quarter would simply rack up bills and issue promissory notes, digging himself deeper and deeper into debt as he waited for his wealthy father to die.

Kit knew that one of the gambling establishments Bartlett attended was owned by none other than Jake Sharp. And so, once Clara had calmed down from her ordeal in the park, Kit went in search of Sharp.

It took Kit a little time to track him down. He tried first the club Sharp had opened near Redford's, where he was told the man had only just left for the Knightsbridge club. When he got to Knightsbridge, he was informed that Sharp had not yet arrived, though he was expected quite soon. Kit gave his name and asked if he could wait. He expected to be turned away, but to his surprise, was invited inside and led into the office of a man who introduced himself as Mr. Tait, the manager of the Knightsbridge club.

Kit wasn't entirely sure what to make of the fact that Tait seemed to know exactly who he was, but he accepted the offer of a glass of port wine with polite thanks, and for the next half hour made pleasant conversation with Tait as they waited for Sharp's return.

When Sharp arrived—throwing the door to Tait's office open without so much as a knock and marching inside—it was evident he'd been informed of Kit's arrival already. His keen gaze went straight to Kit and he grinned wolfishly.

"Mr. Redford," he said with satisfaction, his forceful personality seeming to suck all of the air out of the room. "To what do I owe the pleasure?"

Kit's own smile was pleasant but careful. "I was rather hoping you might be able to help me with something."

Sharp's eyes gleamed, his mouth twisting into a smile that was both sardonic and attractive.

"I will certainly do my best. Come to my office and we can talk."

He beckoned to Kit, who rose from his chair, pausing to thank Tait for his time and the wine.

"You're entirely welcome, Mr. Redford," Tait said. "It's been a pleasure to finally make your acquaintance."

Finally?

Kit kept his expression blank, but he wondered at Tait's words. Had Sharp spoken of him to Tait? And if so, why?

There was no time to puzzle it out. Sharp was already

striding out the room, and Kit hurried after him, following him into another room further down the corridor.

Tait's office had been comfortable and tasteful, but Sharp's... well, it was something else entirely. Fully twice the size of Tait's, it held a large desk, a round table with four chairs, and the largest and most luxurious chaise longue Kit had ever seen, upholstered in deep-red velvet and big enough for two grown men.

Kit raised his eyebrows at the chaise longue and Sharp laughed.

"I spend a lot of time here," he said. "May as well have everything I need." He gestured at the table. "Take a seat, Kitten."

Kit tried to hide his instinctive bristle at the nickname as he pulled out a chair and sat himself down. Sharp opened up a cabinet in the corner of the room and drew out a decanter of amber liquid and two large glasses.

"Brandy," he said decisively as he approached the table. He didn't ask Kit if he wanted one, just set the glasses down and poured out two generous measures, then took the chair opposite Kit.

"Tell me, then. How can I help you?"

Kit sipped the brandy. It was very good, and certainly French.

"There's a man causing trouble for one of my people. I think he may come to this club, and I wouldn't be at all surprised if he owes you money. I was rather hoping to beard the lion in his den—or rather, in *your* den. A public confrontation with the threat of more scandal would be, I think, enough to scare him off."

Sharp sipped his brandy then leaned back in his chair. He looked amused. "This may surprise you, Kitten, but I generally don't allow my punters to be harassed here. It's not what I consider to be good business."

Kit smiled and shrugged. "I thought you might make an exception in this case."

"Why?" Sharp asked, his eyes gleaming with appreciation. "Will you grant me something in return?"

Kit met his gaze. "Possibly."

Sharp's eyebrows went up. "Who is this fellow?"

"Percival Bartlett," Kit said. "Oldest son of Sir Algernon Bartlett."

Even as he spoke, he saw the interest in Sharp's gaze.

"I know of him," Sharp admitted. "And yes, he does come here. His credit's just about up, in fact. I was expecting to have a quiet word with him in the near future."

"That doesn't surprise me," Kit said. "He's an inveterate gambler and entirely lacking in self-control."

"Well, he's not alone in that," Sharp replied cheerfully. "Which is just as well for me, or I'd have no punters. So, you want me to let you cause a scene here, do you? Embarrass the man in front of his friends?"

"That's about the size of it," Kit agreed.

"And what will you give me in return?" Sharp leaned over the table and laid his hand on Kit's forearm. His hand was square with blunt fingers. He had a long scar across three of his knuckles. It was a strong hand. A fighter's hand. He met Kit's gaze with eyes the same tawny-gold as a bird of prey. "I'd give a great deal to have you under me for a night. I think I could show you a thing or two."

Sharp was a compelling man, very attractive in his way, but he could not have said anything less appealing. Kit had no interest in a man who thought he could teach him anything between the bedsheets, thank you very much. Besides, he'd sworn a long time ago never to trade his body again. And he had a feeling there were other ways to gain Sharp's agreement.

"I'm afraid that's not something I'm prepared to bargain

with," Kit said smoothly. He paused then, aware of the enormity of what he was about to do. "But I'll owe you a favour."

He knew it was rash to make so broad an offer to a man like Sharp. But his own request was not small. And since he was refusing what Sharp had asked in return, he had to offer something worthwhile.

A favour—anything—that could be called on at any time.

Sharp's tawny gaze sharpened with interest and he smiled. A slow, dangerous smile.

"Very well, Kitten," he said. "We have a bargain."

It was after six o'clock by the time Kit left Sharp's club and not worth going back home for dinner. He decided to go straight to Redford's and eat there. He'd take the opportunity to do a little work in his office before heading downstairs to mingle with his patrons.

He wondered if Henry would come to Redford's tonight.

By now the man had had plenty of time to think better of his impulse. He'd been overcome by guilt earlier—and perhaps not a little lust. Once his common sense had reasserted itself, he'd have realised it was terrible idea.

He won't come, Kit told himself firmly. But the idea that he *might* kept teasing at the edges of Kit's mind, preventing him from concentrating on anything, and as the hours ticked by, he was unable to control the mounting, squirming excitement in his belly.

It had been an eventful day. As well as Henry's visit, there had been Clara's ordeal and his interview with Jake Sharp. The latter two events were far more significant in terms of Kit's day-to-day life than a visit from the man who had left him destitute two decades earlier. But as he sat in his office reviewing the latest invoices and delivery notes for the club, all he could think of was his encounter with Henry. And as he dined in his small private parlour before going downstairs to socialise with his patrons, he could barely manage a bite of the delicious meal the kitchens had sent up for the nervous excitement fermenting his gut.

Henry.

It had been so long.

Kit had thought he'd forgotten what Henry looked like. He still remembered one night, some years ago now, when he'd tumbled into bed, drunk and miserable, and hadn't been able to summon up the memory of Henry's face. He should have been pleased but instead, he'd wept like a drunken fool, as if his heart was breaking in two.

Except, now it seemed that he hadn't forgotten—not really —because the moment he had laid eyes on Henry, the familiarity of the man's face, his bearing, his expressions—all of it had crashed into Kit like an unexpected wave, knocking him off his feet.

For years, he'd thought of Henry as the man who had cheated him and left him with nothing. The resentment and bitterness he'd felt over that had kept him going for a long time, like red-hot, smouldering coals keeping a fire alive.

But this afternoon, he had seen Henry's unmistakable dismay. His mortification at having wronged Kit. Kit could admit that now—Henry's horror at learning what had happened had obviously not been feigned. There had been real despair in his eyes as Kit had confirmed his worst fears.

All these years, Kit had believed that Henry had just cast him aside, like Kit was nothing. He *had* been cast aside, of course—that remained true—but not as ruthlessly as he'd once thought. And not without regret.

Henry's regret did not, however, undo the past. And it did not change the fact that Henry had seen Kit as little more than an object to be used. One that would not be needed as long as first anticipated, and that could disposed of by an instruction given to a servant.

No need to look Kit in the eye and tell him why he was breaking their arrangement early.

But really was that so surprising? Kit had been of no more consequence to Henry than a tailor, or a footman. It was only that the services he provided were rather more intimate—and that he had made the very great error of imagining that genuine feelings had arisen between them while he was providing those services. He could only be grateful that he had not made the even worse mistake of confessing his foolish feelings to Henry, as he had been on the verge of doing so many times.

Henry had simply never reciprocated Kit's feelings, had he? But then why was he now offering to do whatever Kit demanded to make amends?

Kit stared at his barely-touched dinner, his heart racing as he considered the question... and came to an answer that made his stomach twist.

"If you are making amends, it has to cost you something."

Kit closed his eyes, regret settling in now.

Henry had been genuinely horrified to learn the truth, and Kit could admit now that the Henry he had known, all those years ago, was the sort of man to do whatever was necessary to make good a wrong he was responsible for.

"You, on your knees for me. Sucking me off in front of everyone."

Did Kit really want to do that to Henry? To humiliate him like that? Would it achieve anything? Make anything better?

When Kit opened his eyes again, he glanced at the clock on the wall.

Half past eight.

Time to dress and go downstairs.

Henry probably wouldn't come anyway.

14

HENRY

The entrance to Redford's was very discreet, and only one doorman stood outside. A large man but well-dressed and polite. Henry gave his name to the man, who nodded in recognition and opened the door to admit him.

Inside, there was another door, and another doorman—also large and polite. He directed Henry down a short, well-appointed corridor, which led to a spacious, tastefully decorated room, just like any one might find in an ordinary gentlemen's club.

Some of the patrons sat in groups, their armchairs clustered around low tables, while others stood, talking in low voices. Several discreet waiting staff circulated. Everyone was well-dressed, and there was no sign of any debauchery.

"Avesbury? Is that you?"

Henry turned towards a familiar voice, smiling when he saw who it was.

"Corbett," he said, genuinely pleased. "It's good to see you, man." He moved towards his old friend, his hand extended and Viscount Corbett took it, a genuine smile lighting up his rather forbidding face.

"And you—it's been far too long! What brings you back to town at long last?"

"Family matters," Henry said vaguely. "I am only here occasionally. I don't bother with society events these days."

"Christ, nor do I," Corbett said quickly. "The last time I saw you was at your daughter's wedding, and we didn't get much chance to talk. Before that—hell, Avesbury, it must have been a good few years!"

"I made one or two appearances during Marianne's season a couple of years ago, but happily my sister was only too pleased to deal with bringing her out."

"I'm not surprised I didn't see you then," Corbett said, his expression pained. "I avoid those sorts of events at all costs. Must say though, this is rather the last place I'd have expected to see you turn up. Kit Redford's club?" He arched a brow. "Did he approve your membership?"

Henry noted Corbett's surprise with dismay. How well known was the story of what had occurred between him and Christopher?

"Why do you think he would not?" Henry asked carefully.

Corbett looked momentarily taken aback, then he said carefully, "My apologies. I think I might have spoken rather out of turn."

Henry shook his head. "Don't apologise," he said quietly. "The question was a genuine one. I'd appreciate your honest answer."

Corbett eyed him doubtfully, then he shrugged. "It's not something that is freely gossiped about, Avesbury—you needn't worry about that—but there are a few, like myself, who were regulars at the Lily back then, who remember what happened."

"And what is that?" Henry asked softly.

Corbett looked pained, but he said, "You'd set Kit up—word was with a very nice little arrangement. And then all of a sudden, it was over and Kit was out on his ear with nothing to show for his time with you." He met Henry's gaze. "It was rather assumed he must've done something—some whispered that he had stolen from you, or perhaps tried his hand at blackmail."

"God, no!" Henry interjected, horrified. "You didn't believe that, did you?"

Corbett looked abashed. "Later, I realised it was nonsense, but at the time I didn't know what to think—why else would you turn him off so suddenly? And there was no retribution."

Henry's stomach churned. "Is that why he—is it true he took up with Lionel Skelton?"

Corbett's brows drew together in a frown. "I'd forgotten about that," he said. "Yes, he did. That was a bad business."

"Why? What happened?"

"Well, I only heard about it after," Corbett said, "but the story I got was that Skelton was a brute. Used his fists on Kit and one night went too far—left him in a bad way."

"Christ," Henry whispered. He felt sick.

"I used to make him beg for my cock like a dog."

"Are you all right?" Corbett asked, frowning. "You've gone as white as a sheet, Avesbury."

Henry swallowed and nodded. "Yes. I just—I didn't know any of this. And the thing with Christopher being turned off by me? He never did *anything* wrong, Corbett. That was all *my* fault." Henry took a deep, shuddering breath. "He suffered because of me."

Corbett's frown deepened. "Come with me. You need a drink."

He was only vaguely aware of Corbett steering him towards a couple of armchairs and urging him to sit down. He sank into the comfortable leather, his mind racing, while Corbett summoned a servant and ordered brandy for them both.

"I shouldn't have told you like that," Corbett muttered when the servant had gone. "It must have been a shock."

"It's my fault," Henry said. "I had no idea."

"It was a long time ago," Corbett said gently. "And look at Kit now. He must be worth a pretty penny. He owns this place and dresses as elegant as the finest dandy you ever did see. Whatever bad things might have happened, he overcame them."

When the servant arrived with their brandy, Corbett fell silent, leaning back while the man set the glasses down on the table.

Henry lifted his as soon it was poured and threw back the contents in one go. The spirit burned his throat and a fresh wave of nausea rose in him, threatening to bring up his dinner. He swallowed hard and thankfully the feeling subsided.

"Do you remember Phineas Warren?" Corbett asked.

Puzzled, Henry looked up, meeting his friend's serious gaze. "The name is familiar... wait, was he that old banker who used to go to the Lily with his own boy so he could watch him with other men?"

Corbett nodded. "That's him. Well, that's who Kit took up with after Skelton."

Henry blinked, remembering the elderly banker and his pretty companion very well. It was all too easy to imagine Christopher as he had been then—pliable and lovely—sitting quietly at Warren's feet with a collar around his neck.

Though not so much the *Kit* of today, Henry thought, with his cutting comments and angry green gaze.

"They were together a good few years," Corbett continued. "And Warren left Kit nicely set up, I heard. Nothing in the will—Warren was too smart for that, he made all the arrangements before he died. Wanted Kit to be looked after, he said. Course, he was so rich that what he gave Kit was a drop in the ocean compared to what his nephews and nieces got, but it must have been enough to start Redford's. And Kit's made a great success of the place, I must say."

"So I've heard," Henry said faintly. And looking around he could see it was true—the furnishings were tasteful and expensive. Beyond this room, he could see a glimpse into the dining room next door, which was also bustling with well-dressed patrons. It all looked so respectable—it was difficult to believe there was anything debauched going on anywhere in the building.

It wasn't a bit like the Golden Lily. Christ, the second you walked in that place, you knew you were in a brothel. All those scantily clad young beauties... But Henry could already see that Redford's catered to an entirely different sort of customer.

Yes, Kit had made a success of his life—no thanks to Henry.

"So you see," Corbett said gently, "you don't need to feel so terrible. Kit's done all right. Better than most that come from where he did." He smiled. "And he can't be holding a grudge, or you wouldn't be here, would you? He's very particular about who he lets over the door. You need at least two personal recommendations from existing members, and Kit's own approval to even be considered."

Henry couldn't hold back a laugh at Corbett's assumption that Kit had *approved* him, though he feared he might sound somewhat deranged. Corbett wasn't to know why Kit had really invited Henry here.

It was as that thought crossed his mind that he quite suddenly, and viscerally, realised the full import of what he had agreed to do tonight. To get down on his knees in this place and let the man who had once been his kept boy fuck his face in front of anyone who cared to watch.

Oh God.

Henry groaned and covered his face with his hands. His stomach churned, and his blood ran cold. What had he been thinking to agree to such a thing?

But he had agreed. He *had*.

"Avesbury?"

Abruptly, Henry stood. "I have to find Christopher," he said. "Have you seen him?"

"Kit, you mean?" Corbett said. "He was in here earlier. He may be in the dining room or one of the card rooms now."

Henry nodded. "Thank you. Excuse me, Corbett."

"Of course," Corbett said, but his expression was curious.

Henry found Christopher in the third room he tried, a card room. Not that Christopher was playing cards, or even watching someone else play. He was standing with two gentlemen at the side of the room, talking and laughing, a glass of champagne in hand.

Christopher was turned very slightly away, giving Henry an oblique view of his perfect profile. He was dressed with a sober elegance that Henry did not associate with the young man he had once known. His black coat was perfectly tailored, his black breeches very correct, and his high shirt points and cravat were pristine white.

But when Henry stepped forward and said his name —"Christopher"—he turned to reveal a less sedate picture. His gold silk waistcoat was embroidered with an outrageous snarling sapphire dragon, and his beautifully carved lips were touched with vermillion, while the elegant fingers that cradled his champagne glass bore an array of gleaming and glittering rings.

He was breathtaking.

Christopher raised his eyebrows, his tone disbelieving as he echoed Henry's greeting. *"Christopher?"*

It was only then Henry remembered his words of earlier.

"My friends call me Kit... you may address me as Mr. Redford."

Henry's gaze flitted, unwillingly and uneasily, to the two elegant gentlemen standing on either side of Kit, both of whom were at least a decade younger than Henry, and who were now staring at him with unabashed curiosity.

Clearing his throat, his neck burning with mortification, Henry said, "Sorry, Mr. Redford, I meant."

One of Christopher's companions tittered at that, lifting a lace handkerchief to his mouth, though Henry thought not so much to hide his laughter as to draw attention to it.

Christopher glanced sharply at the man, then back at Henry, and Henry feared he was about to be rather humiliatingly dismissed. Or perhaps ordered to his knees.

But in the end, Christopher—Kit—cast a careless smile at his two companions and said silkily, "Do excuse me, gentlemen."

Stepping towards Henry, he took possession of Henry's right arm with his free hand and expertly steered him away.

Henry could not suppress the smile that tugged at his mouth, though he tried to bite it away.

"Thank you," he said in a low voice.

"Don't thank me too soon," Christopher said lightly, offering a teasing smile to an elderly gentleman walking past them in the corridor. "You've only just arrived."

"Ah, yes. I'm sorry about that."

"About what?"

"Being so late," Henry said. "I had something I had to attend to before I came."

Christopher seemed nonplussed. "You're hardly late," he said. "It's only just past midnight."

"But you said to come at nine."

"I said to come any time after nine." Christopher cocked a brow at him. "We're open till four o'clock, so it's still quite early by my standards."

Christopher led him back into the room where he'd been talking with Corbett. Henry saw that they were attracting some interest. Numerous gentlemen were glancing at them surreptitiously, then murmuring to their companions. He wondered if there was anyone here who recognised him.

There was no sign of Corbett now—he must have gone to one of the other rooms.

Christopher guided Henry over to a quiet corner, pausing on the way to ask one of his staff to fetch more champagne for them both.

"This is where I like to stand," he told Henry. "I can see everything that's going on from here." And it was indeed a good vantage point from which to view the room, especially for Christopher, who was a sight shorter than Henry.

Henry leaned against the wall beside Christopher, reducing the height difference between them a good bit. When Christopher turned his head to look at him, Henry was struck by the strongest sense of familiarity—this was something he used to do in the old days, when they were standing together. Henry had performed the familiar choreography quite unconsciously.

In the soft candlelight Christopher looked younger, and that provocative touch of red on his lips stirred Henry. He used to love the small feminine decorations Christopher employed to enhance his beauty. For Henry, it had never been because it made Christopher seem more feminine—almost the opposite in fact. Something about these decorative little adornments underlined his masculinity in a way that heated Henry's blood and made him impossibly hard.

He stared at Christopher, and Christopher returned his gaze, his own touched with curiosity—it felt almost as though no time had passed at all, as though Henry had somehow imagined all the years between then and now.

"This feels so familiar," Henry murmured.

"Yes," Christopher said. "The memory is a strange thing."

Henry tried to read what he saw in Christopher's eyes. An edge of bleakness perhaps, but something determined too. He wasn't sure what to make of it, how to read him. When he had first seen Christopher this afternoon, the man had been palpably angry. Henry had half expected to see the same fury in his gaze tonight, but Christopher seemed more wary than anything else.

"Ah," Christopher said then, his gaze moving over Henry's shoulder. "Here's our champagne."

Two servants approached, one carrying glasses and champagne on a silver tray, while a second carried a tall stand on which the tray was set. The servant with the champagne removed the cork without fuss and filled both glasses.

"You can leave the bottle," Christopher said, and they withdrew.

Christopher touched the rim of his glass to Henry's with a tiny clink. "What shall we drink to?" he asked lightly.

"Your success?" Henry suggested. "This place is very impressive."

Christopher sipped his champagne and smiled. "What were you expecting? Somewhere like the Golden Lily?"

Henry laughed. "I suppose I was. This is a deal more... restrained."

"Do you remember the first time you were at the Lily? Mabel was having a Roman orgy night and I was wearing this ridiculous garb—" Christopher broke off with a peal of laughter.

Henry did remember that—only too well. Except the memory wasn't having quite the same effect on him. His cock was filling at the mental picture of Christopher's lean, beautiful body, decorated with a few floaty wisps of transparent fabric held together with golden clasps, a pair of golden sandals on his feet, a golden laurel wreath on his head... and very little else.

Somehow Christopher had got even closer—or Henry had —their faces were only inches apart now.

Christopher stopped laughing. He swallowed, then said something too softly for Henry to hear over the babble of conversation in the room.

"What was that?" Henry asked, dropping his head a little lower and offering his ear.

"I looked very silly," Christopher whispered, his warm breath gusting pleasurably over Henry's ear, making him shiver.

He turned his head back, moving his lips towards Christopher's ear to respond—to deny that statement—but as soon as he started to speak, Christopher whipped his head around and their lips grazed, shocking Henry into open-mouthed silence.

Henry's first thought was that Kit had intended to kiss him. But the immediate warm glow of pleasure he felt at that thought died when Christopher jerked back, his cheeks flushing.

"Sorry," he said hastily. "It's just that I—I can't hear in that ear."

Henry stared at him, frowning. "I beg your pardon?"

"I can't—I'm—I'm deaf in that ear. I… had an accident."

His gaze slid away as he was saying the words, and Henry read in the gesture old hurt, old humiliation.

Without thinking he blurted, "Did Skelton do that to you?"

Christopher's shocked expression told him he'd inadvertently hit on the truth.

"He did, didn't he?" Henry said. "I learned today that he was your—" He broke off. Swallowed. "And it seems he beat you so badly, you lost your hearing."

For a moment, Christopher stared at him, stricken, then he tore his gaze away and lifted his champagne to his lips, draining his glass.

"It was a long time ago," he said tightly. "As you can see, I recovered."

But he hadn't. Not fully. He was deaf in one ear.

"God, you must hate me," Henry said thickly. "It was my fault. If I had taken more care—"

Christopher's gaze was impossible to read. There was a hint of the anger from earlier there now, but other things too. Resentment in the thrust of his jaw and, when his green gaze flicked to Henry, a kind of impatient pity.

"Like I said," he said tightly, "it was over a long time ago. I'm not—" He broke off, frowning to himself.

"What?"

Christopher sighed. "I don't know what I was thinking this afternoon, asking you to come here."

Henry's heart sank. Suddenly the thought of being ordered to his knees in front of everyone didn't seem like the worst thing that might happen tonight.

"I thought," he said carefully, slowly, "that you wanted me to make amends to you."

"What I suggested wouldn't be you making amends," Christopher said wearily. "It would be punishment, pure and simple."

Henry stared at him—he didn't know what to say. Relief and disappointment warred in him. He could see that Christopher was working up to letting him off the hook.

"Perhaps," he said slowly, "I want to take my punishment. Perhaps I need to."

Christopher met his gaze. He looked like he was thinking.

After a while, Christopher said, "You don't have the slightest idea what it would be like, you know. You probably think, because you've been to brothels and bought whores and performed acts in front of other people that you wanted to perform, that you know what this will feel like. But you don't."

"Don't I?"

"No," Christopher said quickly, almost angrily. "You don't know what it's like to be used in front of others, with no care for your feelings or comfort or pride. Like a thing."

For a moment, Henry felt like he couldn't breathe, then he said faintly, "Was that how I made you feel?"

Strangely, Christopher looked shocked at the question. "What? *No*, I mean—" He broke off and looked away, closing his eyes, his nostrils flaring as he fought to control himself.

"Skelton then," Henry guessed aloud, and he knew by the shudder that passed through Christopher's body that he was right.

He yearned to reach for Christopher, to pull his slight frame against his own larger body and embrace him, but he had no right to touch Christopher, not now, not ever.

When Christopher finally opened his eyes, he said, "This afternoon I was angry, Henry. I spoke rashly, said things I didn't mean." He sighed. "I don't want to humiliate you in front of my patrons, not really. They may be discreet out in the world, but they gossip amongst themselves. And I don't —" He broke off.

"Yes?" Henry prompted gently when he did not finish.

"I don't want to be a person who would do that, just because I can."

Christopher reached for the champagne bottle and sloppily poured himself another glass, drinking half of it down before meeting Henry's gaze again.

"I'm letting you off," he said. "You made your point. You came here, prepared to do what I asked. Let's leave it at that."

Henry stared at him, unable to speak. Christopher's generosity moved him more than he could say, but still, he felt oddly crushed. Grateful, yes, and relieved, but unmistakably, gut-wrenchingly disappointed.

He levered himself away from the wall, standing straight again and tried to smile, though it felt like feeble effort. "I daresay if I were in your shoes—" he began. He searched for the right words. "Well, let's just say I can understand your reticence to allow me anywhere near you again."

He went to turn away, but Christopher caught his sleeve. "Henry—"

He turned back and gazed at Christopher. At that once-beloved face, the generous, so-often-smiling mouth, the inquisitive green eyes that glinted with intelligence. Christopher looked a little harder now than before, yes, but he still had that deep-down goodness to him. That *sweetness* that had drawn Henry to him just as much as his undoubted beauty and sensuality.

Christopher had every reason to hate Henry, every reason to take the opportunity to humiliate him. Henry would have willingly let him do it.

But, no. It wasn't in his nature.

"Yes?" Henry said hoarsely.

Christopher was frowning. "That's not why I'm letting you off," he said. "It was never bad with you—not once." He let go of Henry's sleeve. "I'm not saying it was exactly how I wanted it, but it wasn't like it was with Skelton or any of the others. I always"—he paused, met Henry's gaze—"God help me, Henry, but I always *wanted* you."

Unbidden, Henry felt tears prickle in his eyes. He swallowed hard.

"Thank you," he said, thickly. "I'd be wretched if I thought you'd hated it."

Christopher smiled then, a sweet curve of his mouth that Henry remembered so well, and that had his heart twisting in his chest.

Impulsively he said, "How *did* you want it with me, Christopher?"

Christopher looked almost comically surprised to be asked. He jerked his head away, lifting his champagne glass to his lips as though afraid Henry might see something betraying.

When he finally lowered the glass, he said, "I suppose, I wanted it to be real."

"Wasn't it real?" Henry asked sadly. "It felt real."

Christopher's gaze was rueful. "It did, didn't it? I thought that too."

"But it wasn't?"

Christopher shook his head. "When you're a whore, your answer to every question is yes. Even when you *want* to say yes, you are always aware that you can't say no. It changes everything. It changes the very nature of who you are."

The heaviness in Henry's chest felt like grief. He blurted out, "I wish I could be with you without that between us, if only just once."

Christopher stared at him for a long time, his green gaze searching Henry's face.

"Do you mean that?" he whispered at last.

Henry nodded. "I do."

Christopher considered that for what felt like a very long time. Then, finally, he said, "All right then, Henry. Come with me."

15

KIT

Kit took Henry upstairs, to his private rooms, where he'd lived before he bought the house in Marylebone. He still used his old bedchamber occasionally, when it had been an especially long night, or he needed to be at the club early the next day, or when he wanted a nap before the evening ahead.

Henry was quiet as Kit led him into the bedchamber, watching as Kit used the chamber-stick to light the candles by the bed. The flames glowed weakly, then rallied, burning a little stronger and higher, casting flickering shadows against the wall.

He turned back to face Henry, excitement and fear twisting in his belly. The realisation of how much he wanted this—how much he still wanted Henry—alarmed him. His old feelings were surging up, like a milk pan boiling disastrously over, astonishing him.

Was it really only this afternoon that he'd first seen Henry again? Henry looked so familiar, standing there in the middle of the bedchamber. Almost as though no time had passed at all.

But things had changed—everything was, in fact, quite, quite different.

Now they stood before one another as equals, and Kit had the sudden, heady realisation that he was entirely in charge of this encounter.

"What shall I do with you?" He mused aloud.

Henry's gaze was steady. He said, "Whatever you want, Christopher. I only want to serve you."

Kit's mouth went dry at that assurance, and his cock hardened. "Is that so?" he said breathlessly.

Henry nodded, and as if to make the point as clearly as possible, he sank to his knees on the rug.

The wave of lust that crashed over Kit at that sight was almost overwhelming. He tightened his hands into fists by his sides and said hoarsely, "You look very alluring like that, Henry, but I only want you to do it if you want it too. This is not a punishment."

"I do want it," Henry said, almost desperately. "Please, Christopher. Tell me what you want."

For several beats, they stared at one another, then Kit stepped towards him and choked out, "Suck me, then. I want your mouth on me."

Henry moaned and the sound went straight to Kit's cock, his already-hard shaft stiffening further in his breeches. *Christ.*

Henry lifted shaking fingers and began unfastening the buttons at the placket of Kit's breeches while Kit stripped off first his coat and then his waistcoat, tossing them aside. By the time he was tearing off his neckcloth, Henry had his breeches undone and was reaching into his drawers to pull out his engorged shaft.

Henry groaned at the sight. He leaned forward and rubbed his face along the length of Kit's cock, before kissing the tip and then taking it into his mouth.

Kit cried out at the immediate pleasure of Henry's tongue curling over his sensitive shaft, then moaned at the velvety clasp of his inner cheeks as he sucked.

Henry feasted on Kit's cock for long minutes, kissing and licking and sucking, before diving deeper, forcing Kit's cock into the warm, tight tunnel of his throat.

"Oh Christ," Kit gasped. "That's too good—I'll be spending in a minute."

It was far too long since he'd had a man on his knees for him like this. And he'd *never* had Henry Asquith on his knees. Kit stared down, tunnelling his fingers into Henry's dark hair and tugging lightly, making Henry moan and look up. And Christ, the lust and the pleasure in that hazy grey gaze...

Henry pulled off Kit's cock and stared at him. His lips were swollen and wet, and Kit wanted to kiss him, but before he could formulate words, Henry was leaning forward again, licking another stripe up Kit's cock that had Kit's thighs trembling.

Henry looked up at him again. "Do you want to lay down while I do this?"

Kit blinked at him dazedly, and Henry added, seeming embarrassed, "In truth, my left knee is getting a little sore."

"Oh!" Kit exclaimed. "Yes, of course. Shall I"—he paused —"undress?"

Henry's smile was sweet and a little uncertain. "Yes. Please."

Kit quickly removed his shoes, breeches, stockings, and drawers. When he was quite naked, he climbed on the bed, watching with rapt attention as Henry completed his own disrobing. And God, but he was a lovely sight. A little bigger in the chest and shoulders than before, Kit thought, and still as powerfully muscled as he'd ever been. His dark chest hair was speckled with grey, as was the nest of hair at the juncture of his thighs. Kit liked it—he liked these signs of maturity and experience in a man. He always had.

He wondered what Henry thought of him. He knew, without vanity, that he still looked good. His body was as slim and lithe as ever, his hair still mostly fair, the silver threads not terribly obvious, but there had been changes. Everyone lost that easy bloom of youth eventually.

Henry didn't seem to have any complaints though. When he clambered up after Kit onto the bed, his grey gaze was hot with lust, lingering on the lines of Kit's body with unabashed pleasure.

"You're so beautiful, Christopher," he whispered, as he caged Kit's body with his strong arms and slowly lowered his own down, keeping most of his weight from Kit even as he allowed the whole length of their bodies to kiss.

Kit made a noise that was not quite a moan and not quite a sigh. Something of both, helpless and needy.

"*You* are," he groaned.

He was saying too much, being too frank, but he couldn't hold the words back—never had been able to with Henry.

Henry's gaze was burning. "I want to make you feel as good as you used to make me feel when you did this for me," he said. "I want to turn you inside out like that."

Kit wanted to tell him he didn't even have to try, but the words escaped him as Henry moved downwards, pulled Kit's cock into his hot mouth again, and began to work him with patient relentlessness.

Henry pressed Kit's thighs apart, giving attention to his tight, quivering balls, his sensitive inner thighs, the soft, wondrous flesh between his scrotum and his hole, and then— oh Christ in heaven—*then*, he kissed Kit's hole.

His lips were soft and warm, and the tip of his tongue, when it delicately probed Kit's rim, was a maddening point of delight.

Kit melted into the mattress, widening his thighs, giving Henry all the access he needed, and when Henry's fingers brushed his hole, his groan was deep. "*Yes.*"

His whole body was singing with pleasure as Henry patiently penetrated him first with one finger, then a second, his mouth still teasing Kit's sensitive rim.

Kit was only vaguely aware of time passing. No one had ever spent so much time simply giving him pleasure. He was undone, a slave to his own lust and need, torn between the desire for more of this, and the desire to topple over the edge and crash through a climax he knew would be shatteringly intense. He cried out as Henry worked his body, heedless of being overheard, demanding more.

And Henry gave him more.

He was plunging his fingers in and out of Kit's body now, and when he lifted his head again, then bent over Kit's groin to take his cock once more into his mouth, Kit grabbed him by the hair and thrust into his warm, clasping depths, his seed exploding from him as he cried out his release.

He came so hard, his vision greyed. Only as the final shocks of it ebbed did he realise he had Henry's hair gripped tightly in his right fist, Henry's head held tight against his thigh.

"Sorry," he gasped, letting go.

Henry raised his head and blinked at Kit dazedly. He was a mess—lips swollen red and eyes wet from tearing up as Kit had fucked his face.

"Bloody hell," Henry said hoarsely. "I've spent all over your bedcovers,"

Kit stared at him for a moment, then slowly grinned. "Have you?"

"I'm so sorry," Henry muttered, his cheeks hot.

"Don't be," Kit replied. "I think I'm flattered."

"Are you?" Henry breathed, blinking at him slowly. He rose up on his knees and repositioned himself over Kit, straddling Kit's deliciously relaxed body, leaning down till their lips barely touched, and Henry's broad, hairy chest skimmed Kit's mostly bare one.

Kit squirmed a little, the intimacy feeling raw again, now that he'd spent and his mind had cleared. But Henry didn't seem the least bit uncomfortable. His grey gaze moved over Kit's face hungrily.

"I can't think why I never did that before," he whispered. "It was glorious. Making you feel like that, watching you come apart."

"Don't tell me you haven't done that before," Kit scoffed, though his voice was a little breathless. "You knew what you were doing."

Henry's mouth kicked up in a rueful half-smile that Kit remembered too well. He felt even more breathless seeing that smile.

"Yes, of course," Henry said diffidently. "But not with you. And not with me—" He broke off, flushing red.

"Not with you what?" Kit asked.

"Not like that… on my knees. Serving you," Henry whispered.

Kit blinked. "Oh," he said slowly. "I see."

They stared at one another for long moments, till Kit began to feel awkward. He was lying here with Henry—the man who had broken his heart so thoroughly, he had never allowed anyone else near it again.

Was he quite mad?

Kit shifted. He forced himself to smile at Henry—though it felt like a very stiff sort of smile—and said, "Do you mind if I get up?"

"Oh—sorry—yes, of course," Henry said quickly, clambering off him.

Kit immediately rose and went to the wardrobe, pulling out a dressing gown—an outrageous saffron yellow one with black trim—which he pulled over his nakedness. He felt suddenly shaky. He wanted to wash and to be alone for a while.

He turned back to face Henry, who was now sitting on the side of the bed watching him with wary eyes.

"Well," Kit said, with a smile that felt horribly stiff. "I

think we can agree that you've thoroughly made amends now."

"Christopher—"

"It's been really quite an odd day, hasn't it?" Kit said, speaking over him. "I certainly didn't expect it to go like this. I daresay you didn't either. But I don't suppose it's turned out too badly, all things considered. Perhaps we can say goodbye properly this time. And part as friends—or as near to friends as a duke and a whore can ever be."

He thought Henry might smile at that. But he didn't. He looked troubled.

"You're not a whore, and I didn't do that to make amends," he said thickly. "Any more than you did it to punish me. I *wanted* to do it. God, Christopher—I spent all over your bedcovers, just from touching you. If that doesn't —" He paused and took a shaky breath. "I'm sorry. I'm making a mess of this."

Kit stared at him. He couldn't think how to respond.

Softly, almost inaudibly, Henry said, "I didn't want to leave you. But Caroline was dying, and I had promised her I would give you up if she asked me." He swallowed. "It was cowardly, sending Parkinson to tell you. I regret that more than I can say."

The sudden prick of tears in Kit's eyes surprised him— irritated him, even. This had happened *lifetimes* ago. It was ridiculous to weep over it now.

And yet, when he looked at the defeated slump of Henry's shoulders, he wanted nothing more than to do just that.

What was Henry's crime, after all? He'd agreed to his wife's dying request. A woman he had made promises to, the mother of his children. Someone he'd always told Kit he truly loved. Would Kit really have wanted Henry to deny her request?

"Did she know about me?" he asked. The question was out before he could second-guess himself.

Henry met his gaze. "Yes. You might remember, we had stopped sharing a bed some time before I met you. She had given me *carte blanche* to take a lover. But..."

"But?"

Henry sighed. "She didn't want it to be someone I had feelings for. I think... I think Caroline saw physical passion as very different from married love." He paused, considering. "I think she was pleased, in a way, that you were a man. She couldn't really imagine what I had with you being anything other than—*bestial*, I suppose."

Kit recoiled. He couldn't help it. There was something so offensive about that. The way it reduced what he and Henry had had. Which really was pretty ridiculous. It wasn't as if there had been anything so pure about him and Henry, was there? He'd been a whore. Henry's kept boy. He'd entered into their arrangement knowing full well Henry was married.

Tentatively, Kit said, "I always assumed she didn't much enjoy the marital bed."

Henry sighed. "Neither of us did."

"Oh," Kit said. "I'm sorry, Henry."

Henry offered a weak smile. "I don't know if it was my fault or if she would have been uninterested even if I had desired her. She said it would have made no difference, so I try to take comfort from that. But sometimes I wonder."

"That's natural," Kit said. "But for what it's worth, there are some people who just don't want that sort of intimacy. I've known one or two in my time."

Henry looked so hopeful at that, Kit could have wept.

"You always spoke very fondly and respectfully of her to me," Kit said quietly.

"In all other ways we were well suited," Henry said. "The best of friends—that's what we always said."

Hesitantly, Kit crossed to the bed and sank down next to Henry, careful to keep a bit of space between them. "You did love her then," he said curiously. "Despite everything?"

Henry nodded. "When she died, I would have gone to pieces if it hadn't been for the children. Caroline was a loving mother. The older ones in particular took her death very hard. When she passed, they needed me in a way they hadn't before. And I needed them too."

"They'll all be grown now, I suppose," Kit said. Henry hadn't mentioned his family a great deal when they were together, but Kit had known he had four children, two boys and two girls—two young men and two young women now —and it had been obvious that Henry adored them.

When Henry said nothing, Kit glanced at him, worried. Had he misspoken?

"Three of them are grown," Henry said at last, staring down at his loosely linked hands. He took a long, steadying breath before adding, "My youngest, Alice, took scarlet fever and passed away when she was five." When he finally raised his grey gaze to meet Kit's, the grief in his eyes was unbearable.

"I'm so sorry, Henry," Kit said, his voice cracking on the words.

Strange how, every time Kit had thought of Henry over the years, he'd imagined him living a golden life in his stately pile in the country. Even when he'd heard about Caroline's death—many years after her actual death, it transpired—he had not, to his shame, considered how much her loss would have hurt Henry. He'd simply imagined Henry casually selecting another wife for himself, siring a second brood of children.

When had he begun to think of Henry in such an ungenerous way?

He'd never had reason to doubt that Henry had loved his family. The fact that he did not cherish such feelings for Kit did not mean that he was incapable of them. After all, why would a man like Henry Asquith think of a paid whore as anything *other than* a servant? Kit had chosen to sell his body for money. He'd put a price on himself, body and soul. He could hardly mind when his customer took him at face value.

It hurt, yes, but it only hurt because Kit had let himself feel things he ought never to have allowed. He'd been foolish, and he only had himself to blame.

Kit glanced at Henry, who was staring down at his hands, his expression still wrecked. Kit wished he could touch him, offer some comfort, but he didn't know how, or if Henry would even want that.

Perhaps he would prefer some privacy, to collect himself again?

Kit stood and stepped away from the bed. "I'll let you get dressed in peace," he said quietly. "I'll be in the parlour when you're ready."

Henry looked up, blinking, as though Kit's words had just reminded him where he was. Without waiting for a reply, Kit left the room, closing the door softly behind him.

He padded through to the parlour, curling up in one of the armchairs to wait. He felt oddly shaky after the intensity of what had just happened with Henry. Stripped, somehow, of his usual self-possession. He wished he could wash up and put his clothes back on. Restore his elegant armour before Henry came into the parlour. But he'd have to wait for Henry to be done now.

After a few minutes, the parlour door opened and Henry stepped inside. His neckcloth looked rather limp, but otherwise he was back to being the elegant, soberly dressed duke. The devastated expression that had shredded Kit's heart was gone, thank God, though Kit could not quite decipher the one that had replaced it. There was something about it that was diffident and determined and uncertain all at once.

When Henry made no move to sit, Kit rose from his chair, uncomfortable to be the only one seated. Immediately, though, he felt the disadvantage of being naked under his dressing gown while Henry was fully dressed.

He was dithering over whether to ask Henry to sit, when Henry said, "I feel that our conversation just now went rather awry."

"Awry?"

Henry cleared his throat. "I was trying to tell you something, but then we began to talk of other things—important things, but still..." He trailed off, frowning.

Kit's heart began to pound in a way it hadn't in a very long time. "What were you trying to tell me?"

Henry rubbed a hand over his face. "I was... trying to apologise."

This again.

Stiffly, Kit said, "Henry, I accept it was your servant who cheated me, not you. You don't need to apologise again."

Even as he said the words—even as he believed the truth of them—they rang hollow in his own ears, and he wasn't even sure why that should be.

Henry said, "I wasn't apologising for that—although I do feel utterly wretched about it." He swallowed visibly, then added, "I was talking about my cowardice in sending Parkinson with a letter instead of going to see you myself."

Kit stared at him, his heart twisting painfully.

"There was barely any time to do anything before we left for Wiltshire," Henry continued, his gaze anguished, "but I should have *made* time. You weren't so very far away from Curzon Street, and if I'm honest"—he broke off, taking a deep breath before he continued—"perhaps I used our hasty departure as an excuse to avoid doing the right thing. The difficult thing." He shook his head.

"Only *perhaps?*" Kit asked, and he was shocked by how clipped and angry his own voice sounded. He had no right to feel so aggrieved by this—he'd just been Henry's whore for God's sake.

But he did feel aggrieved, he realised. He felt aggrieved and hurt and angry.

"I don't honestly know," Henry said, and he sounded frustrated. "It was so long ago, I can't remember how I reasoned it out to myself. I don't think I *deliberately* avoided you, but perhaps I allowed the events of that day to sweep me along in that direction because seeing you—telling you I had to end our contract early—would have been so painful."

Kit's heart ached. Henry would have found that painful? He wanted to demand to know why, but instead he just stood there, with his heart in his mouth, watching Henry.

"I can't stop thinking that if I'd just taken the time—an hour—to go and see you myself, Parkinson would never have been able to do what he did." Henry shook his head. "I'm so sorry," he whispered, and he sounded utterly lost. "I wouldn't blame you if you never forgave me for that. I'm not sure I'll ever forgive myself."

Kit didn't know what to say. Would Henry even believe him if he said he forgave him now?

And would it be true?

He realised that he didn't know the answer to that question. Today had already been far too eventful and Kit needed to let everything just... settle.

"It's been a strange day, for both of us," he said tiredly. "Full of revelations that I've scarcely taken in yet."

Henry nodded.

"Go home, Henry," Kit said gently. He paused, weighing his next words carefully before he uttered them. "We can talk again, if you like. I'm here most evenings."

Henry said tentatively, "Could I return tomorrow evening?"

Kit was taken aback by that—both the request and his own desire to agree to it.

Slowly, he shook his head. "I don't think that's a good idea. I need to reflect on all of this—and so do you." He paused. "Give it a week."

"Next Friday then?" Henry pressed, his gaze hopeful.

Kit's heart was racing now. He suspected this was not a wise course of action. That even a week from now was too soon.

But he did not voice any of those concerns.

"Very well," he said. "Next Friday."

16

HENRY

Henry slept better the night after he visited Redford's than he had in a long while.

Perhaps it was being intimate with someone again. The physical release he had experienced had been powerful. But no, it wasn't just that. He wasn't celibate—he had regular assignations with likeminded men—but none of them ever made him feel like this. Echoes of the deep sense of wellbeing that had suffused him as he and Christopher came together still pulsed through him.

That wellbeing was a feeling he had forgotten, one that came not just from finding release, but from holding someone very dear to you, and touching that person freely. Henry hadn't realised how much he had missed that. How wonderful it was.

The whole of the next week seemed to drag interminably, and all Henry could think of was Christopher.

To distract himself from his thoughts, Henry immersed himself in duty, attending to the pile of outstanding correspondence that had accumulated since he'd come to town and paying a number of long-overdue calls.

Finally, though, it was Friday again.

Henry took his breakfast in his room that morning, then called for a bath, taking a long time over his ablutions. He scrubbed himself till his skin was pink, already anticipating the evening ahead. Of undressing in front of Christopher.

Kit.

By the time he made his way downstairs, Marianne, Jeremy and Freddy had all gone out, and Henry found himself at something of a loss. For the first time in a long while, he was entirely free to do whatever he wanted. It felt both liberating, and at the same time, strangely empty. For the last number of years, his life had been shaped by the needs of his family and the rhythms of life in the country. He was used to the events of his day being shaped around those two pillars. But here, now, there were no estate matters to attend to and no family ones either.

There was only one thing he wanted to do—but it was too early to go to Redford's.

He repaired to the library and tried to give his attention to the morning paper, but was unsuccessful—his thoughts continually returned to Christopher. To how it had been between them all those years ago, when Christopher had been unmistakably his. When he could have gone to the house at Paddington Green any time he chose. Could have spent the whole day in bed if he wanted.

He wished now he had allowed himself that occasionally, instead of religiously keeping to his twice-weekly visits. But at the time, he had been trying to contain what felt like a worryingly uncontrollable desire to spend all his time with the young man with whom he had been so infatuated.

With the benefit of hindsight, his self-denial had been idiotic—what would it have mattered if he'd let himself have a little more happiness? But back then he'd had some idea that, if he tried hard enough, he could control his essential nature. Hell, back then, he hadn't even thought of his desire for men as being *part* of his nature. He'd thought of it as a preference—or rather, a weakness. A self-indulgent weakness that he could set aside if he were only disciplined enough.

Later, he had come to understand how wrong he was. That his desires *were* part of him, deeply and intrinsically. That by denying them, he was denying his very self. But at the time, he had been unable to think of them as anything other than selfish cravings to be suppressed so far as possible.

Leaving Christopher and going back to Wiltshire with Caroline had been a turning point for Henry. His self-denial had become complete as he devoted himself to his family, ignoring his desires entirely and lashing himself with guilt whenever he so much as thought about them—because how could he be so selfish when his family needed him?

As for Christopher, when it became apparent that Henry was never going to receive a reply to his letter, he tried not to think of him at all if he could possibly help it.

But he could not control his dreams, or the idle thoughts that would sometimes catch him unawares.

The year after Caroline's death had passed in a kind of blur—Henry couldn't remember feeling much of anything, except a grinding sort of grief—but as time wore on, his desires gradually came bubbling back to the surface, refusing to be suppressed.

Henry tried everything he could to distract himself. The children took up much of his time during the day, and he filled the rest with busy work he could have handed off to his steward. He began drinking late into the night after the children had gone to bed to avoid his dreams and numb his pain. Whatever he did, though, it made no difference. Despite being surrounded by people, he felt very alone. There was no one who *knew* him—the real, whole man.

After Alice died, his melancholy grew much worse. And on one long and sleepless night, he'd left the house and walked into the middle of the woods at the edge of the grounds. There was a deep pool there, where he and his brothers used to bathe when he was a boy.

He'd stood at the edge of that pool for God only knew how long, staring at the still, black water and thinking how peaceful it would be to slip under that glassy surface and simply... cease to be.

The one thing that had kept him standing on the bank was the thought of the three children back at the house who still badly needed him.

He could not leave them alone in the world.

At last, dawn had broken, and with it the worst of the dark spell that had held him there. He'd turned on his heel and begun a slow trudge back to the house. As he'd emerged from the edge of the woods, he'd looked up to see the sun rising over the turrets and belvederes of Avesbury House, flushing the sky delicately pink. And in that moment, he'd had a revelation: if he was to go on, he had to accept this was his nature and reconcile himself to it.

After that terrible night, somehow, slowly, Henry had managed to crawl out of the pit he had fallen into. It had not happened in one night or one week or one month. It had been a much slower and more painful journey, one that lasted years. But the revelation he'd had that morning had been the first step on a path to some sort of acceptance.

Much later, he'd begun to seek out other men who shared his nature, and who understood the need to be discreet and careful. But there was no one like Christopher. No one who was dear to him in that way. Henry made sure of that.

His encounters were infrequent and forgettable. That was all he wanted. Perhaps, it was all he could bear. There was a very big difference between the temporary physical intimacy those encounters offered and what he'd had with Christopher.

Henry's body may have finally accepted that it needed physical companionship, but his heart remained wary of love.

Even now, Henry's heart urged him to caution, whispering that perhaps he should resist the temptation to return to Redford's tonight.

But there was another part of him, a long-dormant part, that had been wakened to tentative life a week ago.

Wakened by Christopher Redford.

Kit.

And God help him, but Henry wanted more.

Henry decided to while away the hours till evening by calling on Corbett. The man welcomed him warmly, and they spent a companionable day together. After an early dinner at his club, Corbett invited Henry to join him for a few hands of Faro.

"I can't, I'm afraid," Henry said, trying and failing to suppress a smile. "I've a previous engagement."

"Oh? What's this?" Corbett murmured, clearly sensing there was something more to the story. He arched one expressive brow. "Never say you met someone interesting at Redford's last week?"

"Perhaps," Henry said evasively. Part of him wanted to confide in his old friend about his breathtaking encounter with Christopher, but the more sensible side of him warned him to say nothing.

One thing occurred to him, though, that he wanted to talk to Corbett about. And somehow he found himself blurting it out before he could think better of it.

"Corbett, do you—that is, do you ever take the passive role?"

Corbett stared at him, wide-eyed, and Henry flushed hard.

"I'm sorry," he muttered. "You don't have to—"

"It's all right," Corbett said with a short laugh. "It's just, I'm surprised. Especially coming from you."

"What do you mean, *'coming from me'*?"

Corbett frowned, looking as if he was searching for the right words. At last he said, "You were never—" He broke off. Started again. "You were not one to speak frankly of such things. Oh, we'd go to the Lily together and pick up lads"— he gave Henry a half-grin—"you even let your boy suck you in front of me once or twice, but mostly you were quite private. You never spoke of what you liked, or what you'd tried."

Henry smiled. "You thought me very dull, did you not?"

Corbett rolled his eyes. "I didn't mean that," he replied. "Only that the rest of us would joke, and boast and—I suppose it was our way of finding out from one another what we preferred. But you never did that. And then you left town —I don't suppose it's as easy to find fellows like us when you're living in the depths of the country?"

"No," Henry agreed drily.

"That must have been difficult."

Henry nodded. "And not just for the reasons you're thinking about. I missed *this*." He gestured between them. "The company of others like us."

Corbett nodded. "Hence your question," he said, "regarding my views on the 'passive role.'"

Henry flushed and nodded.

Corbett chuckled, though not unkindly. "Do you know, Avesbury, you still blush like a schoolboy sometimes, and you're forty if you're a day!"

"Seven-and-forty," Henry corrected.

Corbett made a rueful chuff at that. "Handsome devil," he complained. Then he leaned forward in his seat and said quietly, "As it happens, the 'passive role' as you call it— though I would refute the accuracy of that particular description—is my preference."

Henry stared at him. Corbett was, like Henry himself, a large man. Well-built with wide shoulders and a deep voice.

To learn that he preferred to receive was surprising. And intriguing.

Henry realised that Corbett was also watching him closely.

"Have you never...?" Corbett began slowly, his eyes widening a little when Henry shook his head.

"No," Henry said, a little defensively. "It's not so unusual, is it?"

Corbett gave a short laugh. "Who is to say? No one has written an etiquette guide on the matter that I'm aware of."

Henry couldn't suppress a chuckle of his own at that, but his amusement warred with embarrassment over his own gaucheness. At his age, he should not need to ask such questions.

Corbett said, "Were you ever curious about it? Before now, I mean."

"Yes, I suppose so, but I assumed—" He broke off.

Corbett raised a brow. "You assumed—what? That because you were bigger—or richer—that you would not be one taking it up the arse?"

Henry flushed at the crude words, his eyes darting around the room anxiously. Not that Corbett was talking loudly enough for anyone to overhear—the club dining room was full, but the tables were widely spaced and the low hum of constant conversation had a muting effect of its own.

Henry forced his gaze back to Corbett. "It sounds a little ridiculous when you say it aloud, but yes, I suppose that was part of it. People make assumptions all the time, and when you're a green lad with no knowledge of anything, you just go along with it. Especially when you're trying to seem like you know what you're doing."

The first time he'd visited a brothel with male prostitutes, he'd been a duke-in-waiting with enormous wealth and a pair of shoulders as wide as a barn door. Perhaps the assumptions everyone made about him were not so strange? And in fairness, it wasn't as though he hadn't enjoyed what had followed... He had enjoyed it very much. It all felt very new, and very wonderful.

But yes, Henry *was* curious now. Curious about possibilities that hadn't occurred to him back then. Doubly curious after getting down on his knees for Christopher—for *Kit*.

"So," Corbett said, quite as though he had just read Henry's mind, "is the man you met at Redford's the reason for this question?" He grinned slyly.

Henry's laugh was awkward. "Perhaps," he admitted.

Corbett laughed too then, but his gaze was kind, affectionate even. "Then I hope you enjoy satisfying your curiosity, Avesbury. Just make sure to use plenty of oil, eh?"

Henry flushed hotly but he grinned too. Pushing his chair back, he stood. "On that note, I think I'll be on my way."

Corbett's sly grin widened. "Good luck," he said softly, and his good-natured laughter followed Henry out of the club.

· 17

KIT

Kit had almost convinced himself that Henry would think better of his supposed wish to return to Redford's, but shortly after nine o'clock the following Friday evening, Henry strolled into the main clubroom looking every inch the elegant and powerful duke. He stood in the middle of the room, searching for Kit, and when his gaze found him, standing with several other gentlemen, Henry's smile was almost... sweet.

Kit could only guess what his own smile was like. It was immediate and helpless, spreading over his face too quickly for him to check it.

"Would you excuse me?" he murmured to his companions, before moving away.

He tried to put away his smile as moved towards Henry, but his mouth would not comply. The corners tugged up at the edges, and even when he tried to bite his lips into submission, they stretched upwards, betraying him.

Christ, was he sixteen years old?

"Good evening, your grace," he said when he reached Henry. "I wondered if I would see you tonight."

"Really?" Henry said, and he looked genuinely surprised.

"I thought my eagerness was rather embarrassingly obvious. I was only worried you might decide not to let me in after all."

Kit couldn't stop staring at him. His gaze ate Henry up, travelling over his strong, appealing features, cataloguing again the changes that time had wrought.

God, he was being pathetic. He gave a sharp little shake of his head, as though to dislodge his thoughts—Henry was here to talk about the past, that was all.

"I won't ban you from the place before you've even had a chance to see it," Kit said. "I didn't give you the tour last week, but I'll rectify that now. Come with me—I'll show you what brings my faithful patrons to my door, night after night."

Kit guided Henry down the twisting corridors that led from the respectable rooms in number fifteen to the scandalous back room in number seventeen.

He paused outside for a moment, his hand on the door knob. "I'll warn you, it can get rather heated in here, but it's early yet—so I doubt it will be too shocking."

Henry gave a soft chuckle. "Don't worry," he murmured. "I promise not to faint."

Kit opened the door and gestured him inside.

The room was reasonably busy, despite the early hour. There were perhaps twenty men scattered around in couples and small groups. Some were pressed up against walls, while others occupied chairs and low sofas. Some of the men were entirely naked, others fully or partially dressed. Most were participating in mutual pleasuring, but a few simply observed from the sidelines. Kit tipped back his champagne glass, watching as an older man rose from knees, kissed the hand of the man he had been servicing, and moved to a second man in the group to offer his mouth.

Kit glanced at Henry. His face was flushed, and he wore an expression of mingled discomfort and arousal that made

Kit's cock harden in his breeches far more effectively than anything else in the room.

Henry cleared his throat. "Are any of these men prostitutes?" he muttered.

Kit shook his head. "This is where my patrons gather to seek companionship from their fellow members"—he winked at Henry to underline the pun—"so to speak."

Henry gave a dry laugh of his own, but his smile was strained.

"Some of them like to perform publicly," Kit went on. "Others will find a partner and use one of the private rooms —I'll show you those in a moment. Others still prefer to pay someone for their services. They'll meet them in the clubroom or one of the gaming rooms in number fifteen, then come through here for their assignation. Why? Were you hoping to engage someone?" He raised his brows at Henry, as though in invitation, even as his stomach twisted sickly.

Henry looked shocked—hurt, even. "I'm not interested in meeting anyone else," he said. "I came here to see you."

It was stupid to feel gratified by that, and Kit felt irritated at himself. He turned away to hide his reaction, saying, "Come on then."

He led Henry out of the back room and down the corridor.

"These are the private chambers I mentioned," he said, waving his hand at four identical wooden doors. "These ones are all occupied. I'll take you up to the next floor and show you one of the ones up there. Those are nicer in any event." He strode towards the stairs.

"You don't need to—" Henry began behind him.

"Oh, but I want to," Kit said, and began climbing the narrow winding steps.

All the chambers on the next floor were empty, so Kit took Henry into one of the larger and better equipped ones, lighting the candles in the sconce on the wall before closing and locking the door behind them.

It was an airy room with a big, comfortable bed and sumptuous drapes. A padded bench at the end of the bed could serve in a number of ways, and the drawers in the armoire were full of items that the patrons could make use of.

"Come and see this," Kit invited, opening the top drawer.

Henry joined him, staring down in silence at the leather straps and crops laid out carefully inside.

"We cater to all of our patrons' needs," Kit said, smiling. He could not help but enjoy the shocked expression on Henry's face. He closed the drawer and opened the second one, revealing three dildos in varying sizes, and some wrist and ankle cuffs.

Kit pointed at the rings on the cuffs. "These can be fastened to the bedframe."

He glanced at Henry, whose gaze was fixed on the contents of the drawer. Henry swallowed hard, his throat bobbing.

Kit's heart was racing. Without thinking it through he said, "Do you want to make use of any of them, Henry?"

Henry was quiet for a moment, then he turned to look at Kit, his grey eyes glittering faintly. "I just want to serve you. It's up to you whether to use any of them."

Kit stared at him, unsure what to say. He hadn't really let himself think about this, since the week before. Henry's willingness—no, *eagerness*—to serve Kit had astonished him but he had not imagined that it would continue.

Kit looked Henry up and down, remembering how he had looked unclothed. Broad-shouldered and rough with hair, his limbs strong and well-formed. A big, beautiful male body, the kind that Kit liked best. It always surprised him, how many men seemed to like his shorter, slender body when his own preferences ran in such a different direction.

Kit thought of Henry's large and powerful body brought to perfect obedience under his hand, and his mouth went suddenly dry.

It was the strangest thing. He had never craved such play before, though perhaps that was because, in his days as a whore, he'd generally been assigned the more submissive role, on account of his physical appearance. But it wasn't as though he hadn't had plenty of opportunity to explore such possibilities since he'd retired his old profession. Yet it was only now, as he considered the possibilities this offered in relation to Henry in particular, that the idea seemed to take hold of his imagination,

He realised that he had picked up one of the wrist cuffs and was idly stroking the soft leather. And that Henry's gaze was on his hands, a stripe of pink scalding his cheekbones.

"Do you know, I think I rather *would* like to fasten you to the bed," Kit said softly, watching with fascination as Henry's flush deepened. "If you really would not mind."

Henry shook his head stiffly and when he met Kit's gaze, his own was glossy with lust. When Kit glanced down at Henry's crotch, the bulge in the man's breeches told its own story.

"Will you fuck me?" Henry whispered harshly.

Kit blinked. After a pause, he asked carefully, watching Henry, "Do you want me to?"

Henry swallowed and nodded.

"You like that, then?" Kit asked, surprised. In all their time together, Henry had only ever seemed to want to fuck Kit. He'd never voiced to Kit any wish to explore the alternative. Or indeed asked Kit what he thought.

But now… now Henry was looking away, unable to hold Kit's questioning gaze.

"I don't know," he mumbled.

"You don't *know*?" Kit echoed. Was Henry really asking him for something he'd never experienced before? Kit tossed the cuff back in the open drawer and stepped towards Henry, reaching for his jaw and gently turning his face to meet Kit's gaze again. "Let me understand—are you telling me you've never been fucked before?"

Henry's face was burning now, but this time he did not look away. He shook his head minutely and whispered, "But I want to—that is, I want *you* to. Fuck me, I mean."

Kit frowned, thinking back to the previous Friday. All those apologies and that desire for service. Henry's horror that Kit would not allow him to gift the house at Paddington Green to him, or pay him money. His apologies. Despite Henry's assurances otherwise, he had a horrible crawling feeling this really was about making amends for Henry.

"Perhaps you should earn the money you owe me the way I had to earn it? On your knees, and on your back, taking my cock like a whore."

Kit dropped his hand from Henry's face as though his skin burned and stepped back.

"You don't need to do that," he muttered, horrified at the thought that Henry was trying to regain his honour in this way. "I don't want you to submit to me as some kind of penance." He swallowed against nausea and turned away.

"That's not—I'm *not* doing that," Henry protested.

"Then why are you—"

"I *don't know.*"

Kit whirled around to find Henry's desperate gaze fixed on him.

Henry said, his voice cracking, "Last week, I—it was different from anything I've experienced before. I just want *more*. If you do, that is."

He held his hand out to Kit. The leather wrist cuffs dangled from his fingers.

Kit fastened the cuffs to the bed posts carefully.

"Can you move?" he asked softly, and Henry demonstrated that he could.

Henry was naked, wearing only the leather cuffs on his wrists and ankles, and his big body was held fast. Being so tall, he wasn't overly stretched, able to maintain a slight bend at both knees and elbows, but my, he was a sight to see. A harnessed beast, tamed and ready for Kit's pleasure. His breath sawed in and out of his chest as he stared at Kit with bright, burning eyes.

Kit laid his hand on Henry's thigh. "I'm not going to hurt you," he reassured him.

"I know," Henry muttered, but he did not relax, his muscles bunched with tension, the cords on his throat standing out.

"Try to find some ease," Kit said gently, "while I get undressed."

He smiled at the sudden interest in Henry's grey gaze, and his hands went to the buttons of his coat.

And suddenly everything was familiar—familiar but different. He was Kit, taking off his clothes for Henry, only he didn't *have* to do it this time, if he didn't want to. This undressing was no act of submission.

He took his time, signalling his power over Henry with the patience of his slow disrobing and the unhurried setting aside of his clothing. He stripped everything away, item by item, till he was—like Henry—fully naked, and Henry was trembling in his bonds, the wet tip of his hefty cock smearing his belly with silvery trails.

Kit rubbed the pad of his forefinger through a sticky patch.

"*Hmmm,*" he hummed, a note of disapproval in his voice. "Messy."

Henry's chest heaved, and his eyes glittered, his gaze fixed on Kit.

"What shall I do with such a messy boy?" Kit wondered

aloud. He smiled at Henry, letting his gaze travel all the way down his body.

"Are you going to fuck me?" Henry gasped.

Kit's smile widened. "You do seem quite fixed on that idea," he said. "Will you be terribly disappointed if I don't? I'm not sure you're really ready for that."

Henry swallowed. "I can take it," he said.

Kit laughed softly, and he sat on the mattress beside Henry. "Oh, I'm quite sure you can," he said. "But you see, I'd prefer to have you begging mindlessly for my cock rather than bravely withstanding it." He leaned over then, till their faces were very close together, and whispered in a confidential tone, "A fellow likes to think he's wanted, you know."

"You *are* wanted," Henry breathed. "And if you want me to beg mindlessly, I can do that."

Kit's cock was beating an insistent pulse between his legs, and all he could do was stare at the man laid out before him. Breathlessly, he said, "Oh, Henry. You really don't know what you're offering."

"I do, I—"

Kit touched his fingers to Henry's lips, silencing him. "Will you indulge me?" he murmured. "By letting me decide what you can take tonight?"

Henry stared at him a moment longer, then he gave a jerky nod. "All right," he said. "But know that I want this, and I want it to be you, Christopher."

"It's *Kit*."

"What?" Henry said dazedly.

"Call me Kit."

"*Kit*," Henry breathed, his grey gaze travelling over Kit's face as he tried to discern why this was important.

Kit leaned down till their lips grazed. "That's right. I'm *Kit* —Christopher was an agreeable whore. I have not been Christopher for a very long time."

Henry frowned at that, but he nodded his understanding, saying, "Kit," again, his breath soft against Kit's lips.

"Good boy," Kit murmured. "I think that deserves a reward."

And with that, he breached the final, infinitesimal distance between their lips, pressing his mouth fully against Henry's for the first time in years and years.

Henry gave a grateful moan, and Kit slid his tongue deeply into his mouth, exploring briefly, slickly, before pulling back to tease his lips again with soft sucking pulls.

God, but Henry smelled good, just like he used to. A natural, masculine smell that made Kit think of leather and wood. Kit couldn't get enough of it. He broke the kiss and dived down to nuzzle Henry's throat, relishing Henry's helpless moans. He felt rather than saw the movement of Henry's arms as he tried to use them, to reach for Kit, only to be restrained by the cuffs. And yes, by God, Kit liked that. Liked knowing that he had Henry held helpless.

Kit climbed onto the bed properly then, covering Henry's leashed body with his own, relishing the roughness of Henry's chest hair against his smoother skin. He began travelling downwards, leaving a feverish trail of kisses in his wake, pausing briefly to suck obscenely at Henry's nipples.

Given entirely free rein to do whatever he wanted, Kit found he wanted map every inch of Henry's glorious body with his mouth.

Henry moaned and gasped in response to Kit's attentions, occasionally muttering his name or pleading inarticulately. His limbs tensed under Kit's mouth, and his cock pulsed and leaked, a thin trail of glittering fluid connecting his tip to his belly.

When Kit reached Henry's cock, he swiped his tongue over the tip, relishing the burst of salt. He played lightly for a while, suckling the head teasingly, tickling the point of his tongue up Henry's thick shaft, stroking Henry's balls with soft brushes of his fingertips till Henry was almost sobbing with frustration.

When Henry gasped, *"Please, Kit,"* Kit lifted his head and grinned.

"Ready to play harder?" he asked. Without waiting for a response, he stretched his lithe body over Henry's to grab a small bottle from the bedside cabinet. Henry groaned again as Kit's body rubbed his own.

Bottle in hand, Kit leaned back on his heels. He showed it to Henry. "Remember using this on me?" he teased.

He rocked the bottle from side to side, and the oil inside moved, slow and viscous.

Henry could only seem to pant. Kit grinned and moved downwards again—this time without the distraction of kisses—and settled himself comfortably between Henry's spread thighs.

Henry was hairy down here too, and God help him, Kit liked it. Liked the way the nest of dark hair around Henry's cock trapped his delicious scent. He kissed Henry's inner thighs, his balls, his perineum, then dipped his tongue, just catching at Henry's rim, making Henry gasp and Kit grin with satisfaction.

He delicately explored Henry with his lips and tongue while he deftly opened the bottle of oil, then leaned back to pour a thin stream onto Henry's body, watching as it trickled down from his balls to his hole.

Kit caught the oil with his fingertips and anointed Henry's hole, relishing every gasp and hiss from Henry's lips. Slowly, he increased the pressure of his fingers, gently massaging the tight, tense muscle.

Henry's moans were fast and rhythmic now, his hips working up and down, his torso arching and twisting with pleasure. He was *loving* this, Kit thought wonderingly.

Kit slowly pushed one finger into Henry's hole—it seemed to greedily suck him in—and Henry's eyes went wide.

"Oh *God*," Henry moaned, his voice thick with pleasure. "More. *Please*, Kit, more."

He took a second finger easily and a third without much trouble, despite the firm tension of his muscles, powerfully gripping Kit's hand.

Soon, Kit was plunging three fingers in and out of Henry's body, and Henry just kept begging for more.

"Give me your cock," Henry begged. "*Please*, Kit. I need it."

And suddenly, Kit couldn't think of a single reason why he should hold back a moment longer.

He scrabbled up onto his knees and found the oil again, pouring another thin stream over his own cock this time, taking a few short but necessary moments to ready himself and line his shaft up with Henry's body.

"Are you sure about this?" he somehow managed to grit out.

"Yes, fuck me, *please*," Henry begged.

So Kit did. He pressed his cock into Henry's body in one long, demanding thrust that made the other man cry out, then breathe hard for several long moments.

Hell, he'd gone too hard.

"Are you all right?" Kit gasped quickly, stilling.

"Yes. Just… getting used to it. Please, that was good—don't stop."

Thank God, Kit thought, because truthfully, he had no idea how to stop. It felt astonishingly good to be inside Henry, to thrust his cock into Henry's big, strong body without holding back anything.

As he began to move again, he became entranced by Henry's uninhibited response. He couldn't believe how open the man was. Other than that initial cry, he'd shown no signs of discomfort or even embarrassment. The panting moans that fell from his lips and the flush that bloomed on his upper chest and throat made it clear he was enjoying this.

"Christ, Henry," Kit breathed, staring at him with wonder. "You were made for this. Made for my cock."

Henry groaned again at that, and his thighs strained up. "I want to—" he began, then stared at Kit pleadingly.

"Shall I free you?"

"Just my ankles," Henry said. "Please."

Kit pulled out, smiling at Henry's swift protest, and quickly undid the buckles on Henry's ankles, massaging Henry's rim for a few moments before pushing inside him again.

Henry's eyes rolled up and he lifted his legs, tightening them round Kit's waist as Kit began to fuck him in earnest, his hips slamming forward.

When Henry came, it was sudden and shocking. His cock had been pulsing between their bellies for a while, leaking a steady stream of fluid, and then suddenly it was erupting in thick, creamy pulses and Henry was gasping, "Oh, fuck! Oh, Kit, I'm coming—no, don't stop, keep fucking me, *please*!"

So Kit did. He kept fucking till Henry's long climax finally ended and he fell back on the mattress, his legs slack now, gasping for air. Only then did Kit let himself go, let his own crisis roll over him, yanking an orgasm from his balls so strong his vision greyed as he came deep into Henry's body, shouting out some sort of absurd war cry of dominance and possession.

The sudden wetness of his own seed inside Henry's body made him feel ridiculously pleased. He found he wanted to stay inside Henry, to keep his seed there, painting Henry's insides, owning him somehow. It was stupid and primitive and made him feel rather silly, but there it was. It seemed that Henry had unleashed something—or someone—quite primitive inside Kit, and he wasn't quite sure what to do with this surprising side of himself.

Eventually, though, as his cock softened and Henry began to shift beneath him, Kit had no choice but to extricate himself. Lifting himself off of Henry, he undid the wrist cuffs, then awkwardly dismounted and wandered over to the jug and ewer on the armoire to wash himself.

By the time he brought Henry a damp cloth and clean towel, Henry was sitting up, blinking dazedly.

"Thank you," Henry mumbled, accepting the offerings, while Kit turned away to fetch his shirt and drawers off the floor.

Once he had his shirt and drawers back on, he found Henry's and handed those over too. Henry blinked, seeming nonplussed. After a moment, he set the bundle of fabric down on his lap, imperfectly covering himself.

"Well," Kit said, aiming for something close to his usual light tone. "That was… unexpected."

He thought Henry might take his cue from that, attempt to put some distance between them, but no. Even as he went to move away from the bed, Henry reached for him, his fingers closing over Kit's wrist, tugging him back.

"Kit," he whispered. "I had no idea."

Kit wasn't sure what precisely Henry was referring to having no idea about, but one thing was clear to him—Henry felt vulnerable in this moment. He needed comfort. And so, half-reluctantly, he let Henry tug him back onto the bed. Let Henry pull him close and settle Kit's head on his shoulder the way he used to all those years ago. Let him stroke his fingers through Kit's hair. So familiar. So intimate. As intimate in its way as it had been for Kit to plunge his cock into Henry's body. And arguably, more dangerous.

After a while Henry said, "That was—astonishing. I don't think I could have done it with anyone else."

Kit snorted.

"I mean it, Chri—sorry, Kit."

Henry fell silent again, but Kit could practically hear him thinking, and he waited patiently for the words he knew would follow. He had learned this about Henry a long time ago—he needed to be allowed a little silence before he would say much.

At last Henry said, "I came to you in hopes of repaying you for my past mistakes. And all I've done is indebted myself to you more."

Kit lifted his head and looked down at Henry, frowning. Henry's handsome face was anxious, genuine regret in his grey eyes.

"If you think I got nothing out of what just happened, I have to doubt your sanity." Kit gave a crooked smile. "I haven't come that hard in years."

Some of the tension went out of Henry's expression and he chuckled softly.

Kit lifted himself up to a sitting position. Looking down at Henry, he said seriously, "Can I ask you something?"

"Of course."

"I asked you this before, but this time I need you to promise first, on your honour, that you will be perfectly honest in your answer."

Henry met his gaze. "I promise, on my honour."

"Did you offer yourself to me like this as penance?"

Henry opened his mouth to answer, then closed it again, and Kit's heart twisted painfully. Henry was having to think about this. Kit had been right to be suspicious.

When he went to move away, Henry sat up too, reaching for him, catching his arm. "Don't look like that," he said, frowning. "It wasn't for penance, but—look, will you let me explain properly without bolting away?"

Kit hesitated, then settled back down. "All right. Go on."

Henry relaxed and let go of his arm. "I'm not sure how far back to go."

"Go back as far as you need to," Kit suggested gently.

Henry smiled at that, for some reason. "You haven't changed a bit, do you know that?"

"God, I hope I've changed a little!" Kit chuckled. "No one

should be as naive as I was when you first knew me." When Henry's smile faded, he added, "Sorry. I didn't mean that—"

But Henry laid gentle fingers on his lips and said softly, "Please don't apologise. You've every right to say such things."

They stared at one another for a beat, then Henry dropped his hand. "Did I ever talk to you about my father?" he asked.

"You mentioned him, from time to time," Kit said. "He knew you preferred men. I know that much."

Henry nodded. "He was not pleased when he discovered it, not by any means, but once he realised I would fall in line with what was expected of me, he didn't care so very much. His primary concern was to arrange my marriage to Caroline before he died—to protect the family line." He smiled at Kit, a little sadly. "And so I married young—as he had wanted—and dutifully produced my eldest son, George, the following year."

Like a breeding bull, Kit thought, though he did not say it aloud.

"I had a few experiences with men before Caroline and I married," Henry said. "All prostitutes, all at the same establishment." He smiled at Kit. "Arnott's, in Covent Garden."

Kit made a face—he knew the place Henry spoke of and hadn't thought much of it.

"When you first went into Arnott's, you were taken to the proprietor. Mr. Arnott, I presume, though he never introduced himself. He always seemed to be sneering, I thought. He'd hand over a price list of what you could have. The men were all young and reasonably well-favoured. Obedient and accommodating." Henry sighed. "It wasn't like this place," he said. "There was no mingling or drinking. No places to gather. Just the ordering of a service, payment up front, then the performance. Arnott would ring for someone to be brought through after you'd paid. You could send them away and ask for someone else, if you wanted, but I never did.

Arnott would tell the prostitute what you'd paid for—never by name, always by number—and you'd go to the room with him and he'd barely speak, just do what was required, then leave you to clean up after."

Kit nodded, watching Henry carefully. He didn't look unhappy as such, but there was something sad in his expression, and Kit could only wonder why he was sharing these memories.

"I remember the rooms were very plain and small, just a bed, and a jug of water. A tiny window at the top, letting in a very little light. It was so gloomy they always had to have a candle, even during the day."

"It sounds rather dismal," Kit said.

"It was," Henry agreed. "But it was better than nothing." He paused. "I stopped going when I married Caroline—I thought that was it for me, with men. And it was, for a few years. Until Caroline had Alice. After that, she asked me not to visit her bedchamber anymore, and said she was happy for me to take my pleasure elsewhere." He smiled at Kit. "I was almost giddy with the freedom of that. It wasn't long before I heard about the Golden Lily, and the very first night I went there, I met you." He smiled, his grey eyes warm. "From the first moment I saw you, I was infatuated. I'd have done anything to have you."

Kit's heart thudded in his chest as he remembered that first night and the young god who had done nothing to disguise his interest in Kit. He'd felt powerful that night, in a way he never had before. The patrons of the Lily usually liked to exercise their power over the men they bought, issuing commands, relishing the eager obedience of the whores. But Henry had looked at Kit with something like wonder in his eyes. It had made Kit feel like a person—a man—in a way he never had before.

"The negotiation was a joke," Henry said ruefully. "The madam gave me a list of demands and I agreed to them all. I just wanted you as soon as I could get you. And then, once I had you, everything you did was so perfect. It never"—he broke off for a moment before continuing—"it never occurred to me to ask for anything different. You would say, *shall I suck you?* or *would you like to fuck me now?* and whatever it was, it would always sound like a wonderful notion."

Yes, Kit recognised the truth of those words. He had gently managed Henry when they'd been together. At the time, he'd thought Henry was indulging him in allowing it, like a favourite pet. Now he wondered if Henry had just preferred being somewhat passive.

"After Caroline died, and I left London, and you, there was a long time when I did not so much as touch another man. Years. At first, there were too many other things to worry about, and I was not inclined anyway. But later, when my desires began to reassert themselves, I tried to suppress them. I told myself I would not return to my old ways. But"— here, his voice cracked—"they would not be suppressed, Kit. The more I tried, the more urgently they loomed in my mind. The more I denied myself, the more tormented I became. I almost lost my mind, I think. One night I considered—" He broke off and turned to look at Kit with despair in his grey gaze.

"*Henry*—" Kit leaned forward, laying his hand on Henry's thigh, needing some kind of physical connection with him. Thinking of Henry enduring such pain was intolerable.

Henry covered Kit's hand with his own. "It was a terrible night," he said. "But I survived it and it was only in that moment of despair that I was able to see the truth."

"The truth?"

Henry smiled sadly. "That, for better or worse, this is part of me. That I could not continue ignoring that and live."

Kit swallowed against the lump that had lodged in his throat.

Henry absently stroked Kit's hand. "I wrote to an old

friend who gave me an introduction to a place in Trowbridge where I could go. It was not a brothel—just a place where one could meet other men and find some relief. Temporary companionship."

Kit nodded his understanding. The thought of Henry being reduced to brief, furtive encounters devoid of any affection, made his heart ache. Henry was not like that.

Henry frowned. "I'm taking a very long time to get to the point, aren't I?" he said.

"That's all right," Kit said softly. "I'm more than happy to listen."

Henry took a deep breath and let it out. "I suppose what I'm trying to say, Kit, is that I *very much* wanted this. That, until now, I've not really had so much choice about what I did in the bedchamber. I denied myself for so very long. And when I wasn't doing that, I took what I could get, what I was offered, what others guessed I wanted. I've not been very good at saying—or even knowing—what *I* wanted."

Kit watched him, saying nothing, but his heart ached for Henry.

"And then," Henry said, his voice almost wondering, "I found you again, and you said those things to me about putting me on my knees and making me take your cock." He stopped. Met Kit's gaze fully. "I *wanted* that. And when I got down on my knees for you last week, it felt like the only place I ever wanted to be. Serving you like that." He let out a long, shaky breath. "When I got home after, I could think of nothing else. Only that and coming back here to ask for more. For *this*."

They stared at one another, and Kit could not look away.

"So, you see," Henry said softly, "I did not offer myself up to you as some kind of penance. If anything, I was taking from you, again. Taking my own selfish pleasure; fulfilling my own desires. You have nothing to feel guilty about." He sighed. "Does that answer your question?"

It answered a great deal more than that single question, Kit thought, but he didn't say so. Only nodded, and leaned closer to kiss Henry's cheek.

"I'm glad—" he began, then stopped. *I'm glad you didn't do whatever it was you were considering that night, when you were in despair.* He couldn't bring himself to say the words aloud though. Instead, he whispered, "I'm glad you came tonight."

Henry turned his head a little, so their lips brushed and their eyes met. "I'm glad too," he whispered, and in that moment, it felt to Kit as though all the years since the end of their long-ago love affair had dissolved to nothing. The man beside him was the same Henry he had fallen in love with, and this was how they'd sat together so many times before, in a nest of tangled sheets, staring into one another's eyes, sharing the very air that they breathed.

"May I say something?" Henry whispered.

"Of course," Kit said.

"You'll stop me if I offend you?"

Kit laughed softly. "Yes."

Henry paused, then he said, "When I call you Christopher, I'm certainly not thinking of you as an agreeable whore."

Kit stared him, shocked into silence.

"I'm thinking of someone rather wonderful," Henry said. "Someone I admired from the first moment I saw him." He paused, then added, "Earlier you said you were naive when I first met you. I wouldn't say so. I would say you were kind and decent and generous. You were entitled to expect the same from others—from *me*—and the fact you didn't get that doesn't point to any defect in you, Kit. I hate that you'd think that."

Kit's throat closed, unexpected emotion gripping him.

"I'll call you Kit," Henry said gently. "I'll call you anything you want. I just want you to know that there was nothing wrong with you when you were Christopher."

To his shame, Kit felt the hot prickle of tears behind his

eyes and he pulled back, turning his head so that Henry couldn't look at him as he calmed himself.

Henry sat quietly, but Kit could feel the man watching him, waiting.

When he felt he had himself back under control, Kit said, "Last week, after you left, I couldn't stop thinking about what happened all those years ago."

"Me either," Henry said softly.

"I want you to know," Kit said slowly, "that I forgive you, Henry, For not coming to see me before you left town. For sending Parkinson instead."

Henry looked anguished. "But I shouldn't have trusted him. I should have—"

"You saying that is like me calling myself naive," Kit interrupted. "You trusted a man you had no reason to be suspicious of—you are not to blame for his betrayal, Henry."

"I should have come anyway," Henry said. "I should have told you myself."

Their gazes locked. It felt as though all the years they'd been apart had melted away. Kit was suddenly very conscious that he hadn't looked at another person so deeply, so intensely, since Henry had left him. This was more intimate than being naked, more intimate than being spread open on a bed for a punter to play with. Kit was gazing into Henry's soul, and Henry was gazing into his. He had no idea what his own eyes betrayed, but Henry's showed old pain and bitter regret.

Kit said, "What did you say in the letter? The one that Parkinson was supposed to give me?"

Henry was silent for several moments. Then he said, slowly, "I said things I'd never expressed to you in person. I told you... how very much I cared for you. How painful it was to leave you."

Kit's heart began to race very fast.

For a moment Henry seemed to wrestle with whether to

go on. Then he said, "I asked you to write back to me. To send me word if you would be willing to see me again, once I had fulfilled my promises to Caroline."

Kit's stomach dropped. "And you never heard back," he whispered, stricken.

"No. At first I hoped you just needed time, to come terms with what I'd done. Eventually I came to the conclusion I'd simply been deluded in thinking you had any fondness for me." He gave a soft, humourless laugh. "*Naive.*"

That word again.

Kit shook his head, a sharp denial, but he couldn't find words. And now he was remembering the long years of loneliness Henry had just described.

"*The more I denied myself, the more tormented I became.*"

Would things have been any easier for Henry if he'd had word back from Kit? If he'd known Kit was waiting for him?

And would Kit have agreed to wait for him?

Yes, probably. He'd loved Henry with all his heart. But Kit hadn't seen the letter. He hadn't responded, or waited. And in the long years since, their lives had diverged down two very different paths.

"*… you were kind and decent and generous…*"

Kit wasn't that boy anymore. He'd become harder, more suspicious and protective. The man he was now was well suited to running a scandalous club—not so much to being on the other side of someone's fireplace.

"Kit?" Henry prompted, and when Kit looked at him again, his grey gaze was vulnerable and uncertain.

"I cared for you too, Henry," he said hoarsely. "When you left me, it felt as though my whole world had broken in two." He shook his head. "But that was a lifetime ago, and we have very different lives now." He sighed and turned away, rising from the bed and reaching for his drawers. "Speaking of which, I should get dressed and get back to the club. I've neglected my duties too long."

"Kit?" Henry's voice was hoarse.

Kit stared at the linen clutched between his hands. He couldn't look at the other man. Didn't want Henry to see how raw he felt.

"Yes?"

"May I come back?"

Kit squeezed his eyes closed.

"Please," Henry said into the silence. "I don't want this to be the end, Kit."

And when he put it like that, neither did Kit. There was something unfinished between them. Something to be settled before he could close the door on his ill-fated affair with Henry Asquith, once and for all.

"All right," he said. "You can come back next week."

18

HENRY

A few days later, Simon Reid called upon Henry while he was having breakfast.

"Do you have some news for me?" Henry asked, once Reid was settled at the table with some tea.

"I do," Reid said. "I've looked into the situation with the solicitors in Lambeth. The rent's been collected regularly since Parkinson's death—I expect it'll turn out to be an associate of Parkinson's, perhaps a family member or friend. The senior partner of the firm is desperate to resolve the matter—he's assured me he'll get the bottom of it, though we may have to wait till the next rent falls due on Midsummer Day if we're not to alert the culprit."

Henry nodded. "What about the tenant? Have you spoken with him."

Reid grimaced. "I have. He's not willing to give the house up, I'm afraid. And having perused the lease, it will be several years before you are able to terminate it—unless you wish to challenge its validity in court." Reid's expression told Henry what he thought of that idea.

Henry shook his head. "No, I don't want to do that. I'm

willing to leave the lease in place as long as he wishes to stay —it's been the man's home a long time now."

Reid looked briefly curious, then nodded. "I'll let him know. I take it you don't need the property back now?"

Henry shrugged. "Kit will have none of it," he said. "I wanted to make good my debt to him but he will not accept any compensation. Nevertheless, the house needs to be taken care of and the rent collected, so I'd be grateful if you would take over its management. And my other city properties, if you are willing."

Reid smiled, plainly pleased with this development. "Very willing, your grace," he said, toasting Henry with his coffee cup.

They talked for a while longer, then Reid took his leave.

Only a short while later, the door opened again. It was Freddy this time, and once again he was looking very much the worse for wear.

Henry watched silently as Freddy made himself up a breakfast plate and sat himself down at the table.

He'd always been the most energetic of Henry's children. Unlike his older brother, and to the despair of his tutors, he hadn't shown the least bit of academic prowess. However, in every physical skill, he excelled. He was a neck-or-nothing rider, a fearless swimmer, an intrepid climber. Henry had long ago resigned himself to unmitigated worry that Freddy might suffer some injury on one of his escapades. He had not, however, foreseen the worries that this new Freddy—the fashionable young man about town—would bring. His enjoyment of prizefighting and racing were entirely unsurprising and of no great concern. But the heavy drinking, and gambling were rather more worrying.

Henry watched in silence as Freddy attempted to eat his breakfast. He soon abandoned the effort, setting down his cutlery and seeking sanctuary in his tea cup.

"Were you out last night?" Henry asked at last, though it was obvious he had been.

Freddy nodded. "A few of us made up a party at Vauxhall Gardens."

"I'm surprised you're up so early, then."

"I'd have stayed in bed, but Fenchurch and Grantham are racing today," Freddy said. "We're going to watch."

"We being you and Bartlett?" Henry asked.

"Yes. I shan't be home for dinner, incidentally. A group of us are going on to Sharp's."

"Sharp's?" Henry echoed, frowning. "Don't you think you're spending rather too much time in gaming hells?"

"Sharp's isn't a gaming hell," Freddy scoffed. "Besides, I'm not going to play. Percy has a game arranged with someone or other, so we're dining there, then after his game we may go on"—he waved his hand vaguely—"somewhere else."

Henry frowned, unhappy, but said nothing. Freddy was only doing the same as any other young man of the ton, but Henry could not help but worry about the idle existence he was presently leading. Despite being born into great wealth, Henry had been expected to play an active role in managing the ducal estate and to learn what that entailed from a young age. He had never been, as Freddy seemed to be, entirely lacking in purpose.

Except, a small voice inside Henry said, *he is not entirely lacking in purpose, is he? You know what he* wants *to do with his life.*

Henry sighed and rubbed at the tense spot between his brows.

"Is something wrong, Father? Do you have a headache?"

Henry looked up at that, and for an instant he caught a glimpse of the old Freddy in his son's concerned gaze. The impulsive, affectionate little boy who had so often cheered Henry in his lowest moments.

"A bit of one," he said. "I think I'll go and have a walk. The fresh air will do me good." He stood and, on his way past Freddy, paused to squeeze his shoulder, wishing he could embrace him the way he used to, when Freddy was little. Things had been so much easier then. "Enjoy the race," he said, and headed for the door.

Curzon Street was located very close to Hyde Park Corner, a circumstance for which Henry had been very grateful since he arrived in town. He greatly missed Wiltshire, where it was his habit to ride or walk most days. But at least he could be in the park within a few minutes, and it was sizeable enough to provide him with some reasonable exercise.

He began a brisk circuit, enjoying the sunshine and the light breeze.

It wasn't long before his mind circled back to thoughts of Kit and their last encounter. Their extraordinary, unforgettable last encounter. Remembering what they'd done together made his cock harden with lust even as a wary anxiety churned in his gut that he'd shared too much, made himself too naked, too vulnerable.

But when he was with Kit, it almost felt as though the last eighteen years hadn't happened. As much as he had changed, at heart Kit seemed to Henry to be fundamentally unaltered. He was the same kind-hearted, perceptive man that Henry had known all those years ago. A little harder, yes. A little more suspicious, certainly. But incredibly, neither bitter nor vengeful.

And that last night together, he had given Henry something that Henry hadn't even known he wanted, no, *needed*. In mastering Henry, Kit had given him pleasure like he'd never known, and brought him peace that he'd never dreamed of.

There was no one else in the world Henry would have trusted to ask for such a thing.

As Henry walked, his mind poked carefully at that thought.

Henry might feel unsure and wary now, but when he'd been with Kit, he'd had no such concerns. He'd trusted him, despite everything that had happened.

Was he a fool to believe that Kit would not wantonly hurt him? When he had done so much, albeit unintentionally, to hurt Kit?

Ah, but the past was a battlefield of old hurts. When he thought back all those years ago to when Caroline had first asked him to give Kit up—that had broken his heart, but he hadn't even felt entitled to acknowledge as much. He'd told himself he was selfish to grieve and buried the pain deep, letting it grow cankerous inside him, a stifled, unacknowledged sorrow.

For years he'd thought his feelings entirely one-sided. But Kit had disabused him of that.

"When you left me, it felt as though my whole world had broken in two."

He wasn't sure if that made matters better or worse—certainly right now it was making his chest ache and his stomach churn.

The wind was getting up. Henry put down his head and walked stoically on. He thought of Kit's bleak expression as he'd listened to Henry's confession about what he'd written in his letter.

"I told you... how very much I cared for you..."

Cared for you.

Such mealy-mouthed words—all these years and he was still limiting himself to careful half-truths. Lying to Kit. Lying to himself.

He'd *loved* Kit.

All of a sudden, hot tears were pressing behind his eyes

and gathering in a solid ball in his throat. He wasn't sure why he—a man who rarely wept—felt suddenly as though he could drop to his knees and soak the earth. All he knew was that something was rising in him, feelings that he'd been pushing down, relentlessly, for too many years. Powerful emotions he had thought were spent were surging to the surface again, as though seeing Kit Redford had lit a flame under him and now everything was about to boil over.

A bird screeched overheard, making Henry glance up. He realised that he'd walked almost all the way around the park, and was now at the other corner next to Edgeware Road, barely a mile from Kit's house.

Kit was not expecting to see Henry so soon—or for Henry to call upon him at his home. When Henry had asked to see him again, Kit had told him to return to Redford's.

He should not go to Kit's house.

But he wanted to see him—and he wanted to see him *now*, while he still felt the rawness of the emotions that had been overwhelming him.

While he might still feel brave enough to share them with Kit.

If Kit wanted to send him away, he would go without complaint—he would always respect Kit's wishes. But if nothing else, he wanted to at least say aloud what his true feelings had been eighteen years before. And he wanted to say those things to Kit. To tell him how important, how *vital*, he had been to Henry's happiness.

With that conviction at the forefront of his mind, Henry set off again, at a more determined pace.

Less than quarter an hour later, he was approaching Kit's front door—a door that, as he drew closer, opened.

The first two figures to emerge were a pretty young woman and a little boy. A moment later, they were joined by an elegantly dressed man.

Kit.

The boy, who looked to be five or six, was talking in a high, animated voice, making both Kit and the young woman laugh. He was holding the young woman's hand, but as Kit drew level with them, he thrust out his other arm, demanding Kit's hand too. Kit laughed, and let him have it, and then they were swinging the boy back and forth between them, making him squeal with laughter.

The fond way Kit looked at the child, his eyes alight with merriment… this was a side of the man Henry had not seen before. Was this child his? Was the young woman his wife?

Henry stood, rooted to the spot, with nowhere to go. Knowing Kit would see him in a moment. Had he made a terrible mistake in coming here? Should he turn on his heel and go? The questions rushed through his mind, but before he could come to any kind of conclusion, the small party was upon him and Kit, looking up from smiling at the little boy, saw him.

His step stalled, making the boy's swing stutter and the young woman's step falter too. The boy began making some piping complaint about Kit's inattentiveness, but the young woman ignored him. She followed Kit's gaze to Henry, her own expression quite curious.

"Henry," Kit said. "I wasn't expecting you."

Did he sound put out? Henry wasn't sure.

"I've come at an inconvenient time," Henry said. "My apologies."

Kit opened his mouth, but it was the young woman who spoke. "Not at all. We were only going for a walk." She glanced at Kit and said, "I can take Peter on my own."

"Clara—"

She smiled ruefully. "Tom can come if it makes you feel better."

The child glared at her. "I want Uncle Kit to come!"

The young woman gave him a level look and he subsided, though not gracefully, kicking at the ground with one foot.

The young woman glanced at Kit then, brows raised expectantly.

Kit sighed, but turned to Henry. "May I introduce my friend, Mrs. Marsden, and her son, Peter?"

Henry's tension eased. Plainly she was not Kit's wife.

Kit looked at the young woman. "Clara, this is Henry Asquith, the Duke of Avesbury."

Henry bowed to her. "I'm pleased to make your acquaintance, Mrs. Marsden."

"Charmed, your grace," Mrs. Marsden said pleasantly with a small curtsey, and a lack of obsequiousness Henry admired. "Peter, say good afternoon."

Peter stared at Henry balefully. "Good afternoon," he said flatly, clearly unimpressed.

Henry bit his lip against a smile. The boy reminded him of Freddy at the same age.

"Good afternoon, Peter," he replied gravely.

Peter ignored him. He looked at the young woman. "May we go now, Mama?"

"We'll go back and get Tom first, but yes," she said. "We may." And with that she nodded to Kit and Henry, and led the boy back into the house.

"I'm sorry to have interrupted your day," Henry said. "I can come back later if you'd rather."

Kit shook his head. "No, no, you're here now. Come in."

He turned on his heel, leaving Henry to follow him.

Was he annoyed, Henry wondered? He didn't seem to be, but then Kit had never been one for shows of temper.

By the time they entered the house, there was no sign of Mrs. Marsden or her son—presumably they'd gone in search of the man called Tom.

"We'll go up to my private sitting room," Kit said, mounting the stairs. After climbing two flights, Kit led Henry down a short corridor and into a small, much less formal room than the drawing room Henry had been shown into before.

"Take a seat," Kit said. "Would you like some tea?"

Henry shook his head. "No, thank you." He settled himself into a small armchair, then immediately wished he'd selected the large chaise longue instead, just to see if Kit would sit beside him. "This is nice," he said. "Very cosy."

"I don't have many visitors up here," Kit said. "It's where I come when I need quiet time."

Henry felt a warm glow at that—that Kit was allowing him access to this private space of his.

"Do Mrs. Marsden and her son live here too?" he asked carefully.

Kit smiled, seeming mildly amused. "They do."

"When I first saw you together I thought—wondered, I mean—if you and she were…"

"—married?" Kit completed for him. "People often assume that. And no. We are merely friends."

"So Peter is…?"

Kit sent him a dry look at the blatant fishing. "Not mine. Officially, we say Clara is my sister, and a widow."

"And unofficially?"

"She works for me—I took her in at the time she most needed help. Now she's a very good friend. I consider her and Peter my family, and he is, officially, my godson."

Henry nodded. "She was an unwed mother then?"

"Through no fault of her own. She's an educated woman. She had a position as a governess but was raped by the oldest son of the family."

Henry grimaced. It was an all too common story.

"I'd put up a notice for a junior clerk for Redford's and she turned up," Kit said. "She seemed to be such a genteel young lady. I was in the process of telling her she wasn't quite what I had in mind when she fainted, and I discovered her condition. When she came around, she confessed that she hadn't been eating, and that her position was quite desperate."

"So, you gave her the job?"

"I did. And then, when I discovered where she was living, I invited her to move into my private apartments in the club. Once Peter was born, I bought this house—Redford's is not a suitable place to bring up an infant." Kit smiled crookedly. "I should know—I was brought up in a brothel."

Henry stared at him, unable to think what to say to that. It was ridiculous to be taken aback—probably many people in Kit's situation had similar backgrounds—but somehow Henry had never considered that.

"Your mother?" he managed at last.

"She was a prostitute. She worked at the Golden Lily."

"The same place—" Henry broke off, and Kit laughed at whatever he saw on his face.

"Yes, the same place where we met."

"Didn't you tell me you ran away from home?" Henry said faintly.

Kit laughed. "I had to tell you something," he said. "And most gentleman like the idea of a wholesome farm lad who comes to the city in search of debauchery."

Guiltily, Henry realised he was one of them.

"Why not just tell the truth?" he asked.

Kit met his eyes, and his own were gentle. "I couldn't have you feeling sorry for me, could I? Better that you think I ran to London town with stars in my eyes, looking for a handsome prince all of my own."

"Would I have felt sorry for you?" Henry asked softly.

Kit sighed. "How do I know?"

"Tell me then—about when you were a child."

Kit made an impatient noise. "Does all that history matter now? It was years ago. Now, I own this house, my own business. Many people born into my circumstances would have ended up little better than beggars. I was lucky."

"In what way were you lucky?" Henry asked, curious.

Kit's smile widened, but his green gaze was oddly bleak. "I was born beautiful."

Henry's heart ached for him.

"How old were you when you first... worked?"

"Again, I was lucky," Kit said. "I had my mother till I was almost fifteen, and she provided for me. Then, when she died, she made Mabel promise to look out for me. So, Mabel kept me till I was sixteen, before I had to earn."

"Sixteen?" Henry said hoarsely.

"Mabel was canny," Kit went on. "She started having me serve in the Golden Lily, dressed provocatively. Got me known amongst her customers, then started up a bidding war." He laughed drily.

Henry closed his eyes. He was beginning to feel queasy.

Kit's hand landed on his knee, and he opened his eyes, meeting Kit's concerned gaze.

"Don't feel bad," Kit said almost angrily. "By the time I met you I'd had my virginity auctioned to the highest bidder and completed my first three contracts. I can assure you, by the time you and I met, I knew *everything* there was to know about my trade."

That didn't make Henry feel better.

"What about after me?" Henry asked hoarsely.

Kit looked away. "You already know about that."

"Not really," Henry said. "I know you took up with Skelton, and that he hurt you."

Kit leaned back on the sofa and stared at the ceiling. "I'm not sure I see the point of this, Henry."

"Is it true that, after what happened with us, some people thought you'd done something untrustworthy?"

Kit's head jerked up. "Who told you that?"

"Is it true?" Henry asked again.

Kit stared at him for several long moments, then he sighed. "Some people assumed you'd thrown me over early because of something I'd done. And then, when I wouldn't let Mabel come after you, that just seemed to convince them more. Mabel and I argued over it—I told you about how I was determined to pay her off. The trouble was, I couldn't get a new protector after you left. So when Skelton made me an offer, I accepted. It was stupid, but it was only meant to be for six months. I didn't realise he would be so violent."

The sudden rage that surged in Henry at hearing that shocked him. He was not a man who was quick to anger, but the thought of Lionel Skelton laying violent hands on Kit was unbearable. "You stayed the six months?"

Kit shook his head. "Three and a half. The violence began after a few weeks, but it was only when I said I was going to leave that he really hurt me."

"What happened?" Henry asked faintly.

"I'd said something he didn't like—he hit me and I decided I'd had enough. I told him I was leaving, and he said I was his till the end of our contract, and if I tried to go, he'd kill me. We struggled, but he was a lot bigger than me. He ended up beating me badly and leaving me locked inside the house while he went out to meet his friends. If I'd still been there when he returned, I suspect he'd have finished me off. Thankfully, he didn't think to lock the kitchen door, and I managed to escape."

"Where did you go?"

"To Mabel. We hadn't spoken for a while, but when she saw the state of me she took me back in. She sorted everything out with Skelton. Then she found me a new contract."

"Another contract for her to profit from?" Henry said bitterly.

Kit raised his brows. "What else was she to do for me? She was the madam of a brothel—it was all she knew. As it was, she pressed my case quite hard with Phin to persuade him to take me. I don't think he really wanted another boy at that point."

"This was Phineas Warren?"

Kit glanced at him sharply.

"How do you know that?"

Henry shrugged. "People talk."

Kit sighed and nodded. "That they do."

"What was he like? Warren, I mean."

"He was very kind to me, actually. He had some rather eccentric ideas, but he was not a demanding man—hell, he wasn't actually capable of much in the bedchamber by then—but he kept me for several years and gave me a very handsome pay-off at the end, including the property where Redford's is located. It was his generosity that enabled me to finally get off the game."

Henry was hit by a hot bolt of shame so intense it stole his breath. Why had it never occurred to him that that might be something Kit would want? Had he really wanted to believe so badly that the man could desire nothing more than to be at his beck and call?

"Henry?"

He looked up to find Kit watching him with a curious expression.

"Is something wrong?" Kit asked and Henry shook his head mutely, unable to find words.

Kit was silent a moment, then he asked quietly, "Henry, why did you come here today?"

Henry gave a helpless, humourless laugh. "I don't really know." He pressed at the spot between his eyebrows where his headache always gathered. "I was walking in the park and thinking about the feelings that have risen up in me since I saw you again. I decided that I wanted—that is, I *needed* to say—" He broke off, staring down at his hands. Was it right to speak these words aloud? None of this probably mattered to Kit. Not anymore.

"Yes?" Kit prompted.

Henry took a deep breath and tried to begin again, more calmly.

"I told you, the other night at the club, that I cared for you, all those years ago."

Kit said nothing, only watched him, a faint frown between his brows.

"But that wasn't the whole truth," Henry said. "I was being careful with my words. Miserly, in fact. But today I realised that I had to be honest with you. Truly honest. Because you deserve to know the whole truth of the past. I wasn't just fond of you, Kit. I loved you."

Kit stared at him, seeming genuinely shocked. "*Henry*—" he began, only to cut himself off and stare at Henry in silence.

Henry smiled sadly, "Don't worry, I don't expect you to reciprocate. I realise that, given what happened after I left, any fondness you ever had for me was probably killed stone dead. But I just wanted to *tell* you. I wanted you to know—to really understand—how much you meant to me, and that leaving you was truly the hardest thing I ever did. You deserve to know that, Kit."

Kit looked anguished. "Henry," he said again. He shook his head and looked away, staring out of the window. After a long pause he said, "I wish I'd known."

Henry felt oddly breathless. "Why?"

Kit turned back to meet his gaze. "Because I adored you, and when you left, it felt like I'd meant nothing to you. Perhaps if I'd *known...*" He trailed off, his expression agonised.

"You loved me too?" Henry whispered in disbelief.

Kit nodded, his eyes shadowed with old grief. "I did. I thought it was pathetically obvious."

"It wasn't obvious to me," Henry said. "Sometimes I wondered, but then we'd part and I'd tell myself I was just another client to you, nobody special."

Kit gave a harsh laugh. "Christ, Henry. You were probably

the most interesting man I'd ever met—you talked to me about things that no one else had before, like I was just as worthy of having opinions as anyone else. And you were affectionate and sweet to me in ways I'd never experienced. Not just in bed, though of course, I loved everything we did in bed—I never had to pretend anything with you."

Henry stared at him, astonished.

"The real question," Kit continued, "is why *you* loved *me* —a common prostitute with nothing to commend him but a pretty face."

"Nothing but a pretty face?" Henry repeated incredulously. He got out of his chair and went to his knees before Kit. "Oh, you were *very* beautiful, Kit—you still are—but you were so much more than your appearance." He took hold of Kit's right hand in his own and pressed a kiss to the back of it. "You were kind and decent and sweet-natured." He swallowed hard. "You still are all of those things. These last weeks, you could have put me through the mill—you know I'd have let you do it—but instead you've shown me nothing but kindness and understanding."

Kit's eyes swam with sudden tears. "You credit me with too much," he said. "I can assure you, I have entertained plenty of unkind thoughts."

"You credit yourself too little," Henry said fiercely. "You always did." He took hold of Kit's other hand and bent his head over it, pressing his lips passionately to the knuckles. "Christopher," he whispered. "*Kit.*"

His throat closed up so completely, he could say no more, but he felt like he might burst with the words inside him. Passionate, reckless words.

I love you still.

Was that true?

Was he still in love with Christopher Redford? Was it madness to be thinking that way so soon? To be wondering if they could build some kind of life together after all these long years apart, when they'd only just met again?

Henry looked up to find Kit gazing down at him warily.

He wanted to ask Kit if he thought he could ever love him again, but his courage was running out, and then—before he could utter another word—there was a knock at the door.

Kit tugged his hands free and Henry reluctantly rose to his feet.

When Kit bid the person on the other side to enter, a maid peeped her head round the door. "Pardon for interrupting, sir, but Mr. Gardiner's here."

Kit hesitated for a moment, then he said. "Show him into the drawing room."

Once the maid had withdrawn, Kit turned to Henry, his expression apologetic. "My neighbour," he said by way of explanation. "It'll be about the roof repairs, I expect."

It was such a stupidly prosaic thing to interrupt one of the most important conversations of Henry's life. Perhaps, though, Kit had welcomed the interruption? Perhaps he did not want Henry grovelling at his feet, invoking the past?

Unsure what to do, Henry stared at Kit helplessly. But then, miraculously, Kit said carefully, "I know it's only been a few days, but do you want to come to Redford's tonight?"

"Yes," Henry said quickly, his tension easing at the knowledge he would see Kit again soon. "What time?"

"I have something I must do this evening, for Clara," Kit said. "But any time after eleven will be fine."

Excitement for the evening ahead buoyed Henry's footsteps all the way back to Curzon Street and carried him through dinner with Marianne and Jeremy, even though Jeremy was unusually subdued, and Marianne was peevish and picky with her food.

"You're not in the best of moods, my dear, are you?" Henry observed mildly when she snapped at him for the third time.

Alarmingly, tears sprang to Marianne's eyes. "I'm sorry," she said miserably. "I don't know what's wrong with me! I've been feeling blue-devilled all day."

Henry met Jeremy's helpless gaze.

Leaning over the table, Henry patted Marianne's hand. "It's nothing to worry about, my dear," he said. "Your mother used to get the same way when she was carrying."

Marianne dabbed at her face with her napkin and gave him a watery smile, which she extended to her husband. "Perhaps I'll go to bed. I don't feel like eating just now. Mary can bring me something later if I'm hungry."

Jeremy stood up. "I'll help you upstairs, my dear."

Left to his own devices, Henry finished his dinner and poured himself another glass of wine. His mind drifted, circling back to his conversation with Kit earlier, and the promise of what would follow later tonight.

A quarter hour later, Jeremy returned to the dining room.

"How is she now?" Henry asked.

"Much happier," Jeremy said. "She'll soon be tucked up in bed with a book, and Mary will make sure she eats something later." He sighed and sank down into a chair. "Did you ever wish you could just have the baby for Caroline?"

Henry nodded, but prudently said no more. There was no need to burden Jeremy with stories of what it was like to hear the screams of one's wife as she laboured through childbirth, and being entirely powerless to help her. That was something he would learn soon enough.

"Henry," Jeremy said, and Henry looked up at the change in his tone.

"Yes?"

"I heard something today that I think you should prob-ably know about." His gaze was unhappy.

Henry's gaze narrowed. "What's that?"

"It's about Freddy. Well, more this friend of his, really, but I gather Freddy will be there too."

"Where?"

"At Sharp's in Knightsbridge," Jeremy said, meeting Henry's gaze. "I know you've been worried about Freddy's gaming, and this Bartlett fellow plays very deep, you know. He's playing Lionel Skelton again tonight."

"*Skelton?*" Henry exclaimed.

Jeremy nodded unhappily.

"I warned Freddy to stay away from him," Henry said. "And for that matter, I warned Skelton to stay away from Freddy."

Jeremy watched him, carefully. "Skelton may not know Freddy will be there. It's Bartlett he's due to play."

"But he knows Freddy's part of Bartlett's circle," Henry said. He pushed his chair back and stood. "Thank you for telling me."

"Are you going to Sharp's?" Jeremy asked. "Do you want me to come with you?"

"I'm going, yes, but there's no need for you to come. You concentrate on looking after Marianne. I can take care of this. Skelton's nothing more than a wastrel and a bully."

And, Henry thought, if he got the chance to deliver some punishment to the man for his old sins against Kit, he would not be holding back.

19

KIT

Kit dressed carefully for his confrontation with Bartlett at Sharp's that evening. No colourful waistcoats tonight, and no jewellery, only soberly elegant black and white. He wanted to look entirely, irreproachably respectable.

When he arrived at the club, he was taken to Mr. Tait's office. The man greeted him pleasantly enough, but he was rather less friendly than the last time Kit had met him.

"Jake told me of the favour you asked of him," Tait said. "I must say, I'm not happy about it, but this is Jake's establishment, not mine."

"Do I take it Mr. Sharp is not here?" Kit asked.

"He'll be along shortly," Tait said. "He rarely comes by before ten though. Still, he was clear that if you arrived before he did, you were to be allowed onto the floor and left to conduct your business with Bartlett."

Kit nodded. "I'm grateful. I do understand your concerns, Mr. Tait, but this is something I require a particular sort of audience for. I do not envisage it will disrupt the evening overmuch."

Tait made a *hrrmphing* sort of noise which indicated his

disbelief. And fair enough, given Kit was hoping his accusations against Bartlett would attract considerable attention.

"He's at a table in card room two. The staff will direct you if you ask."

Kit rose from his chair. "My thanks, Mr. Tait. I hope to be out of your hair very shortly."

Tait just shook his head and turned his attention back to the papers on his desk.

As Tait had promised, one of the staff directed Kit to card room two. Kit was gratified to see it was a reasonably large room with a half dozen tables and a good number of gentlemen playing. He stood in the shadows for a minute or two to get his bearings and soon spotted Bartlett on the far side of the room. He was sitting at a table with two other men, neither of whom Kit could see well. Thankfully Bartlett was in the most visible seat, facing the entrance to the room where Kit was hovering. Kit could only see the backs of the other two players. A fourth chair was empty.

Kit took a deep breath, then strode forward, raising his voice as he approached the table. "Mr. Percival Bartlett?"

Bartlett looked up. "Yes?" he said, irritation in his voice. His shirt points were so high, they obscured half his sideburns and forced him to hold his chin up at an artificial angle. "And who are you, sir?"

"My name is Redford," Kit said. "And I have something to say to you, sir."

Bartlett frowned, glancing uneasily at his two companions. "As you can see," he said shortly, "I am busy. And I do not know you, sir. I suggest you call upon me at my place of residence where we can speak in private."

"I do not seek privacy," Kit said in a loud, clear voice. "The reason I came here was to say my piece in front of witnesses."

The men at the other tables were turning in their seats to see what was going on. Bartlett cast a panicky look about the room, searching for one of Sharp's staff, no doubt, to throw this upstart out. But of course, there were none to be seen.

"Now, look here," he said to Kit, his colour beginning to rise. "I don't know who you are, but—"

"I told you, my name is Redford," Kit said flatly. "I'm here because you have been harassing my employee, a defenceless young woman."

Bartlett paled. "I don't know what you're talking about!" he exclaimed, but Kit could see he had a sense of what this was about.

"I think you do," Kit sneered. "Let me help you remember: she was a servant in your father's house and you ravished her and got her with child—"

Bartlett surged to his feet. "*How dare you!*"

"—and when she asked you for money to raise that child you sent a thug to warn her off with his fists," Kit continued relentlessly, his voice rising. "What kind of *gentleman* does such a thing?"

The room was silent now, but for hushed murmurs at the neighbouring tables.

Bartlett was puce, his slightly protuberant eyes wild.

"If anyone lays a finger on that young woman again," Kit said in a loud, clear voice, "I will hold you responsible, sir, and I will make it known, far and wide, what you have done and what kind of man you are."

No sooner had he finished speaking than a voice behind Kit—a horribly familiar voice—said silkily, "Are you going to let this low-born milksop insult you like this, Bartlett?"

Kit whipped around, and there, looming over him, was Lionel Skelton.

His gut roiled, and his heart began to thud in a panicky rhythm. Without meaning to, he stepped backwards, and Skelton's thin, cruel smile widened into a nasty grin. He always had enjoyed Kit's fear.

"No, by Jove," Bartlett snarled, emboldened by Skelton's

intervention, and surged to his feet, his chair screeching against the wooden floor. Kit whirled back to face him, only to realise that Bartlett had already swung at him. An awkward blow landed on Kit's chin, which, despite its lack of elegance, had enough power to send him to the floor in an ungainly sprawl.

Baring his teeth in a nasty sneer, Bartlett strode towards Kit, while Kit tried to scrabble to his feet and glance over his shoulder at Skelton at the same time.

And then, astonishingly, help came from an unexpected quarter—one of the other two men at the table, who threw his own chair back and strode into the fray, pushing Bartlett roughly back.

"Percy, for God's sake!" he exclaimed. "You can't brawl in here!"

"Fine!" Bartlett cried. "Let's take him outside and thrash him!"

"Capital idea," Skelton said, chuckling.

Kit was on his feet now. He cast a look of dislike at Skelton then turned his attention back to Bartlett.

"I'm not thrashing anyone," the intervener said flatly. "And neither are you, Percy."

Kit frowned then—the young man's profile was oddly familiar.

"Get out of my way, Freddy," Bartlett said in low, dangerous voice.

"I don't think so."

And that was when Kit realised who he was—the young man who had escorted Clara back home on the day she'd been attacked.

"I said get out of the way!" Bartlett roared. He tried to push his erstwhile friend aside but when the young man wouldn't budge, Bartlett tackled him to the ground with a yell of fury, the two of them landing in a twisted tangle of bodies right next to the neighbouring table.

All around the room, men got out of their chairs and began to gather around to watch the brawl, some shouting for calm while others encouraged the fight, even shouting out wagers.

Head swimming, Kit tried to push his way through the swiftly gathering crowd, but before he could make any headway, he felt himself being grabbed. Twisting in his captor's hands, he looked over his shoulder to see Skelton's furious face staring down at him. Skelton yanked him around and shoved him up against a wall, then pushed his face against Kit's. His breath was sour with brandy.

"I *needed* that fucking idiot's money," he hissed, raising his fist.

Kit looked around desperately for help, but everyone was crowding around the other brawl. He opened his mouth to yell out but before he could make a sound, Skelton's fist connected with the side of the head. An instant later, a second blow to his stomach knocked all the air out of him.

He'd have fallen to the ground, but Skelton was holding him there, against the wall, and raising his fist again while Kit gasped for breath and tried to make his limbs move, his vision swimming alarmingly, his right ear ringing in a way that was horribly reminiscent of the last time Skelton had laid hands on him. And then, quite suddenly, the hands holding him fell away as Skelton was yanked away from him.

Without Skelton holding him up, Kit dropped to the floor, only just catching himself on his hands before he landed on his face.

He heard Skelton cry out and the sound of scuffling and blows. Another familiar voice, cursing and angry.

Henry?

Kit managed to open his eyes briefly—just in time to see Henry's fist connect with Skelton's jaw and Skelton fall backwards, arms windmilling—before he had close them again to stop the world spinning.

HENRY

No sooner had Henry felled Lionel Skelton than a loud voice shouted, "That's quite enough! Back to your seats, gentlemen."

Henry glanced up from Skelton's satisfyingly crumpled form on the floor to see that the voice had come from a dark-haired, well-dressed man that he suspected must be Sharp, the notorious owner of the club. Flanked by two enormous fellows with grim expressions, Sharp strode towards the larger group of men at the centre of the room, where clearly some other drama had begun to unfold before Henry arrived.

Henry wasn't interested in that though—he needed to take care of Kit, who was now sitting with his back against the wall, his head in his hands.

Henry rushed to his side, dropping to a crouch beside him.

"Kit, are you all right?" he asked urgently, placing a hand gently on his shoulder.

Kit nodded, though he didn't raise his head from his hands. "I'll be fine," he said. "I'm just a bit dizzy. Can you give me a moment?"

"Of course," Henry said gently. Now that the immediate panic of seeing Kit being assaulted by Skelton had worn off, his mind was racing. What was Kit *doing* here? He almost asked, then decided Kit wasn't fit to be questioned right now. "Sit quietly and don't move, all right? I'll be back in a moment. I'm just going to make sure Skelton doesn't slip off."

Kit murmured something that sounded like assent.

As Henry rose to standing again, he saw that the larger group of men was now dispersing. They'd been watching another brawl, he realised. And then, as the final stragglers moved aside, he stopped in his tracks, shocked to see that his own son appeared to have been one of participants—Freddy's clothes were rumpled and his hair was wild. A red mark on his cheek showed where a blow had landed. But he looked perfectly calm. He was speaking to Sharp, while one of the big bruisers hauled the other combatant—Oh Christ, that was Percy Bartlett!—to his feet.

Freddy looked more or less all right. He was a little mussed to be sure, but other than that one red mark on his cheekbone, he appeared unhurt. Bartlett, on the other hand, was very much the worse for wear. His lower lip and left eyebrow were both split, and the area around his left eye was swelling. The bruiser handled him ungently, his expression unimpressed as Bartlett spluttered outrage.

There was a story here, but it would have to wait a little longer. Henry couldn't risk Skelton leaving before he'd spoken to him and left him in no doubt of the danger he was in if he ever so much as looked at Kit again. But when Henry glanced Skelton's way, it was to see that the other bruiser was already hauling that sorry specimen to his feet with the same disregard for comfort that his colleague had shown Bartlett, and was pushing him towards Sharp.

Henry strode towards them.

"Mr. Sharp, I presume?" he called out, and the dark-haired man glanced his way.

"Pleased to make your acquaintance, your grace. That was quite a punch." Plainly, he already knew who Henry was.

"*Father?*" Freddy exclaimed.

"Good evening, Frederick," Henry replied coolly, inclining his head.

"What are you doing here?" Freddy said weakly.

"Punching my customers, it would seem," Sharp said. "Is that an Avesbury family trait?" He raised a brow, and Freddy flushed.

Henry did not. "If you don't want your customers punched, then don't allow Lionel Skelton in the door," he said tightly, adding in a lower voice, "the last time he was here he was using his own marked cards."

Sharp's gaze narrowed angrily at that, and he glanced at Skelton. "I think we need to have a talk, Mr. Skelton," he said. His voice was not unpleasant, but there was a note in it that was somehow chilling. Skelton paled.

Sharp glanced at the bruiser who nodded and led the unprotesting man away.

Sharp turned to Bartlett then. He smiled, but his eyes were flat and dangerous. "As for you, Mr. Bartlett, I think it's about time we discussed your account, don't you? Join me for a glass of brandy in my office. Ackroyd here will show you the way. I'll be with you in just a few minutes."

Bartlett went red with angry mortification, but he too was silent as the other bruiser escorted him from the room. Given his docility, he must owe Sharp a fortune.

Sharp turned to Henry, meeting his gaze. "Thank you for the information about Skelton," he said. "I don't tolerate cheats in my establishments—you can rest assured that I will deal with him. As for the other one, I'll make sure he doesn't come near Kit or his friend ever again." His smile was tight. "He's in considerable debt to me, and I can make his life extremely uncomfortable."

Henry wasn't sure what Bartlett's connection to Kit was, but he nodded, resolving to ask Kit later.

Sharp sighed. "I should have insisted on dealing with Bartlett myself. Kit's got balls, to be sure, but not much by the way of muscle to back up his heroic tendencies." He jerked his head in Kit's direction. "So, are you planning to take him home, your grace? He's not fit to find his own way back—if you can't—"

"I'll take him home," Henry said firmly.

"Who's *Kit?*" Freddy asked, then, looking in the direction of Henry's gaze, said wonderingly, "Wait, do you mean Mrs. Marsden's brother?"

Mrs. Marsden? Wasn't that Kit's friend, Clara?

Sharp glanced between them. "I can see some explanations are required, however, I really do think Kit needs to be taken home without delay."

Henry nodded.

"And he'll need to be watched tonight," Sharp said. "If you can't stay with him, tell me now and I'll—"

"I'll stay with him," Henry bit out.

Sharp looked faintly amused at his tone. "Very well."

Henry felt himself flush. Trying to ignore the betraying heat, he turned to Freddy. "Can you help me get him out to the carriage?"

Freddy nodded, though his puzzled expression did not fade, indeed, it had changed now into something more wary.

"Good night, gentlemen," Sharp said. "I'm sure all will be well by morning."

Henry nodded his thanks then returned to Kit's side, Freddy on his heels.

Kit now had his head leaning back against the wall, his eyes closed.

"Kit?" Henry said worriedly, crouching down again. "How are you?"

"Other than a headache and feeling like I'm about to cast up my accounts, I feel as fine as fivepence," Kit mumbled without opening his eyes.

"Don't worry," Henry said. "We'll get you home and into bed."

"*Hmmm*," Kit replied, eyes still closed. "Is that a promise?"

Henry's face flamed. Christ, what must Freddy think? He couldn't even bring himself to look. Instead he cleared his throat, becoming all business. "Let's get you up then," he said heartily. "Freddy, you take his right arm and I'll take his left."

Kit's eyes flew open at that and he stared at Henry then Freddy in horror before quickly masking his expression.

"Sorry," he said. "Am I talking drivel? It's that punch to the head. Please ignore my ramblings."

"It's fine," Henry said reassuringly as he gently helped Kit to stand.

Freddy said nothing, but he was equally careful with Kit, and for that, Henry could only be grateful.

They took him outside, walking slowly, and at length got him into the carriage.

"Kit's house is in Marylebone," Henry said to Freddy, once he'd settled a blanket around Kit and wadded another up into a pillow for his head. "Do you want me to drop you back at Curzon Street? It's on the way."

Freddy shook his head. "No, the sooner you get Mr. Redford home, the better. I'll make my own way, Papa."

Henry smiled helplessly at the old name—he still preferred it, even now that the children were grown. Freddy usually called him Father these days.

"All right. We can talk tomorrow."

"Are you—are you staying at his house then? To watch over him?"

Henry blinked. "I—"

"It doesn't matter," Freddy said quickly. "Tomorrow is fine. To talk, I mean. Get your—get Mr. Redford home."

He lifted his hand, patted Henry's shoulder awkwardly, then turned on his heel and walked quickly away.

An hour later, Henry folded back the sheets on Kit's bed.

"In you get," he said firmly.

Kit—looking absurdly fetching in a plain white nightgown—said, "I'm fine now. I don't feel sick or dizzy anymore. I've just got a bit of a headache left."

"Even so," Henry said, patting the mattress. "The rest will do you good. I'll watch over you."

Kit pressed his lips together, but eventually he said. "Fine, but only if you come in beside me."

Henry was only too happy to agree to that condition. "Very well. You get in while I get undressed."

He quickly removed his clothes, only stopping when he was down to his drawers. By the time he turned back to the bed, Kit was tucked under the covers waiting for him, his gaze unashamedly travelling over Henry's mostly naked body.

Henry smiled and extinguished the candles before climbing in next to Kit.

He didn't reach for Kit, not yet, but settled his head on the other pillow facing him. His eyes had not yet adjusted to the darkness, so he could not see Kit's face. "We have much to talk about," he said gently. "But perhaps in the morning? You must be exhausted."

"Actually, I'm not tired at all," Kit said. "Remember, I'm up half the night most nights and sleep late into the morning. This feels like a very early bedtime to me."

"Not to me," Henry replied. "At home—in Wiltshire, I mean—I'm usually in bed before now."

"Bumpkin," Kit said, but his tone was affectionate. "So, what do you want to talk about? I suppose you want to know why I was at Jake Sharp's club tonight?"

"Yes, and what that brawl was about," Henry said. "And I must admit, I'm curious as to how you know Sharp."

Kit's eyes gleamed in the darkness. He shifted, settling one hand under his cheek as he looked at Henry. "I have questions too," he said.

"Such as?"

"Such as why *you* were there," Kit replied. "And why your son was."

"Freddy?" Henry said. Then, "He knows you—how?"

"He doesn't really," Kit replied. "But a couple of weeks ago, he saw a man set upon Clara while she was out walking. He chased off her attacker and brought her home. He didn't mention his name, or of course, I'd have made the connection —he's very like you."

"He mentioned that incident," Henry said.

"You should be proud of him," Kit continued. "He came to Clara's aid that day, and to mine tonight—his friend was intent upon giving me a beating, but Freddy stepped in and stopped him."

"I am proud of him," Henry murmured. And he was. Freddy had not only stood up for Kit tonight when he obviously needed assistance, he had done so against his own friend.

"I hope he wasn't hurt?"

"He seems to have come out of the scuffle more or less unscathed," Henry said. "Which is more than I can say for Bartlett—Freddy inflicted a black eye and a split lip on him."

"Good," Kit said with relish. "He deserves that, and a great deal more besides."

"So, Bartlett was the man who wanted to give you a beating?"

"He was."

"Why?"

Kit sighed. "You remember me telling you that Clara was a governess in a wealthy household? And that the son of the house forced himself on her?"

"That was Bartlett?" Henry asked, horrified.

Kit nodded "Peter is his natural child—not that he'll ever recognise the boy. Clara recently approached Bartlett and asked him to contribute money to Peter's upbringing. He didn't take it well."

Henry stared at Kit. He could just about make out his features now that his vision had adjusted to the darkness, and Kit's expression was tight with anger.

"She shouldn't have approached him," Kit said. "She knew what he was like."

"Then why did she?" Henry asked curiously.

"Peter has a weak chest. The doctor told Clara she needs to move him to the country and she realised she would have to stop working at Redford's to do that. So, she decided to try to get the money she needed from Bartlett—and he reacted by sending thugs after her."

"And is this where we come to why you were at Sharp's tonight?" Henry guessed.

Kit's soft laugh was rueful. "It is."

"You went to see Bartlett? Why? To ask for the money for Clara?"

"Christ, no!" Kit exclaimed, rising up on his elbow. "I would not sink to the level of that slug by blackmailing him. I've already told Clara not to worry about money again—she and Peter are family to me, and I will always provide for him. I went to Sharp's tonight with the sole intention of forcing Bartlett to leave Clara alone by publicly confronting him." He gave a dismissive snort then. "Besides, he's got no money. His father has some wealth, it's true—though it's mostly tied up in land—but I expect Bartlett will run though that within a year or two of his sire passing on."

Henry gazed at Kit, who was now settling himself back down onto his pillow. His strategy had been well thought out. He was a clever man, and a principled one. Brave, too. He didn't need to stick his neck out for Clara and Peter, but he did it because he thought it was the right thing to do—and because he'd taken responsibility for a little boy who was not his own son.

Henry was rocked by an unexpected wave of emotion that had him swallowing painfully against a sudden lump in his throat.

When he had himself under control again, he said, "Clara and Peter are very lucky to have you."

Kit's expression softened. "I'm lucky to have them," he said. "Given how Peter was conceived, one might think—" he broke off, shaking his head minutely—"but despite everything, Clara's devoted to him. She is the best of mothers."

Henry watched Kit, fascinated, trying to interpret his expressions. After a moment, he said, carefully, "Was your mother... not like that?"

Kit made a soft noise of amusement. "Actually, my mother was very indulgent—very affectionate." He smiled. "But she was also rather..." He trailed off, as though unsure how to finish.

Henry stayed quiet, waiting as Kit thought.

"Life was not kind to her," Kit said at last. "And it is hard to be strong when life always beats you down." He paused, and again, Henry waited, sensing there was more to come. There was something about the darkness that made it easier to share one's thoughts.

"She conceived me with a client," Kit said at last. "She didn't ever tell me who the man was. She may not have known. She'd been pregnant before and got rid of the babe, but for some reason, she decided to keep me."

Kit must have seen the shock on Henry's face, because his eyes gleamed, hard like polished stone in the darkness. "In the world I grew up in, women like my mother had to make all sorts of decisions you would disapprove of, Henry, just to survive."

Kit's anger surprised Henry a little—Kit might as easily have been the babe that was got rid of, after all—but what did Henry know of the life Kit had been born into, or the choices his mother had made?

"Tell me," he said gently. "What was she like?"

Kit's anger faded and his lips stretched upwards in a smile that was sweet and a little sad. "She was very beautiful. I suppose everyone thinks that about their mother, but mine really was breathtaking."

Henry reached a hand out to touch Kit's face, brushing his thumb over the fine line of Kit's cheekbone. He was filled with a soft, familiar affection, and it struck him that he had missed feeling like this. It was a different sort of feeling than the one he felt for his children, but with the same sort of tender ache to it.

"I'm not surprised to hear it," Henry murmured. "If she was anything like you."

Kit's eyes flickered to Henry's. After a few moments, he said, "Beauty is a strange thing. It can be a gift, and it can be a curse. If you're lucky, it can be the means of lifting you out of the gutter, but it attracts people, ruthless people, who only want to exploit that beauty for their own gain. Who don't care where you end up."

"Is that what happened to your mother?" Henry asked gently.

Kit nodded. "Her father sold her to a brothel when she was twelve years old." He swallowed, hard. "Can you imagine?"

Henry shook his head, his heart aching. Helplessly, the picture of Marianne at twelve came to mind, followed a surge of anger so intense, it took his breath away.

"She was lucky," Kit said, the bitter edge in his voice

giving lie to the words. "One of the patrons was so taken with her, he wanted her all for himself. She was with him for a few years, before she was moved on. She was mistress to a number of men after that until she fell pregnant with me." He sighed. "I don't know why she kept me—it wasn't a very sensible decision."

"Why not?"

"She could not keep me with her and live as a man's mistress, at his beck and call. But she didn't want to live apart from me, so she went back to brothel work—that was when she started at the Golden Lily. It was a fancy place but still, she was servicing multiple men every day, exposing herself to all sort of risks."

"And you grew up there? In the brothel?"

Kit nodded. "I think I told you before—my mother left me in Mabel's care when she died. Mabel wasn't what you'd call sentimental, but for some reason, she loved my mother, so she agreed to look after me."

"Until you were sixteen," Henry pointed out.

Kit looked faintly amused. "I had to earn my keep at some point. Even then, she treated me differently from the other whores. I was not made generally available to patrons of the house. She only offered my services to certain clients."

Henry winced. He remembered his own discussion with the madam after he first saw Kit. "*Christopher is a rare beauty. I am only offering his next contract to a very few select patrons.*" She'd had several wealthy men vying to become his protector. When Henry's bid had been accepted, he'd been triumphant.

Was that Kit's idea of being looked after—being put to work in a brothel at sixteen? Repeatedly sold to the highest bidder?

Even as he had the thought, Henry was filled with self-loathing. Who was he to judge? He'd never questioned how Kit had become a prostitute, or doubted Kit's eagerness to serve him. At the time, he had been only too happy to take him at face value—a beautiful, pliable young man with a seemingly endless appetite for pleasure. A man who was always available to Henry, never complaining.

A man who'd seemed to be free of any desires or thoughts of his own, and conveniently devoted to fulfilling Henry's every whim.

How Henry now regretted not looking beyond Kit's endlessly accommodating nature. Never questioning whether Kit really was as agreeable and obliging as he had seemed. He was so lost in these thoughts that Kit's next words near passed him by.

"I like your boy, Freddy," Kit said. "He seems to be a very decent young man."

Henry blinked, startled by the sudden change of subject, then he smiled, his heart swelling with affection and pride. "He's always been like that. Even as a very small boy, Freddy would always speak out when he thought something was wrong."

"You raised him well," Kit said. "When he came here, the day he rescued Clara, I was so absorbed with looking after her, that I didn't even think to ask his name. I feel rather foolish that it didn't occur to me how similar he looks to you when I first knew you. Tall and handsome and—"

Henry placed his fingertips on Kit's lips, silencing him. "Please," he said. "Do not say any more admiring things about Freddy."

Kit's laughter was muffled under his fingers, the vibrations ticklish. When Henry moved his hand away, Kit said, "I'll restrict my admiration to his actions, then. He seems to be a man of action."

"He is rather," Henry admitted. "Growing up, he cared for nothing but horses and joining the cavalry."

"Ah. Is that what he wishes to do?" Kit asked.

Henry sighed. "Yes, unfortunately. I've tried to persuade

him to consider another path—hell, any other path, but it's all he wants and every time we discuss the matter, we fight."

"Why do you want him to consider another path?" Kit asked curiously.

"You may not have noticed," Henry said shortly, "but life in the military is not exactly safe."

"Is anything?" Kit asked carefully. "Life is… very unpredictable."

Henry was quiet a moment, then he said, "My younger brother died in Portugal. My mother never got over his death."

Kit stared at him a moment, then he reached his hand out and stroked a lock of hair back from Henry's face, his touch unbearably gentle. Henry wanted to press into his hand, like a cat, but somehow managed to hold himself back. They stared at one another.

At last, gently, Kit whispered, "You realise—I know you do—that it's Freddy's life. And that means, as difficult as it is for you to accept, it's his decision to make."

Henry opened his mouth to argue, but no words came out.

He thought of Freddy in Sharp's tonight, bruised and dishevelled and absolutely calm. His boy—his energetic, happy, sometimes angry boy—who seemed to find the best part of himself whenever he was tested.

Kit was right. Henry knew he was right—and it made his heart feel like a lead weight.

He closed his eyes.

"Oh, Henry," Kit said, his voice brimming with sympathy. He inched closer and his fingers stroked through Henry's hair again. The tenderness of it was almost unbearable. Over the years, Henry had grown so used to being alone—in this way at least—that he had begun to think himself immune to isolation. It was galling to learn that all it took was a few brief gestures of affection to have him so undone.

"I just want to protect him," he said hoarsely. "For him to be *safe*."

"I know," Kit said. "You're a good father, Henry. But your boy is a man now, and he seems to me to be an independent one. I wager he'll go his own way in the end, with or without your consent. Wouldn't it be better to at least be able to help him, so far as you can?"

Henry shook his head mutely, but when he spoke, it was to agree. "I know you're right," he said. "But Kit—I'm afraid. I have lost a child before and it's a terrible, terrible grief. I don't think I can—" He broke off, unable to go on, unspeakably grateful when Kit put his arms around his shoulders and pulled him close.

Resting his forehead against Kit's shoulder, he said in a muffled tone, "I'm supposed to be looking after you, not the other way around."

"We can look after each other," Kit said gently.

Henry pulled back a little, enough so he could meet Kit's eyes again. He whispered, "I would like that more than anything, and not just for tonight, Kit."

Kit just stared at him, wide-eyed.

Henry had balked at this fence earlier today, but now he gathered all his courage and made himself leap.

"The truth is," he said shakily, "I still love you, Kit. Despite all the years that have passed."

"*Henry*—" Kit shook his head mutely, as though denying Henry's words.

"I know this is hasty and that it probably feels too soon to you," Henry added urgently, cupping Kit's cheek. "But I also know my own heart, Kit. And I want... I want *something* with you. A life, Kit. Together."

Kit's eyes welled with sudden tears, and he dashed them away with the back of his hand impatiently.

"We're too old, and too much time has passed," he muttered. "Our lives are different now. *I'm* different."

"If you don't love me, just—"

"It's not that!" Kit flashed back angrily, and despite his fury, Henry's heart filled with elation.

"Do you then?" he pressed. "Do you love me, Kit?"

Kit groaned. "Yes, God help me, I do, but I'm"—he broke off and shook his head, frustrated—"I'm not the carefree boy you once knew. I have responsibilities, obligations. And so do you—you have *children*, Henry."

"Grown children," Henry replied. "Grown children who are living their own lives now."

"But you are still their father. And I have a business—a scandalous business that you cannot afford to be associated with. I have Clara and Peter, and others who rely on me for their livelihoods."

"You don't need to worry about any of that," Henry said gently. "I'm a very wealthy man, Kit. You don't need—"

"*No*," Kit interrupted. "One thing I am very sure of is that I am never going back to that."

"To what?"

"To being kept."

"It wouldn't be like that," Henry said. "I wouldn't be *keeping* you. I would be providing for you. I provided for Caroline. It would be the same thing."

"So I would be your *wife*?" Kit said flatly.

"No—yes." Henry made an impatient sound. "Oh, I don't know! I only know that I want you with me—the real you, I mean. Not a pleasure servant. I don't want to be your master ever again, Kit. Hell, that's the last thing I want!"

"If you keep me, or provide for me, or whatever you want to call it, I'll be beholden to you. That's what money does, Henry. I don't want that. Never again."

"But money shouldn't matter between us," Henry said. "We don't even need to think about it."

"You only say that because you have it," Kit retorted. "But it *does* matter. Maybe not to everyone—maybe not to you,

JOANNA CHAMBERS

Henry. But it matters to *me*. I had too many years of being kept. I won't live like that again. When I gave up the game, I promised myself I would never be financially dependent on another man again. I make my own way now."

"God, Kit—" Henry said, but he didn't finish the sentence. The fact was, he understood why Kit felt that way, given their history. And in truth, he too would prefer it if money never came between them again. He liked the proud, independent Kit who said whatever he wanted; who was brutally honest with Henry; who demanded things of him—hell, who could make Henry his *slave* if he wanted to.

Henry didn't want dominion over Kit. He just wanted to be part of his life.

After a few moments, he said quietly, "It comes to this: I love you. I think I've always loved you. When I left you, my heart"—he paused—"I was going to say it broke, but it was more like it *shrivelled*. It closed in on itself, around the emptiness where you were meant to be. I don't want to go back to living like that again, Kit. I want another chance with you. Just—tell me you'll consider it."

Kit went very still, his gaze tangling with Henry's. "This is absurd," he muttered. "To still feel like this—giddy as a boy, after all these years."

Henry's laugh was shaky. At least Kit admitted he felt giddy. That was something.

"Love's not absurd," he murmured, smiling.

Kit just sighed. "I'm old enough to know better. We both are." He rubbed at his ear. "And my head aches like the devil."

A pang of guilt speared Henry. "Hell, I'm sorry," he said. "I said I'd look after you tonight, and here I am forcing you into a discussion you're not fit to have. Why don't you try to sleep now? I'll be quiet, I promise."

"I don't think I can," Kit admitted wearily.

"You can," Henry encouraged. "Just close your eyes." He

stilled his own body and began breathing deeply, concentrating on being a calm, steady presence.

At length, Kit relaxed. His breathing slowed and became more regular until finally, he drifted into sleep.

Henry lay and watched him for a long time before he too closed his eyes.

2 1

KIT

When Kit awoke the next morning, it was to find Henry almost dressed.

"Are you leaving?" he croaked as he sat up, and Henry turned, seeming surprised to find him awake.

"I need to speak to Freddy," he said. "He'll probably have questions about last night."

Kit nodded. The young man undoubtedly would have questions, and they would not be easy ones for Henry to answer—though he did not seem too worried.

As Kit watched Henry tie his cravat, he wondered if Henry remembered his foolish words of the night before. His sweeping declarations of love.

He was probably regretting them now, Kit thought bleakly.

Satisfied with his cravat, Henry adjusted his cuffs then crossed to the bed, perching beside Kit on the mattress. He leaned forward and smoothed Kit's messy hair back from his brow. "I have not changed my mind about what I want," he said, smiling gently. "Last night you told me you still love me, and I intend to find a way for us to be together. One we can both be happy with. It may take me a little while to persuade you, but I warn you, I plan to do it."

Kit just stared at him, astonished.

Henry leaned forward and kissed Kit gently on the mouth, then rose from the bed.

"May I come back later?" he asked. "For supper, perhaps?"

Kit frowned. "Here?"

Henry chuckled. "If you don't mind. I can come to the club, if you prefer."

Kit bit his lip. He should not encourage this foolishness.

He opened his mouth to say something of that nature but somehow found himself instead saying, "All right. Seven o'clock?"

Henry's smile was sweet. "I shall look forward to it all day."

Kit would too, he realised, as he watched Henry depart. He would look forward to it far too much. It was terrifying how much he already wanted to see Henry again. Loving Henry had nearly destroyed him once—why was he even considering repeating that disaster?

Determinedly thrusting his unproductive thoughts aside, Kit got out of bed, wincing at the aches and pains that assailed him as he did so. Skelton had landed a good few punches and between those blows and falling to the floor, every bone felt bruised and aching.

For now, though, there were things to do, and the first of them was to speak to Clara. He needed to tell her about last night, and set her straight on a few things.

He washed up, gingerly tended his bruises with ointment, then dressed and went looking for Clara. He found her in the parlour downstairs with Peter, playing dominoes.

"I'm winning, Uncle Kit!" Peter announced excitedly when he entered. "Two games to one. But it's best of five. Mama could still beat me!"

"Can I watch?" Kit asked, pulling up a chair.

"Yes, but you must be quiet," Peter said, very seriously. He bent to study his tiles, and Kit met Clara's gaze over his head.

She eyed his bruises, frowning, but said nothing. She proceeded to lose the game quickly though, then sent Peter to the kitchens, saying he might have a biscuit, if cook let him. He trotted off happily, and Clara closed the door behind him.

"What happened to you?"

He told her all of it, holding nothing back.

"Oh, Kit," she muttered when he was finished. "You shouldn't have put yourself in that position... but I'm very grateful, I hope you know that."

"I know," he said, patting her hand. "You and Peter should be safe now."

"Your plan worked then."

Kit's mouth twisted in a self-deprecating smile. "Well, I believe my bringing Bartlett's behaviour to public attention was certainly of *some* use, as was Lord Frederick Avesbury's intervention, but in all likelihood, it's Jake Sharp's participation that will prove to be the most persuasive. I suspect he practically owns Bartlett's soul now."

Clara bit her lip. "I don't deserve you, Kit. I was so stupid to approach him."

"Not stupid," Kit said firmly. "I understand why you did it, my dear."

Clara dashed away her tears with the heel of her hand.

"You need not worry about Peter," Kit continued gently. "You know I regard the two of you as family, my dear. And since I have no other, and find myself a rather well-to-do fellow, you may take it from me that I will provide for Peter." He smiled. "But since I know you *do* worry, I have decided to put a sum of money aside for Peter now. That way, you have the certainty of knowing that it's there and it cannot be lost in future. I will put it into trust for him, to be held safe until he is old enough to take care of it."

Tears brimmed in Clara's eyes. "Kit, you are too kind. We cannot—"

"Yes, you can," Kit said, patting her hand. "I want to do this, my dear."

She squeezed his hand back, swallowing back her tears with effort. "Th-thank you," she managed at last in a tight, emotion-filled voice.

"And now," Kit said. "While I am on the subject of Peter's future, there is something else we must discuss."

"And what is that?"

"It is time you moved to the country, my dear. The air here in town is terrible."

Clara swallowed and nodded. "I know, but Kit, my work—"

"As I've said, I will make provision for you," Kit replied gently.

"It's too much," Clara said, and her expression was distressed. "I could not impose on you so. And then, to go somewhere new again, somewhere we know no one." She rubbed at her forehead wearily. "It would be a big change, for both of us. And for you, Kit. We would both miss you terribly."

Kit smiled, touched. "And I would miss you too, but... I have had a hankering to move to the country for a while. It's difficult with the club, of course, but if I purchased a property, you could live there with Peter, and I could visit from time to time." He smiled fondly. "Your beloved brother. And if you wanted to look for teaching work, you could do so."

Her eyes brightened a little at that, and he saw her begin to consider his words.

Well, he had sown a seed at least. It would do for today.

"Just think on it for now," he said, and Clara nodded.

Peter came back then, with a large, half-eaten biscuit in hand.

"What happened to your eye, Uncle Kit?" he demanded, noticing Kit's bruises for the first time. He approached and set his sturdy little fingers gently on Kit's face, tracing the bruise beneath his eye. "It's red and purple *and* blue. Is it sore?"

"A bit," Kit said, smiling.

"How did it happen? Did you get in a fight?"

"Yes," Kit said simply, at the exact same moment that Clara said, "Of course not!"

They looked at one another and laughed.

"Sort of," Kit said, by way of compromise, then swiftly changed the subject. "Do you want to play me at dominoes? I warn you, I'm *much* better than your mama…"

Needless to say, Peter did want to play.

They had just finished their fourth game when Tom swept in.

"You'll never guess who it is, Kit," he said. "Only bleedin' Jake Sharp!"

———

Kit wasn't sure if he should be surprised to see Sharp so soon after the previous evening's events. And he certainly wasn't sure what mood the man would be in. On any view, last night had not gone precisely as planned. Sharp had agreed to Kit confronting Bartlett in his club—not to a full-scale brawl.

However, when Sharp was shown into the parlour, after Clara and Peter had left, he seemed perfectly relaxed, greeting Kit pleasantly and declining his offer of tea.

He watched Tom leave the room with undisguised interest.

"Ogling my footman?" Kit said, amused.

"I remember him," Sharp said, one corner of his mouth

quirking up. "That arse is unforgettable. He was selling it up at your club, wasn't he? What's he doing here?"

"He wanted a change of direction," Kit replied.

"That so?" Sharp nodded. "Still, I'm a bit surprised at you keeping a footman. And with all the fancy livery too. Don't seem like you, Kitten."

"It's a temporary arrangement," Kit said. "Tom is… gaining experience with me before he looks for a permanent position."

Sharp raised his brows. "If he's looking for a position, there might be one directly under me"—he cleared his throat —"so to speak."

"That's precisely what he *doesn't* want to do anymore," Kit said drily.

Sharp chuckled. "I was only jesting anyway—I've got someone else in mind for that post."

"Have you?"

Sharp's smile was wolfish.

"How about last night then?" he said after a moment.

Kit felt his face heat. "I'm sorry things got so out of hand. I wasn't expecting that. I don't think it would have happened had Skelton not been there."

Sharp only shrugged. "There was always a risk of fisticuffs. I wouldn't have let you do it to a good customer, but Bartlett was on his way to being banned anyway. As for Skelton, your duke friend did me a favour with that one. Turned out he'd been using marked cards in my club."

Sharp leaned forward, his tawny gaze oddly intent on Kit. He looked unusually serious with no hint of amusement or sarcasm in his expression. It was a look that said he meant what he was about to say.

"Don't you worry about them coves, Kit," he said quietly. "I'll be taking care of both of them. You don't need to give 'em another thought, and neither does your friend, Clara."

Kit blinked.

Perhaps he shouldn't have been surprised. Sharp had already been remarkably decent about the whole thing.

"Thank you," Kit said at last. "I appreciate that more than I can say, and Clara will too."

Sharp acknowledged his thanks with a brief nod. "So," he said after a pause. "This duke of yours. Avesbury."

"He's not my duke," Kit replied quickly. He might be grateful to Sharp, but he wasn't about to give him any information about Henry he didn't need.

"No?" Sharp said, raising a brow. "I heard he was your keeper?"

"That was years ago," Kit said with a careless shrug. "And he's not the only keeper I ever had."

Sharp was silent for a long time, then he leaned back in his chair and said, "Well, that's good to know, Kitten, because if there's a position free as your keeper, I'd be very interested in applying."

Kit laughed softly and shook his head. "There's no position. As I think I've told you before, I don't do that anymore. And even if I did, I'm too old for you."

"Bollocks," Sharp said, grinning. "You're not much older than me."

"Whether or not that's the case, the fact remains I swore to myself a long time ago that I would never take money for that again."

Besides, I'm in love with someone else.

He wasn't stupid enough to say that last part aloud though.

Sharp sighed. "Well that's just a damned shame," he said. "The way I see it, money keeps things simple between two people. And I need things simple."

Kit could have told him he was wrong. That far from making it simpler, money complicated everything. That it changed the balance between two people in ways that couldn't be easily rectified.

But he didn't say any of those things.

"If you recall, you do owe me a favour," Sharp said, canting his head a little and quirking a smile.

Kit gave him a look. "I do recall—and I also recall that I told you that doesn't include *my* favours. Ask for something else."

Sharp laughed. He leaned back in his chair, watching Kit with unconcealed curiosity. "What have you got to offer me, Kitten?"

Kit opened his mouth to make some flippant comment in reply, but then he stopped himself. Paused. Let the idea that had just occurred to him expand in his mind.

What he was contemplating terrified him, but he made himself say it anyway.

"How about I sell Redford's to you?"

Sharp's eyes widened

And it was then that Kit realised something.

He really did want to sell Redford's.

He wanted to be done with it.

"The members value the discretion I provide," Kit said. "So we would have to find a way of reassuring them on that score. I could not sell without being satisfied that they were fully protected."

Sharp's gaze searched his face. "I understand," he said at last. "It only makes sense after all—that's where the real value lies. Your members pay through the nose for safety. It's a nice little earner, Kit, and I admit, it would fit well with my other businesses."

"So," Kit said, "can you guarantee their safety? It all rests on that."

Sharp met his gaze. "Guarantee? No."

Kit's disappointment at that response was crushing. He tried to hide his reaction but feared it must be obvious to Sharp.

"In that case," he began, "I don't think we can—"

"The real question is not what I can or cannot guarantee them," Sharp said. "It's whether they can trust me. So, we'll ask them."

"Ask them?" Kit echoed.

"Yes," Sharp said simply. "You'll tell them you're selling up and I'm buying and we'll give them the choice to leave or stay. If they want to leave, fine—and you'll destroy all their membership records. Or, they can stay with me as the new owner. I'm reasonably well known now, with my own clubs, so they can judge for themselves whether they're prepared to trust me." He paused. "I'll give you seven and a half thousand for the club regardless of who stays, and another two and a half if more than two-thirds stay."

Kit swallowed hard. It was a very fair offer.

"Fifteen thousand," he said coolly, "Guineas, not pounds. Plus the extra two and half if you get over two-thirds of the members, *and* you keep on all the staff at the same wages."

Sharp laughed. "You cheeky sod," he said wonderingly. He thought for a moment. "Ten thousand guineas then. Two and half more if two-thirds stay—if nine-tenths do, I'll make it fifteen all-in. And I'll keep the staff, but you won't remove so much as a stick of furniture from the reception rooms or a single spoon from the kitchens."

Kit's head was swimming. "Done," he said faintly.

Sharp held out his hand, and Kit took it.

"Pleasure doing business with you," Sharp said.

22

HENRY

When Henry arrived home, his butler advised him that Lord Frederick was in the breakfast room and had asked to be informed as soon as his grace returned home.

"Shall I inform Lord Frederick that you are back, your grace?"

"No need," Henry said. "I'll go and speak with him. I could do with some breakfast in any event."

Freddy looked up from his plate when Henry opened the door.

"Good morning, Freddy," Henry said. "Did you sleep well?" He went to the sideboard and filled a plate before returning to the table and settling down.

"Tolerably well," Freddy said. "You?"

Was there a note of challenge in that question, or was Henry imagining things? Mildly he said, "I did, thank you. Could you pour me some tea?" He pushed his cup and saucer towards Freddy who lifted the pot, poured him a cup, and pushed it back.

"How is Mr. Redford?" Freddy asked.

"He's fine," Henry said. "And very grateful to you for your intervention last night."

Freddy shrugged. "Anyone would have done the same."

"No," Henry said. "In point of fact, no one did—only you." He smiled. "I can't tell how proud I am of you for that."

Freddy flushed, his mouth curving briefly into a smile before he cleared his throat and said, "May I ask you something?"

"Of course," Henry said.

"How do you know Mr. Redford?"

Henry had been expecting this, and he'd had time to consider his answer on the way home. Even so, it was not easy to speak the words.

"We knew each other a long time ago," he said. "But until very recently I hadn't seen him for many years."

"So you're... friends?" Freddy asked.

Henry set down his cutlery. "Freddy—"

Freddy blurted, "Are you like George?"

"Like George," Henry repeated slowly. "Your brother George?"

Freddy swallowed. He nodded.

Henry frowned. "I'm not sure what you mean."

Freddy paled. "Don't you—?" He broke off. "I thought you *knew*. George did too."

"Knew what?"

Freddy's eyes widened, his gaze horrified. "I—nothing, I—"

Henry had never seen him so flustered.

"Tell me," Henry insisted. When Freddy just stared at him, he added, "Freddy, please. I know George has been unhappy for a while. If you know why—" He broke off then, remembering what Freddy had just said before panic set in.

"Are you like George?"

Faintly, almost disbelievingly, Henry said, "Are you telling me that George—that he prefers men?"

Freddy swallowed and nodded. "I thought you knew," he whispered. "I would never have mentioned it otherwise."

"How would I know?" Henry said helplessly. His heart was racing, his gut in turmoil. The thought of George suffering in silence the way Henry had suffered for so many years made him hurt all over.

"Fletch's father caught them together at Dinsford Park, when George was there for the holidays." Freddy said. "Don't you remember when George was sent back in disgrace? We were sure Fletch's father had told you what happened."

Henry did vaguely remember an occasion when George had been sent back early from his friend's house—he would have been sixteen or so. Back then, he'd spent most of the holidays with his best friend, Oliver Fletcher, sometimes at Avesbury House and sometimes at Fletch's family estate in Surrey. On that last occasion, George had been sent home with a terse but vague note from Sir Joseph Fletcher alluding to unacceptable behaviour and suggesting that Henry ask George for an explanation.

After reading the note, Henry had taken one look at George standing on the other side of his desk, his expression miserable and defeated, and had thrown the note on the fire. Henry had always liked Oliver Fletcher, a scamp of a lad who was the one person who seemed to have the power to bring out George's more frivolous side.

Henry had decided then and there that George had been punished enough. Instead of asking George to explain himself, he'd dismissed him, saying only, "Take yourself off—just don't do it again."

"Don't do it again."

Hearing the words again in his mind, he wanted to weep. He hadn't even known what he was telling George not to do.

"I didn't know," Henry said, his tone agonised. "God, if I'd known…"

It all made a horrible kind of sense. George's low moods had begun a year or two before the incident at Dinsford Park, and they only seemed to have got worse since then. Henry ought to have recognised them for what they were, given he'd suffered from the same malaise.

"Papa?"

Henry looked up, meeting Freddy's worried gaze.

What if George had known that Henry was like him? God knew this world did not make life easy for their kind. Would that knowledge have helped?

"Yes," Henry said hoarsely.

Freddy just waited silently for him to go on.

"Yes, I *am* like George," Henry said. "And, yes, that is how I know Christopher Redford."

There was a moment of profound silence, then Freddy said, "Was he your..." He trailed off, seeming unsure how to finish the sentence.

Henry nodded, watching his younger son carefully. "He was, yes." Henry's stomach hollowed with fear and dread, but he made himself continue, made himself say the next words. "I loved him. I still do."

Freddy closed his eyes for a moment, taking that in.

When he opened them again, he said quietly, "When were you and he together?"

"A very long time ago." Henry paused then added, "And I'm afraid that's all I'm going to say about Kit for now, Freddy."

"All right," Freddy said quietly, but his brows were drawn together in a frown and he stared down at the table as though he couldn't bear to look at Henry.

"Are you disgusted?" Henry whispered. That was an unbearable thought, but he had to ask.

Freddy shook his head and looked up again. "Confused mostly. You and Mama—" He broke off.

"I loved your mother," Henry quietly. "We loved each other. That's all that matters."

Freddy didn't say anything to that, only went back to

staring at the table. After a while, Henry said desperately, "What are you thinking?"

Freddy shook his head. "All this time, I've been so angry at you, because of George. Because he started being miserable after you learned about him." He shook his head disbelievingly. "Except now it turns out you didn't actually know at all and, in fact, you and he are the same and... oh hell, everything's topsy-turvy!" He sighed and rubbed a weary hand over his face. "I'll get used to it eventually, I suppose. I can hardly accept this in George but not in you, can I?"

He offered Henry a watery smile and Henry wanted to weep, because Freddy was proving to be far more understanding than Henry would ever have imagined. His younger son could be brash and recklessly neck-or-nothing, but he had a solid core of decency that ran through his character like a seam of gold.

"Thank you," Henry said. The words were inadequate. He felt so much profound gratitude in this moment, for Freddy's understanding towards himself and his loyalty to his brother. And he felt relief too, overwhelming relief that, having bared this part of himself to his son, he seemed—against all his expectations—to have been accepted. Shown kindness, even. He would never have dared hope for such a thing, yet here it was, being given to him.

"You need to speak with George, Papa," Freddy said.

Henry nodded. "I do. I'll make arrangements to return to Wiltshire soon." He paused, then added, "But before then we must speak about you."

Freddy frowned. "What about me?"

Henry took a deep breath. "Last night, Kit made me see it's time I stopped standing in the way of what you want to do with your life—though I hope I'd have realised that for myself by this morning anyway."

The suspicious look fell away. Suddenly Freddy looked both hopeful and scared to hope.

"I'll buy your colours," Henry said roughly. "If that's what you still want."

Henry despatched Freddy to Simon Reid's offices later that morning with a letter of introduction and instructions to ascertain what commissions were available. It was the first definite step towards Freddy embarking on a military career, and Henry had mixed feelings as he sealed the letter and handed it to his son.

The anxiety he already felt over Freddy's future career was something he sensed he was going to have to learn to live with. But as Freddy took his leave, Henry saw many things in his son that weighed on the other side of the scales: joy, excitement, and that steely determination that was so much a part of Freddy's character.

Kit was right, he thought. It was Freddy's life, not Henry's. It had not been fair of him to stand in Freddy's way. Even if this was a mistake, it was Freddy's mistake to make.

And hopefully it would not be a mistake. After all, it seemed that Freddy had more kindness and human understanding in him than Henry had ever realised. That made him feel both proud—of Freddy—and ashamed—of himself. He had not judged his son generously.

Well, he would have to do better at that, and at other things too. He had another son to apologise to—which was going necessitate leaving London—and he had a daughter to say farewell to, before he spent the next few months worrying incessantly about her till her baby was born.

His children might be grown and fledged, but they would always occupy every corner of his heart. No matter how old they grew, he would never escape the endless, daily work of worrying about them.

And nor would he want to.

But now—now he had someone else to occupy his heart too. Someone who had never really left, truth to tell.

That was the thing about hearts, Henry reflected. They looked quite small, but they could hold a lot—and all kinds of love at the same time, some of which could not be neatly boxed and labelled.

"I loved your mother. We loved each other. That's all that matters."

It *was* all that mattered, Henry decided. Really, when all was said and done, what else was there?

Kit had said that Henry could return to him at seven o'clock. He glanced at the clock.

Not quite noon.

Hell.

Well, there other things he could do in the meantime— spend some time with Marianne, plan his return to Wiltshire, and of course, come up with some way of persuading Kit to spend the rest of his life with Henry.

23

KIT

"I'm selling the club," Kit said.

"You never are!" Mabel exclaimed, sitting forward in her chair and making Nell Gwyn—who had been perched on her shoulder—squawk and rise up in a fluster of outraged feathers.

"I am," Kit confirmed.

"To that Sharp fellow?"

Kit nodded. "What do you think?"

"Depends on the price," Mabel said promptly, canny as ever.

Kit told her the arrangements and was relieved when she nodded her approval.

"You've done well, my lad," she said, and her eyes grew a little misty. "I wish your mother was here to see this. She would be that proud."

He smiled, touched. Mabel Butcher was a tough woman, but even now, all these years on, she got a tear in her eye when she mentioned his mother. Kit had been thinking of Minnie Redford more often lately, remembering how much fun she had been when he was small, how proud he had been of having a mother so much lovelier than everyone else's.

Remembering too, less happily, the first time he'd seen her with a bruise on her face, and the times he'd seen her sadness, her exhaustion, her worry.

He wished he could have had just one chance to lighten her load, instead of making it always heavier.

"She knows," a soft voice said, and when Kit looked up, it was to find the usually silent Gracie watching him with a calm expression. "She's looking down on you from heaven, Mr. Redford."

Kit was embarrassed to feel a lump rise in his throat at her gentle assurance. He didn't believe in angels and heaven, but something in Gracie's certainty made him at least want to do so.

"Thank you," he murmured.

"What will you do with yourself now, then, ducky?" Mabel asked. "A comfortable retirement? Your mother and I always used to say we'd retire to Southend. She fancied the seaside." She sighed.

"You could still go there," Kit said, but she waved that off.

"I'd only have been going for Minnie," she said. "I'm London born and bred, and I plan to die here too."

"You'll live forever," Kit said scornfully. "You and that bloody parrot."

Nell whistled loudly. "*Bloody parrot! Don't be rude!*"

Mabel chuckled, affectionately stroking the parrot's head with the crook of her finger. "Ah, Nelly, my clever darling." Then glancing at Kit, she said, "So? Retirement?"

"I'm too young for that," Kit said, smiling.

"Another business then? Or the country? There'll always be money in land."

Kit cleared his throat. "You remember how you said I needed to find someone? For the other side of my fireplace?"

"*What?*" Mabel shrieked, sending Nell Gwyn squawking yet again. "You've finally got yourself a new fancy man?"

Kit shifted uncomfortably. "It depends what you mean by new."

Mabel's gaze narrowed speculatively. "Someone you already know…" she mused, tapping her chin. "One of the boys at the club, is it?" But already she was shaking her head. "Is it someone I know? Wait"—she clapped her hands, grinning—"is it Jean-Jacques?"

"No!" Kit exclaimed, offended. "He's married, and I'm friends with his wife!"

Mabel scowled. "Shame," she said sourly, and went back to tapping her chin. "Who then? I can't think of anyone. You've never been one for romantic feelings, Kit, despite being so soft-hearted. Not since that bloody duke—" She broke off at the expression on his face, her own transforming into one of pure disbelief. "Oh, no, Kit! Never tell me it's *him* after all these years!"

Kit said, "I'm afraid so. Henry found me and—"

"That lying, cheating—"

"*And* he's explained what happened in the past," Kit spoke over her. "He had no idea, Mabel. It was all the fault of his man of business."

"And you believe this rubbish?" Mabel hissed.

"Just listen," Kit insisted, and proceeded to tell her the whole story—or at least, most of it.

By the time he was finished, she looked somewhat mollified, though her mouth was still tight with disapproval.

"I can't believe you wouldn't let him give you the money!" she exclaimed. "I think you're touched in your top loft, Kit. He owed you that."

Kit laughed softly and shook his head.

Nell Gwyn whistled noisily and hopped from Mabel's shoulder to the arm of her chair.

"*Woo-hoo!*" she shrieked. "*He loves you; he loves you not.*"

"You should listen to Nell Gwyn." Mabel told him sternly. "I swear this old girl's practically a prophet."

The parrot launched herself from the chair in a lazy flap of wings, landing on top of her cage.

"*He loves you,*" she intoned flatly, then hopped from the cage to the top of a wooden glass-fronted cabinet where Mabel kept her best china. "*He loves you not.*"

Next was the sideboard. "*He loves you.*"

The mantelpiece. "*Woo-hoo! He loves you not.*"

She paused on the coal scuttle to whistle tunelessly, then shrieked, "*He loves you,*" only to hop to the tea table and intone mournfully, "*he loves you not.*"

Finally, Nell Gwyn did something she had never done before. She landed on Kit's shoulder and rubbed her feathered head against his hair, whistling again. "*He loves you.*"

And fell silent.

For a few moments, no one said anything, waiting. Then Nell Gwyn flapped back over to her cage and hopped inside, picking up a nut from the floor of the cage, which she began to tear open.

Kit looked at Mabel, wide-eyed. She had tears in her eyes.

"Well in that case," she said, "you'd better have your duke, I suppose."

Henry arrived at five minutes to seven.

"He's keen," Tom commented unprofessionally, leaning in the doorway of Kit's private sitting room. "You should let him kick his heels for a while."

Kit chuckled. "I'm too old for that sort of nonsense. Show him up."

"I thought you were having supper with him?" Tom said, surprised.

"I'll have a supper tray sent up later," Kit said casually.

"Oh, it's like that, is it?" Tom crowed.

"Oh, be quiet," Kit said crossly, but his mouth twitched and Tom was laughing as he left.

A few minutes later, Tom was back, swinging the door open and announcing, "His grace, the—"

"That's enough, Tom, thank you," Kit said. "Let Henry in."

Tom bit his lip, "Very good, sir," he said, his voice thick with suppressed laughter. He stood aside and Henry passed him, walking into the room.

Kit was already on his feet and walking forward.

They came together in the middle of the little sitting room, both smiling. Kit was vaguely aware of the door closing, but he did not look away from Henry's dear, smiling face.

"Kit," Henry murmured, "*Christopher*. I've missed you."

"It's only been a few hours," Kit scoffed, but his tone was fond.

"Has it? I've been wretched without you," Henry said. He set his hand against Kit's cheek and tilted his face up, his expression soft with affection. "I have things to tell you," he said.

"And I you," Kit replied. "But you go first."

"All right," Henry said. "May I kiss you before I begin?"

Kit grinned. "You may."

Henry grinned back and bent his head, capturing Kit's lips in a warm, soft kiss that made Kit's legs go weak.

When they broke apart, Henry said happily, "I told Freddy about you."

"*What?*" Kit exclaimed, shocked.

"In fairness, he had guessed," Henry said. He was smiling.

He was *happy*.

"Now you," he said.

Kit shook his head. "No, wait. What did you tell him about me exactly?"

Henry smoothed his big hand over Kit's hair, his expression fond. "That I love you."

Kit stared at him, amazed. "He must have been shocked."

"He... surprised me," Henry said. "Turns out that Freddy knows more than I could ever have guessed." He smiled. "Now tell me your news."

Kit gazed at him, staring at those familiar grey eyes, loving the happiness he saw there. "I'm selling Redford's," he said simply.

"*What?*" Henry exclaimed. "But you—wait—you'll be free, and financially independent?"

Kit grinned. "I will."

"And does that mean that you're willing to consider some other changes in your life? So that we can be together?" Henry said breathlessly.

Kit nodded, his smile feeling irrepressible. "I want to be with you too, Henry."

"Bloody hell!" Henry whispered. He blinked hard, then dropped to his knees and pressed his face against Kit's stomach, clutching him close, his arms strong bands around Kit's waist.

Kit's stared down at him, stupefied. Slowly, carefully, he stroked Henry's dark, silvered hair with gentle, careful touches.

At length, Henry raised his head, meeting Kit's worried gaze with damp eyes. "I was afraid," he said hoarsely. "I thought you might palm me off with some kindly nonsense about seeing me every once in a while when you had time." He shook his head. "You seemed so uncertain this morning."

"I had some sense talked into me by a parrot," Kit said, laughing when Henry blinked. He stroked Henry's hair again, and said gently, "I don't quite know what our future will look like. We need to think about that. I want to see Clara and Peter well settled, and I have to make sure the sale is properly taken care of and all my staff are provided for—

JOANNA CHAMBERS

including my over-familiar footman who just isn't cut out for that sort of work." He paused. "And then we have your family to consider."

"My family will be—"

"Given all due consideration," Kit interrupted.

Henry opened his mouth and closed it again.

"We don't need to rush anything," Kit said softly. "We have time to plan our future."

"But you *do* want a future with me," Henry said urgently.

Kit smiled. "I do. More than anything."

"Then the rest can wait," Henry said.

"You should get up," Kit said. "Before your knee starts playing up."

Henry grinned. "Chaise longue?" he suggested, clambering back to his feet.

When Kit nodded, he pulled him over to the long sofa, pressed him down, and settled his big body down next to Kit's.

"This is nice and roomy," he said. "Easily big enough for both of us."

"Believe it or not, I've seen bigger," Kit said idly.

"Have you?"

"Jake Sharp has an absolutely *enormous* one."

Henry scowled, "How do you know that?"

Kit just laughed. Maybe one day he'd tell Henry how often Sharp had tried to get him into bed—but not tonight. "Size isn't everything," he said sweetly instead.

"I hear it's what you do with it that counts," Henry replied, beginning to shuffle his way down the length of the sofa.

"What are *you* going to do with it?" Kit asked breathlessly as Henry rubbed his cheek against Kit's crotch, making his already semi-hard cock stiffen to full hardness in his breeches.

"I scarcely know," Henry whispered, rubbing his face back and forth. "Tell me what you want."

"Take my cock out," Kit breathed. "Suck it."

Henry did as he was bid, his fingers working frantically to open Kit's breeches and gently extract his painfully hard cock.

He licked a stripe up the shaft, from balls to tip, then swallowed Kit down, taking in his whole length.

"Oh God!" Kit groaned, palming the back of Henry's head. "Yes, like that."

He let Henry suck him for several minutes, then grabbed a handful of Henry's hair and pulled him off.

"Such a good boy," he breathed. "Will you serve me tonight with your cock?"

Henry seemed to shudder all over.

"I want it inside me," Kit added lewdly. "So get your clothes off."

Henry's cheeks flushed, grey eyes glittering with pleasure as he clambered to his feet.

Kit rose too, and they both quickly undressed.

"Lovely," Kit said, walking around Henry once he was naked, admiring the powerful planes of his body. "Are you ready to serve me?"

"Yes," Henry whispered.

"Good," Kit said, smiling. "That's what I like to hear." He strolled over to the bureau and removed the bottle of oil from the top drawer that he'd stashed there earlier.

On his way back to the chaise longue, he picked up Henry's shirt, tossing the linen down on the sofa before he laid himself down on top of it. "You can wear this tomorrow," he said. "You'll smell of my spend."

Henry moaned and Kit laughed softly. "Come here. I want your tongue on my hole."

Eyes shining with lust, Henry dropped to his knees and moved closer.

"Hands behind your head," Kit said lightly. "I want to see you work for this."

Henry groaned again but he did as he was bid, clasping his hands at the back of his neck as he inched forward.

At the first touch of his tongue, Kit sighed with pleasure and spread his thighs further apart. "Yes," he moaned. "Just. Like. That." He dropped a hand to his cock and began to lazily tease it, rubbing the head with his thumb, then stroking the length.

Henry's eager tongue was exquisite against his sensitive rim, dipping inside, hot and squirming.

Ah fuck.

After a while, Kit tugged at his hair.

"All right you lovely beast," he said hoarsely. "I want you inside me now."

Henry let out a groan that was abjectly grateful and clambered up onto the chaise longue while Kit opened the oil and covered his fingers, liberally spreading the warm, viscous liquid over his already quivering, desperate hole.

"You too," Kit breathed, reaching for Henry. He loved the easy glide of his oiled hand over Henry's desperately hard shaft, and Henry's gasp of pleasure at his touch.

"Come on, then," Kit said when he was done. "Let's get that lovely big prick inside me."

But when Henry reached for his hips, Kit gave him a quelling look.

"Ah-ah," he admonished. "Let's keep those hands out of the way."

"No, Kit, please," Henry begged.

"Oh, but *yes*," Kit said. "It will help you concentrate on my pleasure rather than your own. Come on. Hands behind your head again. I'll help you get in."

Henry groaned almost painfully this time, but he did as he was told, linking his hands at the back of his neck while Kit took hold of his shaft and lined him up perfectly to sink deeply into Kit's warm, welcome heat.

"*Yes,*" Kit hissed, throwing his head back as Henry sank inside him. "God, yes, like that. Fuck me."

Henry did his best.

Without his hands for purchase, he was all at sea, trying to give Kit what he wanted with powerful punches of his hips, his expression hazy with lust.

Kit lifted his legs, pulling his thighs back with his own hands, splayed and open and needful.

"Yes, right there," he panted. "Pound me hard, Henry."

And Christ, but Henry did, as best as any man could with his hands out of the way.

"Good boy," Kit gasped, insinuating a hand between them to grasp his own cock and begin stroking it in time with Henry's thrusts. "Fuck me, Henry. Make me spend."

Henry redoubled his efforts, hips snapping, chest heaving, eyes glittering—and Kit came like a fountain, his eyes rolling back in his head as the world went grey for long, blissful moments.

When he opened his eyes, he smiled, taking in Henry's flushed, desperate face, hard, bobbing cock, and the hands that were still clutched behind his neck.

He opened his arms and smiled. "Time for your reward. Come here."

Relief suffused Henry's expression as he lowered his arms, then draped his big body over Kit's smaller one, carefully keeping his weight off Kit.

Kit wound his arms and legs about him, rubbing himself against Henry's hard length.

"Fuck me," he whispered against Henry's mouth. "I want to feel your spend leaking out of me when you're done."

Henry's moan was deep. He wasted no time, pulling back his hips and adjusting his angle to sink deep into Kit's body.

Kit was sensitive still, but he didn't care—he wanted this. Wanted to welcome Henry into his body and give him pleasure. Wanted to reward him for the pleasure Henry had just granted him with his willing, perfect obedience.

Henry was close already, so it wasn't much more than a minute before his thrusts began to stutter. He pushed deep, holding Kit close as he emptied himself, mouthing his throat and moaning low as he came, long and hard.

They lay entwined for several minutes after, breathing slowly returning to normal as Henry's cock softened and their mingled spend dried stickily between them.

Kit sighed contentedly. "I wish I'd known this was how you liked it when we were first together," he murmured into Henry's ear.

"I could say the same to you."

Kit laughed softly. "True. Did you know back then?"

Henry lifted his head and met Kit's gaze. "Back then, I couldn't even admit it to myself, never mind to you." He shook his head, regret in his soft grey gaze.

Kit's heart ached, but it was a joyful sort of ache. The pain of the past was still there, but it was part of the joy of the future. What they had once lost, they had now regained, and this time they were older, wiser, kinder men.

Kit had once despaired at how much he loved Henry—the young god who looked certain to crush his heart.

Who had indeed done so.

But this Henry was a man that Kit could trust with his heart. This Henry was a man who had already set his own bruised heart on a silver tray and handed it to Kit, without knowing what damage Kit might do it. Trusting that Kit would not hurt him, but willing to be hurt if it came to that.

This Henry—softer, more vulnerable, and entirely less godlike—was so very much stronger than he had once been. So very much braver.

Kit laid his hand against Henry's cheek, meeting his gaze.

"Better late than never," he whispered, smiling.

Henry's answering smile was sweet.

EPILOGUE

KIT

Avesbury House, June 1827
14 months later

It was a beautiful morning, so Kit decided to walk down to the green and tranquil pool in the middle of the woods

It was one of his favourite spots in the sprawling grounds of Avesbury House. The canopy of trees over the clearing shaded it from the sun, only letting through gentle, dappled sunlight that glinted on the smooth surface of the water. Kit liked to sit at the base of the willow tree that peered into the pool, listening to the insects drone, and the frogs croak and topple into the water.

Sometimes Kit brought a notebook with him, and sometimes he just sat and looked at the water. Sometimes he came alone, and sometimes with Henry—sometimes they kissed under the tree, like boys. Today, though, Kit was alone. Henry was spending the day with his steward, and Kit was only too happy to leave him to it. He had no interest in estate business —agriculture bored him senseless.

But he loved the countryside.

He loved long, vigorous walks, exploring his new home

and learning about the flora and fauna of the area. He was growing quite a library of books on the subject. He had even begun taking his own samples home to study under a microscope that Henry had bought him, and his notebooks were full of drawings.

"You're turning into quite the gentleman scientist," Henry had teased him just the other night, as they lay in bed.

"Perhaps I should do something more productive with my time," Kit had said, frowning.

"Oh, I think you're quite productive enough with the school," Henry had said, then distracted him from his thoughts with a deep kiss.

Had he not been distracted, Kit might have pointed out that the school did not, actually, take up a great deal of Kit's time. Clara and Tom did most of the work: Clara teaching and Tom dealing with everything else. Kit had only provided the money to set it up. Well, that and he financed five annual scholarships —and of course, he helped Clara select the scholarship pupils. Oh, and he *did* help teach literacy and numeracy to the local villagers two evenings a week. And took a turn teaching the local children at Sunday school every other Sunday too.

But all these activities still left him with plenty of time to indulge his own interests to the full. And Kit was trying to teach himself not to feel guilty about that. He was allowed to enjoy some of the fruits of his labours. He had plenty of money carefully invested. As for the rest, he'd used a good portion of it setting up Clara and Peter—and Tom too, who, having fallen in love with Clara, persuaded her in short order she ought to return the favour.

Well, he *was* a handsome devil.

And entirely unsuited to being a footman.

Kit smiled to himself as he walked the uneven path to the pool, thinking of his friends, and the unexpected happiness they had found together. Gentle sunlight filtered through the leaves overhead. A bank of wild garlic gave off a warm, spicy scent.

As he approached the clearing where the pool was, Kit realised there was already someone sitting beneath his willow tree: a tall, rangy figure with an oddly pensive droop to his shoulders, staring at what looked to be a letter.

George.

Kit stopped walking, but he must have made some noise, because George turned his head and looked at him. For a moment, their gazes locked, and Kit felt as though he should apologise for interrupting what seemed to be a private, quiet moment. But already, George was rising to his feet, and folding the letter up.

"Kit," he said. "Are you out for a walk, like me?"

There was something about George Asquith that made Kit's heart ache a little. He was such a serious, sober-minded young man.

Kit sensed a rare sweetness in George that reminded him of Henry years ago. In George, though, that sweetness was both a little more tender and a little less obvious, buried beneath a stiffness of manner that made George seem always distant somehow. Almost stern sometimes.

Kit was keen to know George a little better, but he was wary of scaring him off, like a skittish horse.

"I am indeed," he said. "I'm sorry if I interrupted you— you looked very peaceful, sitting there."

George shrugged. "I was only reading." He lifted the hand holding the letter.

"It's a nice spot to sit and read," Kit said. "My favourite, I think, in the whole park."

George smiled. "Yes," he said. "It is." But his smile was wan.

If it had been anyone else, Kit might have asked him if something was wrong.

"I'll get out of your way," George said. "And let you have your turn sitting under the willow tree."

As blissful as that sounded, Kit didn't want to chase him off. "Not at all," he said. "No need for you to vacate your spot. I wasn't planning to sit here today. I'm heading back to the house now."

"Are you?" George said, tucking the letter into his pocket. "I'll come with you, then."

"Oh," Kit said, surprised—he'd rather got the impression that George avoided his company.

They set off back through the woods, walking the narrow path in single file as they made stilted conversation about the weather, and how pretty the woods were, and how they'd been prettier still before the bluebells had died off.

Once they emerged out of the woods into the wild garden, they were able to walk side by side, and it became a little easier to talk.

"What was it like for you, growing up here?" Kit asked, glancing at him.

George kept looking ahead but his expression softened. "Idyllic," he said. "We had all of this, you see. And Papa was —well you know how he is." He sent Kit a slightly awkward smile.

"Tell me," Kit urged.

"Indulgent," George said. "Affectionate. Kind. Far nicer than any of my friends'—"

He stopped walking suddenly and covered his mouth with his hand, as though to stop something coming out. He turned quickly away from Kit, but Kit saw the flash of torment in his grey eyes before he did so.

Kit stepped closer, laying a careful hand on George's shoulder. "George," he said softly. "Is something wrong?"

George shook his head, but Kit sensed he wasn't so much answering Kit's question as expressing some kind of deep denial.

"What is it?" he prompted. "Was it the letter?"

George gave a choked cry, and his shoulders trembled with the depth of his emotion. He choked again then, a horrible repressed sound. The sound of grief being pushed down and buried deep.

Sensing George's discomfort with his touch, Kit let his hand drop, even though it felt like the wrong thing to do.

At length, George turned back to him. His eyes were red-rimmed, and his gaze was hopeless, but he was back under control.

"I'm being absurd," he said. "It's happy news. My friend Ollie is getting married."

Ollie.

Oliver Fletcher.

"You don't have to be happy," Kit said carefully. "Especially if you have a fondness for the person yourself."

George looked at Kit and in that moment, Kit saw all his misery. How hard this blow really was.

"Why don't you talk to your father?" Kit said gently. "If there's anyone who'll understand how you feel, it's him."

George stared at him for a few moments, saying nothing, then he nodded. "All right," he whispered.

They walked the rest of the way back to the house in silence.

They were nearly at the door when George finally spoke.

"Kit," he said.

Kit turned to him. "Yes?"

"I'm glad Papa has you. He's much happier now." George smiled and there it was, that rare sweetness. "I used to worry about him so," he said.

The sudden lump in Kit's throat took him by surprise, and then he was blinking back tears, feeling like a perfect idiot.

George clapped him awkwardly on the shoulder and stepped ahead of him, heading for the door.

"I'll speak to him," he said. "Thank you, Kit."

Later that evening, Kit was reading in bed when his bedchamber door opened.

Flustered, he pulled off the spectacles he'd only recently begun to wear, causing Henry to chuckle.

"Why do you take them off as soon as I arrive?" Henry said as he began to remove his clothes.

Kit wrinkled his nose. "They're ugly."

"Nonsense," Henry said. "Actually, I rather like how strict they make you look." He grinned. "I keep hoping you'll threaten to give me six of the best."

Kit chuckled. "That can be arranged."

Henry began undressing again, and after a moment, Kit said tentatively, "How was George?"

Henry's expression grew pensive. "Sad," he said. He sat down on the mattress, clad only in his drawers now. "I feel as though he has been sad for a long time, Kit. Sometimes I wonder if it is events, or his nature." He paused. "Or both."

"This Oliver," Kit said. "He is the one whose father caught them when they were boys?"

Henry nodded. "He's marrying. An arranged match. The estate needs money, and the father of the bride wants her married to a titled gentleman." He shrugged. "It's common enough."

That was certainly true.

"Perhaps George should expand his horizons," Kit said gently. "A stint in town might do him good. Or a trip abroad."

"He avoids London like the plague—he voluntarily exiled himself here as soon as he respectably could after university, and it's nigh on impossible to get him to leave." Henry sighed. "He hides it well, Kit, but he's very shy."

Kit nodded. He'd guessed as much.

Getting up on his knees, he shuffled closer, pressing his front to Henry's back and kissing the nape of his neck.

"It'll be all right," he said soothingly. "He has you—and there's no better father in all England."

Henry huffed a laugh. "Hardly," he said drily.

"The best," Kit repeated, insistent, pressing more kisses to Henry's neck, and all the way around the shell of his ear. "Kindest, most affectionate, and tender."

"Tender, eh?" Henry said, squirming a little with pleasure. He twisted, catching Kit up in his arms, making him shriek as he rolled them both till Kit ended up lying on top of him, giggling hysterically.

"Lout," he accused breathlessly.

"What?" Henry exclaimed, feigning offence. "But you said I was the kindest, most tender—"

"All right, I spoke too soon!" Kit gasped. His stomach hurt from laughing, and his cheeks ached from smiling so hard. His heart felt good.

They gazed at one another, smiling like lovesick fools, and as the bubbling mirth melted away, Kit felt the warmth of a deeper, quieter joy.

"Kiss me, Henry," Kit said.

And Henry obliged.

The End

THANK YOU, DEAR READER

Thank you for reading this book!
I hope you enjoyed Kit and Henry's story.

I love hearing from my readers. You can:

~ Email me at authorjoannachambers@gmail.com
~ Visit my website at www.joannachambers.com
~ Connect with me on social media through those
cute little icons below.
~ Sign up for my newsletter at my website or on https://
tinyurl.com/joannachambersnews for up to date
information about my books, freebies and special deals.

If you have time, I'd be very grateful if you'd consider leaving
a review on an online review site. Reviews are so helpful for
book visibility and I appreciate every one.

Joanna Chambers

ACKNOWLEDGMENTS

Enormous thanks to Sally Malcolm, Annika Martin and Amy Pittel for beta-reading this book and providing such valuable insights.

ALSO BY JOANNA CHAMBERS

CAPITAL WOLVES DUET

Gentleman Wolf

Master Wolf

ENLIGHTENMENT SERIES

Provoked

Beguiled

Enlightened

Seasons Pass *

The Bequest *

Unnatural

Restored

* exclusive bonus stories for newsletter subscribers

WINTERBOURNE SERIES

Introducing Mr Winterbourne

Mr Winterbourne's Christmas

WITH ANNIKA MARTIN

Enemies Like You

PORTHKENNACK SERIES (RIPTIDE)

A Gathering Storm

Tribute Act

OTHER NOVELS

The Dream Alchemist

Unforgivable

GENTLEMAN WOLF, BOOK ONE IN THE CAPITAL WOLVES DUET

He must master the wolf within...

Edinburgh, 1820.

Thirty years after leaving Scotland, Drew Nicol is forced to return when the skeleton of a monster is found. The skeleton is evidence of werewolves—evidence that Marguerite de Carcassonne, the leader of Drew's pack, is determined to suppress.

Marguerite insists that Drew accompany her to Edinburgh. There they will try to acquire the skeleton while searching for wolf-hunters—wolf hunters who may be holding one of their pack prisoner.

But Drew has reason to be wary about returning to Edinburgh—Lindsay Somerville now lives there.

Lindsay who taught Drew about desire and obsession.

Lindsay who Drew has never been able to forgive for turning him.

Lindsay who vowed to stay away from Drew twelve years ago... and who has since taken drastic steps to sever the bond between them.

Marguerite's plan will throw Drew and Lindsay together again—and into a deadly confrontation with Lindsay's enemy, Duncan MacCormaic. They will be tested to their limits and forced to confront both their past mistakes and their true feelings.

But it may be too late for them to repair the damage of the past. The consequences of Lindsay's choices are catching up with him, and he's just about out of time...